To
|
Helen
and
David
and
Ray
and
Tony
|
Thanks!

1

Blood pumping scarlet from below the left eyebrow and snot sliding down from the burst nose. Spit and a curse from the mouth as the big cunt staggers back against the wire mesh — put up to keep the crowds out and the fighters in. Above in the starry sky the darkening night-quiet contrasting with the mad fucking pandemomium down here on the ground. November birds all gone to bed if they hasn't already fucked off to the warm safety of the western Sahara or some other sanctuary. Away from the coming winter cold and the murderous mayhem. The meshed arena is speckled with blood as the big cunt against the wire stumbles back into the centre. Eyes glazed and hardly seeing. The Yella Lad waits for him to come. Then sends a sickening blow full on into his mashed-up face. He sinks slowly. Looking down at his teeth and seeing the stars converge to make a blinding light and then fade away to oblivion.

Crowd cheering and breaking through the mesh and the Yella Lad is carried shoulder high from the arena. Money made and lost. Minor scuffles breaking out around the clearing. Air full of loud voices and praise and threats and cheers and curses and dogs barking and bottles breaking. Almost unnoticed, the unconscious pav is carried away with all attempts to revive him failing. And to most Gorgios this little scene of bare-knuckle buileam would be cause enough to call the fucking wobs. But to my people it's all part of the sweet sketch of life. Even though they're not really my people any more.

With darkness now dropping from the listless sky and the mob dispersing, I decides I've seen enough and starts away across this piece of gauche wasteland towards the anaesthetic lights of Manchester. Soft November rain unexpectedly falling to wash away the blood and bitterness. Caressing my face like gentle tears and telling me I has no real alternative but to be here. Despite the fact that I lives in Collins' caer and could try to draw on the benefits if I wanted to. But they don't make it easy for us people with their cagmags and cross faces and new deals and fucking nonsense — making things even tighter than they was before.

Anyway it's not really my road. Maybe because some buried instinct makes the yawney little five O level faces seem so sneering. With their probing and prying and purges. And what did you do for work this week? Wanked myself sick! Often felt like leaning in over the safe counter and dragging one of the cunts out by the nose. Quick poke of a freshly sharpened pencil into the eyeball. Just for fucking spite. But I suppose it's not their fault. Or maybe it is. Life's such a confusing cunt of a thing altogether. Especially if you can read and write. And it's all shite like the single European currency and shrinking international markets and commodities flying up and down and fucking sideways too. Zillions of digital dollars zooming through the air all around us and everybody shiteing on themselves to be a millennium millionaire.

As well as all that every day some new story showing the total lack of any morals amongst the rich and powerful — and the fucking poor as well. O'Connell would call it a complete load of bollix and say we're all media morons in this country. Reckons we'd believe even the Lord's fucking Prayer if we read it in the fucking tabloids. And imitate every patronising po-face we sees on the television box. Young stocky cunt called Myles Cashin appearing beside me and stepping into my stride.

'You coming with us, Owen?'

'Where to, Myles?'

tribe

'Into town for a drink. The Yella Lad's buying.'

'Isn't he barred from all the fucking pubs in these parts?'

'The man in the Rose and Crown serves him sometimes.'

'I don't know about that place ...'

'Come on, Owen.'

O'Connell is bound to be in there. Might be better to stay away because the cunt'll only start heckling me again. But bollocks to him — I'm entitled to go where I wants without being harassed by that fucking gavvers-nark turncoat shite. Be good for the cunt to see whose side I'm on.

After a clean-up and some stitches the Yella Lad bullying his way into the public bar and buying the drinks all around. Local consumers a bit crowded by these irritating fucking itinerants. Cunts with bandannas of bright colours round their necks and some in leather with long hair and others in vests and the odd few fuckers bare-chested as if they themselves had won the fucking fight. Redundant scrap dealers and horse handlers and crooks and cheats and motor traders and tarmac men. All the cunts imagining themselves to be the best fucking bare-knuckle boxer in the whole world. Reliving the fight in its aftermath. Bobbing and weaving and throwing rights and lefts and simulated skelps.

Regular customers wary and leaving as soon as we blusters in with mutters of poxy fucking pikeys and they should all be fucking barred. Not fit to drink with decent people. None of the cunts wishing to articulate their opinions too loudly and the landlord glad of the extra trade in these days of speculative serendipity. O'Connell staring in at me over the counter from the saloon bar.

'Owen!'

'Oh Christ!'

'What are you doin' in there with the go-boys?'

'Fuck off, O'Connell.'

'Will you get yourself in here to civilised company, this very minute!'

I suppose I'll have to — now that the cunt's seen me. Won't fucking leave off unless I do. Finish this Guinness first. Make the higgler buy me another for his intrusion into my privacy. Down the hatch and through the swing doors. O'Connell the great hairy bull. Sitting up at the bar on a stool.

tribe

'Where have you been?'

'Get me a pint and I'll tell you.'

O'Connell beckoning to the barman with his red hand. Grinning at me out of the red face with the red whiskers and the red freckles on the back of the red neck.

'Why aren't you out there, Con, blowing bits out of the ground?'

'I never work in bad weather, Owen — or in the dark for that matter.'

'You professionals is so fucking particular.'

'Ah now, enough of the ould sarcasm. I've done my share of skivvying. Skilled man now. You still fart-arsing about with them fucking Tinkers?'

'I *am* a fucking Tinker, and so are you — you fucking yawney.'

'I never was, you dirty liar! I come from the dispossessed aristocracy.'

'Magairles! Anyway, we can't all be good with the gelignite.'

'I've put the word about for you, Owen, but y'know how things are.'

'Wouldn't matter, Con, I knows nothing about the demolition.'

'You ought to learn. A growth business these days boy. Tearing down the old, to make way for the new. Structural evolution, that's what it is. Two thousand and ten, and all that bollix.'

'Fuck two thousand and ten. All you hobbledehoys does is blow the shite out of the whole fucking countryside for the cony-catchers and fill in the holes with plastic money-boxes and portable fucking lavatories.'

'Not my fault the scrap game's fucked, Owen.'

O'Connell getting the hump and slipping into a sulky silence. Face falling as the cunt downs the pint of Guinness and orders two more. Waits without speaking for the next drink to come and then flings half of that down his great gaping gullet.

And he's right. It's not his fucking fault. No money in bits of fucking metal any more. All plastic and polythene and vinyl and vassly! Every fucking cunt wants to be in the block-paving

tribe

10

business these days. Soon won't be a blade of fucking grass left. My daddy was a dealer and I followed in his footsteps while I could. Even though my mother made me go to school and learn a few things. Believed her when she told me metallurgy was the scientific side of the scrap trade and that's where the future lay. Nothing left now. Even the lorry itself sold to the breaker's yard — and I'm qualified for fuck-all else.

Some might say good riddance to the dirty piles of shite all over the caravan sites. And the Gorgios complaining about the rats and the rubbish — and that's when they're talking about the people. But it was a handy little world and I misses the shadowy cunts of the scrap game. It was mine. And nobody asked me if I wanted it to go. It was something I knew — following after the old pavs. Slipping along the path of their profession. I felt it touch my frightened heart. Watched it claim me as its own. Then it died. And I said to myself what the fuck will I do now? Stay at home or stand on street corners and cry myself down into the fucking dust?

But a good horse is never a bad colour and I feels fresher lately after getting a little tarmacing work with these Cashin conyas. Keeping me from becoming a right cunt altogether. And we can't all have everything we wants. Can we?

'Better times is on the way, Con.'

'So they say, Owen. Anyway, all this is the direct result of giving the working classes the vote. Get away from them fucking Tinkers, Owen. They'll have you in trouble.'

'You natchy cunt — and your people all push-cats and hedge-mumpers!'

'Who told you that?'

'You did!'

'Keep it up and I'll give you a fucking clatter ...'

'For what?'

'For being such a fucking trimmer!'

'See — I knew I was right!'

'Think what you like. *She's* putting you up to this, isn't she?'

'I wants to work, Con. Can't live on the fucking benefit — and I don't need your lectures.'

Leave O'Connell tut-tutting with his head scowling down into his pint. Push back into the public bar where the singing and dancing is reaching a fillyhoo and Myles Cashin pulling my arm across to meet Tom Lee — a small dark-skinned Romany Chal they calls the Blackberry Gypsy. The cunt wears a broad-brimmed hat and grins at me with a wide row of yellow teeth. And when he walks he has the hotchel from some younger infection of polio. Which they says is a dead disease now. Unless the fucking politicians decides to exhume it. Along with a few others.

'Myles tells me you wants work.'

'That's right.'

'What can you do?'

'Anything. Tarmac, groundwork, block-paving — whatever.'

'Any experience with horses?'

'No.'

'That's unusual, for a pav.'

'I knows that, but I never had much dealings with the grais.'

'You'll get some tomorrow. What's your name?'

'Owen.'

'Welsh?'

'English. Father was Irish.'

'Was?'

'He's dead.'

And fucking buried. Light years ago. Don't know a horse's head from its arse. And he's right. It's unusual for a Traveller — whether he's still on the drom or stuck in a caer. But I never liked the big fuckers and was always a bit afraid of them. It's not something you admits to and anyway I've been settled for some time now. I'll try anything once though — if the fucking money's right.

Air full of smoke and swears and obscure outlines. Cunts drinking and talking and laughing. Some making deals and money crossing palms after the spits and slaps. Wanted to run back when my mother first took me to live in the Gorgio world — after daddy died. Didn't want the soul to show. They laughs at souls — them who don't have any of their own.

'A travelling man?'

'Who?'

'Your father!'

'He was a conishfein. What's the pay for tomorrow?'

'Fifty a day. Maybe more when you knows what you're doing. That's fair.'

'Fairer than some.'

'You wants it then?'

'Aye!'

Arrangements made with the Blackberry for a pick-up at five in the morning. Quick off the mark this conya. Didn't reckon on working with the grais and it's something I've always avoided. But never look a gift horse in the mouth and if I don't get on with the game I can always scarper. The Blackberry limps away into the harlicking and haggling and I suppose I could have found something else to do. Tried a retraining course or even the Open University. Or become a mugger or murderer — sell my serial to the fucking tabloids.

But who's to say even that's a safe bet these days? Maybe when you wakes up it might be gone and you'd have to start all over again — like a new-born chavvy. Better to play safe and take my chances with Tom Lee for now. Work for his wages but keep myself just a little apart. Not to take the backward step and become one of these pavs again. Ann wouldn't like that at all.

Last bell ringing in our ears and the landlord won't have any fucking truck with afters — even in the face of threats. A few glasses broken on the floor and the panic button pressed to the local wob station. Bottles and things thrown at the cunt for this premature and hostile action but the strategy succeeding as the fuckers breaks ranks. Some racing away at high speed in their four-wheel drives with shouts and whoops and bottles out through the windows.

Back to the caravan site on a piece of gudgell real-estate between the Manchester ship canal and a now-derelict industrial site where some of the wives waits in holy fucking terror — but others well able for these drunken ruillefeins and capable of giving the cunts a good clout round the fucking ear for their unruliness. Other Travellers dispersing away to whatever part of the country they've come in from to attend the fight tonight.

tribe

This section of the city will be glad to see the backs of them. Gathering for the past three days in their trucks and cars and vans and terrorising the local community and barred out of all the pubs except for this one. Some streets closing down altogether and putting up the steel shutters. Which is an insult as our money is as good as any other cunt's. We pays for what we can't naif and something's better than nothing these days.

Rain easing slightly on the walk home. Sky jet-black and the stars beginning to peep out again. Be glad to get inside for once. Shake off this uneasiness that's feeling round my heart — to see if it's still warm. Go away you wishful thinking. I'm not dead yet. Neither am I done for.

Maybe Ann will come round to cheer me up. With her starry-eyes and her happy hands and her deadly devastating dreams.

'It's time you got away from those people, Owen. Twenty-eight isn't young you know.'

'You sounds just like O'Connell.'

'I don't care. Why won't you talk to father?'

'If you'll pardon my profanity ... fuck your father!'

'He's not as bad as you make him out to be, Owen.'

'Butter wouldn't melt in his mouth, but a hard chunk of cheese'd choke him!'

Logic is Ann's forte. She's some kind of software storcher who might for all I knows be at the sharp end of this molecular manufacturing. She understands all the docity about the information super highway and cyberspace and talks in terms of web addresses and net sites and a new virtual way of life for us all.

Shouldn't be too much against it I suppose because that's where the money is these days. Danger is some smart cunt might identify your password and intercept your stash before you retires to your rocking-chair. Or else the fucking fundamentalists could unleash some sort of deadly disease or the racists and ethnic cleansers might come along and creep up on you in the middle of the fucking night. Burn us all to death in the name of normality.

We met at the technical college where my mother sent me to study metallurgy and Ann was a trainee programmer. Ann liked me for some reason and I also liked her. Didn't seem to think of me in terms of the Tinker — although she still has the fucking Gorgio prejudices. We just sort of grew together over the few years we've known each other and takes each other now just a little bit for granted.

I couldn't find any work after college because there's no fucking iron foundries nor steel mills left. So what was the fucking point of it all?

Went back to my father's trade — while it lasted — and then on the gaff in the summer seasons which was cushti enough because it was only two days' work in a week to put up and pull down. The rest was rolling the rides and dinking the skippers.

But even that game's all hydraulics now and anyway there was always too much trouble with the wobs. Blaming us for all the burglaries and pickpocketing and pilfering and worse crimes being committed when we weren't there. In any case Ann likes to pretend I'm not a Traveller. Says she can see something else in me — a complete cunt altogether? And despite her advanced state of technical development she's still quite a conservative — as far as all this family stuff and settling down is concerned.

She wants us to marry. When we have enough money. And she's right, twenty-eight isn't fucking young these days. Wonder what it would have been like if we'd met back in the old days — on the drom. I'm not Irish. My daddy was. My mammy is.

'He can get you a proper job, Owen ...'

'Doing what?'

'Working for the newspaper, selling advertising space or something.'

'What do I know about all that kind of stuff?'

'You've been to college, you could learn!'

'I don't even read your father's pimmocky little paper.'

'Don't be such a defeatist. You won't even try. We could get married ... maybe even next year!'

Not too keen on maybes at the moment. Or marriage. Nothing to stop her from moving in here with me and living in sin. Except her deadinthebed fart of a father — says he objects to shiftlessness in all shapes and forms. The shite-arsed cunt! I'll end up fucking killing him. She's twenty-two for Christ's sake!

tribe

'We'd have to get a house, of course.'

'What's wrong with this place?'

'Too poky. This is a poky little flat, Owen.'

I happens to like this poky little flat. As caers go it's not the worst. Just a place to sleep in — that's all. And it's mine — sort of. Compliments of the Greater Manchester Council. And Collins, when he absconded to Australia. It's still in the cunt's name. Should have went with him. They says a man can travel out there for weeks at a time without seeing anyone else. And them Aborigines seems like OK conyas if the red-necks and reverends would leave them alone. What with genetic cunting-around and child-killers and smokers' civil liberties being shat on everywhere — this country's turning more fucking sinister by the day. Maybe next year!

'Don't think I'm pushing, Owen. I just want us to be comfortable.'

'I'm comfortable here, and you could be too. Tell your father that.'

'I know he's a little old fashioned ...'

'He's a little old ferrucker!'

'I expect that's another insult?'

'Sorry.'

'Sometimes I wonder if you really want me.'

I does Ann. But does you come without the mortgage? Can I have the basic model with no dada and no baba and no fucking neurosis? You're a great girl Ann. In more ways than the obvious one. Sex and sensibility can't be a bad basis for lifelong commitment. I loves Ann. She loves me. You can go a great length with something like that in common.

'I can't stay very late.'

'What are we waiting for then?'

'Christmas?'

'Too far for the feick.'

'You mean fuck.'

'I do ... that too. But leave the bad language to me.'

Glide gently down onto the mat in front of the smokeless fire. And is this your tongue Ann that's trying to lick out my eardrum? There can't be more to life than lust. Or more to marriage than madness. She folds her clothes neatly in an elegant little pile. Lending respectability to this sordid

tribe

scene. Descending slowly onto my face first and then inching across my chest and stomach. Turn her over onto her back and someone run the jolly roger up that fucking flagpole.

Why do I sometimes feel so sad when I'm with this woman? My guilty eyes reflected in the light now licking at her golden thighs. It would be so easy to submit — to concede. To give in and talk to her God and her father. Why don't I do it? I'm an easy type and hates to hurt. But it would mean the cutting of the last tenuous thread still holding me to the old ways. And I'd be fucking corbed. Although they says that all minority groups poses a threat whether real or imagined to the collective well-being and it wouldn't be fair for her to be criticised because of me. Easy now angel! Balls bursting between the warm walls and wanting to send their silver stream high as the moon.

'Jesus Ann ...'

'Oh Owen ...'

'Jesus Ann ...'

'Oh Owen ...'

Hands heaving at my arse. Fingers digging and pulling the cheeks apart. Bury me in this position when I dies. Face down and arse in the air. And who the hell is that fidgeting at the fucking door? Can't stop to find out.

'Mother o' Jaysus ...'

Take a glancing squint back over the shoulder at the wide open red eyes.

'Fuck off, Con!'

O'Connell retreating with a slamming sound of the door. Be praying in the fucking hall now. For the salvation of selfish souls.

'Who was that?'

'Nobody.'

'Who was it, Owen?'

'I don't know. Ignore them.'

'Let me up.'

'No.'

'Owen ...'

'Ann. Don't move.'

Hold tight onto her shoulders in this moment of crisis. Coming fast! Blood draining down from the head. Sense

flying from whatever cells are still left in the fucking brain.
Up from the balls at full belt comes the singing stream.
Shooting into her elegant estuary. Everything! Even the air
rushing out of my ears. Nothing left inside now.

Empty and trembling. Lying there with Ann heaving
under me. Don't want to ever fucking move again. In my
whole life.

'Owen ... let me up.'

'Wait a second.'

'Now!'

'It was only O'Connell.'

'Did he see us?'

'He closed his eyes.'

'Don't be flippant ...'

'Don't be foolish.'

'Let me up!'

'He won't tell a soul.'

Great heave of the tóin muscles and I goes rolling across
the floor. No consoling her now. That little prudishness
there in the background. Coming through as the clothes goes
quickly back on. Straightening hair and hem — panties and
pride.

'How did he get in?'

'I must have left the key in the lock.'

'I'm going now, Owen.'

'Wait ...'

Gone! With the hump and a heave of the hall door —
slamming hard in my head. Can't help thinking there would
be more hump and heaving of fucking doors if we was
married. Has to be considered as part of the larger picture.
O'Connell returning with a sheepish look across the cunt's
puss — and a red eye.

'What the fuck's up with her?'

'Bad hormone day.'

'She give me a box in the fucking eye. I never said a word,
just stood in the hall. "Peepin' fucking tom", says she, and
up and hits me a box in the fucking eye.'

'No self control. What d'you want?'

'Nothing. Just thought I'd drop in to see how you were.'

'At a quarter to one in the morning?'

'Sure the night is young yet! Why don't you get up off the floor and put your fucking trousers back on?'

O'Connell slinking off to the kitchen as I collects my clothes. Returning with two glasses and producing a bottle of Glenfiddich from an inside coat pocket. He sits, spreading out his legs in the chair opposite me. Scratching his red head as he rolls up a cigarette from the tin balanced on his knee.

'Thought we'd have a drink and a chat.'

'Did you now?'

Pouring the whisky and pulling this chair up to the fire. Slip it down slowly and let it tingle a while in the throat. Savour the taste like a sin. Nice little glow in the hearth now and another starting in the belly. Uneasiness still icy on the back of my neck.

'I worry about you, Owen boy.'

'No need for that, Con.'

'You're beginning to show signs of stress.'

'What signs would they be, Con?'

'All this hanging about with fucking Tinkers — and fornicating on the floor.'

3

Didn't sleep easy last night despite O'Connell's whisky. Tossing and turning into the rare hours for no apparent reason. Fretful dreams of mutilated mammals and crop circles and interstellar abductions and strange fucking lights in the sky. Alarm clock making a noise like a demented dilling at five. Feels like I've only just fallen asleep and don't want to get up because of this fucking headache.

Dark and cold outside. Am I the only cunt alive at this cock-crow hour? Light from the paper shop and a few more lost souls coming out of the murk like drugged moths. Wind sharp as a knife through my jacket and in between the ribs.

'Half ounce of Holborn.'

'Can't serve you if you're off the gyppo site.'

'Why not?'

'Fucking bunch of thieves, that's why not, especially the kids.'

'What if I reports you to the race relations board?'

'Be my fucking guest!'

Only one thing for it. Reach over the counter and grab the gavver by the throat. He screams and soon flings the baccy at me. I throws two pound on the counter and tells the shiteing wanker to keep the change. Dirty discriminating drotchel. Hope they catches the cunt with his fingers in the fucking till.

Smell of the stagnant canal reaching me before the smoke sight of the trailers. Orange lights of what's left of the industrial estate over on the left — searching for survivors. Away to the right the motorway traffic already down to a crawling standstill. They built Gypsy sites in places like this back when councils had to find somewhere for us to poove down.

Legislation forced us off the tramp so we had to be given a hatch. The cunts looked for the worst fucking pieces of real estate they could find. I was born on a shite-heap site like this — only worse. It felt like being in starry. And that was just for a chavvy like me. The old people must have fucking cried.

'Hey you!'

Shout from the site entrance frightening the shite out of me. Haven't been up here for a while and a lot of strange cunts about. The Cashin pavs usually picking me up from the flat whenever they got a day or two. Some fucker in a donkey jacket sitting on the open gate with a definite look of craziness round the cunt's squinty eyes. Clench my fists and be ready to fleece him.

'Owen McBride?'

How comes the cunt knows my name?

'Who the fuck are you?'

'They calls me the Duck.'

'The what?'

Must be on account of the way he walks. God bless the mark! And Myles Cashin sent him to wait for me in case I tried to sleer away. Through the gate the low spread of caravans and mobile homes and trailers reaches out. Each on its individual concrete pad. Showing off their status in the pecking order of the place. The bigger the trailer, the more cushti and respected its owner.

Winter flowers hanging in coloured wooden baskets from the fences and grass growing tall round the wheels of a few ornate old vardas that will never see the road again. Some of the beors already up and sitting out on their cold steps chatting and chopping food. Conversations cut short as I approaches with the Duck waddling before me. Faces peering through trailer windows and gawking at the neo-Gorgio. Whenever I've come up here in the past I've always found the fuckers to be a bit stoachy — sort of friendly and aloof at the same time. An atmosphere of private pride and public squalor — like a ghetto. Forced to live in these gudgell conditions and it's us Gypsies who considers the Gorgios to be the dirty ones — with their shitty cities and their slums and their sotchel.

Dogs growling and barking at me out of dark recesses under the caravans. Wiry little terriers with their warnings and mad-eyed lurchers trying to take lumps out of my fucking ankles. A fire burning bright down at the other end of the site with a few faint shadows warming their hands.

We steers ourselves in that direction. A milieu of other cunts around me now — heading for their moulders and pick-ups and Land Rovers. Some a sort of black colour and others off-white. Brown and half-baked. Slushy skinned and shite stained. The air full of Shelta and Cant and Gamon and Romany and spitting on the ground and no good mornings or general greetings of any kind — for fucking Gorgios.

Light stretching its faint fingers in the desolate sky. God laughing down at me. The Duck taking me over to the broomdashers round the yog. Myles Cashin pumping my hand and saying you turned up then Owen. I said I would. And sure you can take the man out of the Tinker but you can't take the Tinker out of the man. If you has anything valuable Owen leave it in my trailer. Half these fucking hawkers would take the whites from your eyes. Especially that Duck fein.

'I got nothing valuable, Myles.'

Except my sense. And I left that at home in a safe place. Introduced immediately to these other cunts who look deep into my eyes before reluctantly taking the shake I offers them in all good fucking faith. Big Bill, the Irish Tinker with hands the size of coke shovels and ears sticking out like a fucking taxi with the doors open.

A small wiry Gypsy called Louis dressed in brightly coloured clothes who Myles tells me is a lazy bastard and what's even worse Owen he's one of them things the Gorgios calls a quare. Louis limp-wristed taking my hand with a small squeeze and a smile in the cunt's impudent eyes. The last in line a surly Scotsman called Black Jake —

with one eye that winks and blinks while the other stares permanently ahead. Hope the cunt's not a fucking Oráisteach!

The story's told round the camp fires that Jake went once with Louis to the Leather Bottle public house where the barman wore pink chiffon shirts and Jake's eye would wink all by itself and no matter how busy the barman was Jake always got served first. Rumour has it that the odd free double brandy became involved until one night the barman follows Jake into the gents to negotiate terms. The black Scot — not being too sophisticated in the subtleties of these circles — lays the cunt out on the piss-stained floor. But a scandal like that is difficult to live down and there are some who still has their doubts.

And have a cup of weed Owen while you're waiting. Don't mind if I does.

Tom Lee coming from his trailer with a brisk hotchel and a bright red bandelero round his neck and over to this crew of motley cunts. He looks at me up close and says some turns up their sleeves at work Owen and some turns up their noses. Which sort are you?

'Why don't you tell me at the end of the day?'

'Good enough. Let's be away on the drom then!'

He climbs into his Land Rover and leads the way as Big Bill drives behind in this blue pick-up. Jake and The Duck in beside him on the seat with me, Myles and Louis in the cold breeze of the back. Don't know why I agreed to take on this fucking job.

Always had a private fear of large animals and what if one of the cunts kicks me? In the fucking bollocks? I huddles down as far as I can and shivers while the other two farts like automatic fucking cannon-guns. Stink forcing my head up again into the flying wind-chill. Out along the M62 towards Warrington and Tom Lee's rented fields down by the river Mersey. Greyness of the day reflected in the river water and also in my humour. And Myles telling me the Blackberry has five clover fields of a couple of acres apiece and some stables and a few sheds and suchlike. And the river water running away in the opposite direction as if it knows something I doesn't and chuckling as it flows with little cross-currents and bits of broken water and backwashes and whirlpools and the whole world wearing me down into the ground. Will I ever again be able to hold up my head? Or will this job be the last one and the death of me down here in the soft green countryside and away from the hard city hinterland.

Light drizzle falling on my heart. And these conyas gabbing away in Gamon about this and that and the fucking other and the Blackberry up ahead thinking his own thoughts in Romany about the five stages of prejudice — and wondering when the local authorities will finally embrace the fifth like the fucking Nazis did and try to exterminate his entire race. Plenty of them cunts left around despite Nuremberg! Even so in my own defence I has to say the Gypsy cultural imperialism is a match for its racial cousin and has encouraged the fucking Gorgios' ignorance and fear. In retaliation they offers us the choice of assimilation or criminalisation. And we've all seen the signs in the shop doorways. No dogs or Tinkers!

We arrives at the long clover fields with the cold horses grazing in the early rain. Cunts jumping from the pick-up and drifting away into the gloom of their work. Left standing on my own in the middle of a puck-ring and afraid to move out of it in case it brings bad luck — like a whistling woman. Until Tom Lee at last approaches. Lighting up a fag and looking me straight in the eye.

'This mungy fucking weather mommers me, Owen!'

'Me too.'

'McBride ... a Scottish name?'

'I already told you — English. Father was Irish, and grandfather Spanish.'

'Good blood-line.'

He thinks I'm one of his fucking horses!

'Come along with me, young hobbledehoy.'

While I explains. The Romany pav walking away up the field. I must follow him and try to stay out of the animals' way while he tells me he keeps about thirty grais at any one time here. As well as a pace of donkeys and the odd stubborn mule. The fields is rented from a local farmer who allows the stock to poove down on his land. The Blackberry explaining that most of his horses is American Shetlands which is slightly taller than their Scottish cousins and good for pulling the benogs and also the pacing. There's one or two traumatised thoroughbreds that's shit out on the racetrack and also a couple of cobs.

Although all Travellers has replaced their vardas with motor vehicles, Tom says he still likes in catchy weather to go for trips along the lanes in his trap. Listen to the mistle-thrush and watch the swallows fly high in the mackerel sky.

Constantly looking over my shoulder and barely fucking listening while he tells me how he buys his horses at the various fairs around the country — like Epsom and Appleby and Barnet and Banbury. Even across to Ireland and places like Ballinasloe and Spancilhill and the great Puck Fair in the Kingdom of Kerry. And only a few of us deals in horses these days Owen. But as you knows most Travellers keeps one or two — like a hobby. We've always known grais and would go insane without one. Even if only to lie down in the grass on a summer's evening and watch 'em graze. You falls asleep Owen and they'll graze all around you. But all the horses now is silky little beauties and no-one needs 'em for work anymore.

'The lorry is more respected these days than the horse.'

'That's progress for you.'

'And every generation gets weaker and wiser.'

'So they says ...'

'My heart is in the horse, Owen. I loves 'em.'

'Mine's in my fucking mouth at the moment.'

'Don't be worrying. I usually buys unbroken grais, Owen .. apart from the thoroughbreds.'

'What's that?'

'I goes to the sales and buys 'em unbroken. Then we flag 'em out and make 'em tame.'

'I don't know about ...'

'Them riding stables takes two or three months to break a horse. I can do it in a couple of hours. A conventionally broken horse treats man as his enemy, Owen. My grais is my friends.'

'You won't be expecting me to do that? If you are, you can fuck off with your fifty a day!'

'Not everyone can do it. Let's see how you gets on first, before we says any more.'

'I'm just telling you in advance.'

'And not every horse will have it done to 'im either.'

The Blackberry saying how the grais must bond with their breakers. And how body position and speed and direction of motion all contributes to what he calls horse language. Horses don't understand English Owen — nor Russian nor Chinese. They only understands body language. And there's no need to hurt a horse to break it. Some ropes 'em up and hits 'em with lead pipes. I doesn't believe in hurting grais and any pav that does won't be working for me long. He says he'll teach me horse-talk and warns me as well to be careful because a grai can kill with a kick — from back or front feet and they can break limbs with their teeth.

'See that banner over there, Owen?'

'The what?'

'The claybank cob, little heavy feller about fourteen hands ...'

'That cunt there?'

'He's a wicked peevish pony, Owen. Don't go near him 'til you knows a bit more.'

'Don't fucking worry about that.'

'Then there's the donkeys ...'

'They're not so big, them buggers.'

Tom Lee laughs as he takes me by the arm and tells me that his donkeys are shipped for pets all over the world. To the European Continent and the United States and recently even Russia. Donkeys can see the wind Owen. And they originally come from Africa and Asia and were brought over here by the Romans. They doesn't like being on their own and needs to run with their kind or with other animals. And no I never realised that cattle ranchers says it's lucky to keep a couple running with their herds.

'If a cow falls into a mire, the donkey will bray 'til help comes, Owen. Or if a cow calves, the donkey will protect the young 'un from dogs and other animals. They can keep skittish horses calm and comfort a lonely foal.'

'Well I never knew ...'

'Donkeys is not stupid. They're cunning pretenders.'

tribe

'I always thought the fuckers were thick.'

'Not at all. They're intelligent and learn quickly and you'll never see a dead 'un. They're full of curiosity, Owen and likes to know what's going on all the while. If a donkey don't want you on its back, he'll buck and leap and jump to get you off. If that fails he'll pretend to be broken. Then, when you're not expecting it, you'll be dumped into the ditch.'

The Blackberry wearing his heart on his sleeve for these yawney little beasts. And after all Owen — God loves the crow as well as the nightingale! Standing suddenly in front of us is a huge shire horse which makes me almost shite on myself with fright and try to hide behind the Blackberry.

'This is my baby — Juno. I keeps her as a pet. Just for the novelty. And she wouldn't hurt a fly Owen.'

The great animal being led along like a lamb by this tall olive-skinned conya with jet black hair and oriental eyes. He hands the bridle and bit to Tom Lee and stands back soundless.

'This here is Tolui, Owen. He's my best man. Do as he says.'

The Blackberry trots off patting his percheron on the neck and stretching up to kiss the fucking thing on the cheek. Leaving me standing face to face with this yellow-coloured conishfein who stares at me in a sinister way and says. I am Mongolian and my forefathers were known. As the *Mangüdai*.

4

Morning moving lightly along and this job not nearly as fucking bad as I thought it would be. Maybe the Blackberry cares about my phobia because I finds myself sitting in the warm dry tack shed out of the cold. Buffing up the bits and bridles and polishing the saddles and stirrups. Happy in here among the numnahs and neckstraps — curbs and cruppers and cavessons and chambons. Collars and catching sticks. Not that I knows what half the stuff's for and this Tolui rooker in and out and telling me this and that.

Not all pimmock-time as I must also distribute feed and haul hay out around the field as the sparse grass at this time of the year is not enough for the stock. Needs other stuff like barley and bran and wheat sorghum and molasses for the lactating mares. Some likes a lick of salt and others the haychaff oats and all must have a bucket of the fresh clean water in their troughs — greedy fucking guzzlers. Back to the barn again as quick as possible and a fag butt for a few minutes in among the smells of saddle soap and metal-polish and neat's-foot oil and mutton fat. Before Tolui appears with his oval eyes to stare down at me in a superior fashion.

'Breakfast!'

'Where?'

He turns without telling me and I follows him up the long field 'til we comes to the rest of the crew. Crouched round a cast-iron cooking pot over a friendly fire. Tolui takes a bowl and sits aside and aloof from the rest of the cunts.

'Does you know what a pacer is, Owen?'

'Some sort of horse ...'

'It's a high-stepper, you know.'

'That's mostly what we're doing today.'

'What is, Myles?'

'Getting the pacer ready for the race.'

'As well as weaning a few foals.'

'What race?'

'In a couple of days' time.'

'On that piece of straight carriageway down the M6, near Chelford.'

'Horse-racing don't really interest me all that much ...'

'It's more than just a horse race, Owen!'

'What is it then?'

'It's a tradition!'

'That's what I was afraid of.'

'And we travelling people is entitled to our little pleasures, like every other pav.'

'That's what you think!'

'We is, you yogger-shite!'

'Don't come if you don't want ...'

'To make some money ...'

'How?'

'On Tom's horse, hug-a-fucking-day!'

'Can I bring my girlfriend?'

'You can, Owen, but ...'

'It's illegal.'

'And the fucking wobs might get wind of it.'

They laughs and smokes and swills down jogray from the big pot which tastes fair enough but I've seen how they makes the stuff and wouldn't recommend it for any cunt with fucking ulcers. I also knows how some of these pavs eats hotchi and hare and other horrible shite. That's another part of the appanage I can live without. Give me a fucking beefburger any day. Honeymoon's over and after this little break I'm told to go help Tolui with the horses.

Cunt sees my fear but doesn't force me into it. Lets me take my time and explains that the grais is herbivores and herd animals and feels safest shabbing in a string. And horses Owen are not angry or wicked or vicious. If they behave badly it is because they are frightened. If a horse is not frightened it is easier to train and young colts are like children and do not concentrate for very long.

I'm listening and letting it all in one ear and out the other until the cunt calls me over to where a quarter-horse is tethered in the paddock. He gets me to pat the beast and then rub it down with round movements. Then he unties the rooker and it looks at me through a suspicious eye. Tolui tells me to lower my shoulders and turn away because this is horse language and it means I won't hurt it. And soon to my surprise the animal follows me and I can get the grai to go or stop or turn to left and right. Tolui smiles and says you're doing well — for a *kalmück*.

In the afternoon he explains how to look for weak links in an animal — shite like splits and marin bones and spavins and how quidling in the feed bins means teeth needs attention.

Even surprise myself how quick I can spot a capped hock or blemished leg and soon I'm talking like a cunt with counterfeit credentials about turned toes and crib biters and wind suckers and bad-tempered bloods.

And he tells me he comes from a place called Müren on the great Mongolian Plain. All the other fuckers thinks he's Chinese and that suits Tom Lee — who smuggled the cunt into this country because his race are known to be the best handlers of horses in the entire Universe. And his country was the land of the Tus and the Tengri and the Eryn Gurvan Naadom before the Communists came. His people were the Halh and the Dorvad and the Dariganga.

And he says a blue wolf and a fallow doe were the ancestors of all the Mongols. His history is a history of blood and savage conquerors and wandering tribes and prophets and shamans and mystic kings — with eighteen inner hells and eighty-four thousand outer hells. A land where the wolf and the wild horse still run free and eagles hang in the blue sky and wild argali sheep graze on the bare mountains.

He tells me a blanket of darkness hung over his country for seventy years and was lifted only when the Communists left. But then there was hunger Owen amongst the hills and shortages of everything in the cities and the road to a free market economy is long and difficult. So he was forced to leave for a while to make some money for his family. But now he says *bi ovchtei baina* and he wants to put his soul on the soles of his feet and return to his *onghon* and his *aimag*.

He needs to see his wife and small sons but the Gypsies keep telling him tomorrow Tolui. Tomorrow we'll send you home from this alien ground. But the world is an unequal place with many ups and downs. And certainly isn't round!

The further minutes of this day moving like little white mice and my anxiety over these big animals subsiding as Tolui takes me among the cunts and tells me there's nothing to fear from these beasts Owen *aanda*. They are your friends and will be better to you than any of these two-legged *cumans*. I helps out with some shoeing and shovelling of donkey shite and suddenly the day is over and we're on our way back. To the trailers.

'Where's Tolui?'

'He stays with the stock, Owen.'

'What is he, a fucking slave or something?'

'No, no. It's his own choice.'

'He could live with us.'

'At the hatchintan.'

'But he won't.'

'His people lives with their livestock.'

'And we respects things of that type.'

'Sure, he has his own bunk and his grub and the grais ...'

'What more could any cunt want?'

Company? Tom Lee pays me fifty pounds for the day and says he's happy with my work and would I like to come out on a regular run? I certainly would and count me in. We sits round a long table in his Gypsy trailer with its lustre and candlewick and brightly coloured cushions. And the crown derby china cascading down the elaborate cupboards and the family pictures and decorative lace all over the place and cut-glass mirrors and a baroque little display of bowls. The Blackberry's wife Lóla giving out bottles of beer and we drinks and laughs and the talk is of the imminent death and demise of the Travelling people.

'Fucking designation was the beginning of our downfall.'

'That's too true, Tom.'

'Then it was the Public fucking Order Act.'

'And the fucking Criminal Justice Act ...'

'And other illegal acts of harassment and holy fucking terror!'

'Pedantry has become policy now ...'

'We can't travel and stop where we wants to ...'

'Romany means we is romantic ... did you know?'

'And the local authorities don't have to provide these slawmy sites no more neither ...'

'If we uses a stopping place, the wobs can knock us up with only ten minutes' notice.'

'Travelling is the oldest way of life on earth!'

'And it's a basic human fucking right ...'

'Prejudice would die out tomorrow if only pride would do the same!'

'D'you know, we comes from Egypt, Owen?'

'My daddy told me it was India.'

'The first Traveller was called the Lord of Little Egypt.'

'India!'

'Egypt!'

'India or Egypt ... no one fucking knows.'

Trailer door thrown open and stepping into the immediate silence the Yella Lad. Bruises still black round the cunt's eyes from the recent fight and he smiles and sits and after a cool introduction shakes my hand.

'What d'you think then, Felix?'

'About what?'

'Us Travellers.'

'Sooner we all settles in caers the fucking better. Let the chavvies get a proper education and take their place in the Gorgio world. There's nothing left for us in places like this.'

'Some's doing well for themselves.'

'Them cunts is stealing cars and selling drugs. D'you want to do that?'

'All Gypsies is not travellers and all travellers is not Gypsies.'

'We was once fortune tellers and dancers. The women made lace and flowers and pegs. Baskets at Easter, for the primroses, elderwood flowers at Christmas. We was crop-pickers, never came near fucking towns.'

'God made the country and man made the city!'
'Then the farmers got machines ...'
'There's no mending any more.'
'And plastic's destroyed the fucking scrap game.'
'We're saulked if we camps anywhere ...'
'Except on these shitty fucking sites — for as long as they'll last.'
'We're persecuted from the cradle to the grave!'
'All things must change, I suppose ...'
'That's the certain truth and the truth needs no study!'
'And the worst mistakes is made in bed ...'

And ethnic cleansing is a fucking euphemism in which language disguises official violence — like holocaust and apartheid and clearances and final fucking solution. And Travellers over the years has been subjected to everything that could be thrown at us. Murder and enslavement and imprisonment and extermination and sterilisation and seizure of the chavvies and expulsion and laws restricting intermarriage and forced conscription and the banning of our languages and them all hoping we would just disappear altogether from the face of the fucking earth. And the travelling races is an ethnic minority — a mobile community surviving in a settled world. On the receiving end of an endless series of fucking bye-laws and acts of parliament and private bills and codes of good practice and all kinds of other legislation.

Hounded by town councils and district councils and county councils and borough councils and rural authorities and urban authorities and sanitary inspectors and agents and landowners and vigilantes and local residents' committees and an assortment of wobs and gavvers and muskras.

'They doesn't want us travelling, but they doesn't want us settling beside them neither.'
'The ould ones are used to fire and scared of electric. The young ones can't light a fucking fire but knows everything about computers.'
'And television is a tragedy!'
'What you never had, you never misses. But, once you've had something, you gets used to it.'

tribe

'Marry a big woman, Owen and live in a small trailer. That way you'll not need much furniture.'

'These sites killed the Gypsy way of life.'

'And more people rusts than wears out these days ...'

'Can't cook outside anymore ...'

'Can't travel anymore.'

'Young ones listens to that twipper music, goes to Gorgio schools ...'

'Don't know how to live on the roadside.'

'Don't need to fucking know that anymore!'

'Just moves from one site to another.'

'Won't even be able to do that soon ...'

'The Romany Roads is all gone.'

'We're like the American Indians on their reservations. They've taken everything away from us ... gradually, like a creeping death.'

'They should make us a country, like they did the Jews.'

'They couldn't give us a country, because we need the Gorgios.'

'We survives off them higglers.'

'Not for much longer.'

Should just come out with it and tell these pavs that there ain't never been no fucking common identity with us. No dream of a central unifying nexus of belief and heritage to unite Gypsies through time and space. But I don't.

And later on and half dibby I wanders home. Up through the south Salford area of town into the evening breeze that carries with it the smell of snow from the northern regions of this little spinning-top world. At last along Anchorage Quay and stick the key in the front door of the flat. Poke the dead fire with the toe of a boot and collapse into a chair. Never mind making tea. Too tired.

Thoughts running back a hundred years to the hopfields and hazel branches of the bender tents and 'tilters and the roadside verges and the broomdashing and colourful vardas drawn along at a leisurely pace by the little banners and the gift of the gum-sha-lack. Head dropping and eyes half-closed and don't even notice the soft little paws of sleep stealing.

5

Muffled voice niggling away at the back of my brain. Can't tell where the fuck it's coming from. Open the eyes slowly to see Ann standing over me with a shaking hand on my shoulder. Fire out and feet on the cold floor. Head spinning slightly and heart sunk.

'Circling rooks is for rain, but the tawny owl calls for a starlit night and a morning fair....'

'What are you talking about, Owen?'

'It's you ...'

'Of course it's me. Who else would it be?'

'I must have been dreaming.'

'Sounded a bit sinister to me. What did you do today?'

'Make some tea and I'll tell you.'

Sink back into the chair and scowl at the dead grate. Ann putting the kettle on to boil up for a cup of weed. It's the only fucking thing at times like this. She bounces back in from the kitchen.

'Well?'

'Well what?'

'Tell me.'

'Learned a lot about horses.'

'Owen ... talk to father ...'

'They've taken me on regular-like.'

'Owen ...'

'Want me to come back to the old life.'

'Make your own bloody tea then.'

'Wait, Ann ...'

'No.'

'I'm pulling your leg ...'

With hero's hands. Ann looking alluring in her business suit and short skirt and hair pinned back behind her head. And maybe I could still pull some satisfaction from the jaws of this grey little bastard day. Amazing how quick you can fucking recover. But it's only early evening and not nearly time for that sort of thing. Father would go wild if he found out she was fucking before dinner. So put the hands back in their place until the appointed hour approaches and then we'll do it in the time-honoured Tinker way — in front of the fire.

'You won't go back to them, will you, Owen?'

'On my mother's scapulars.'

'Then why not have a chat with father?'

'I'll think about it.'

'Will you, Owen? Will you?'

'What about the weed?'

'Why don't we go out and get something to eat?'

Ann looking at me with her smiling eyes which she knows I'm a sucker for. Maybe we're not really meant for each other. Perhaps we should pursue separate and quite distinct directions in our speeding little lives. Meet up again in fifty years' time and confide to each other all our regrets. But I'm a firm believer in the opinion that opposites attract. And I'm in now far deeper than you'd naif in a pitchmot. Her voice driving the doubting-Thomas thoughts from my mind.

'Where shall we go, Owen?'

'Rose and Crown.'

'No!'

'Why not?'

'That O'Connell will be in there — and those filthy Tinkers. Sorry ...'

'Seems suitable enough to me.'

'Let's go somewhere we haven't been before. New ground ... let's be symbolic.'

'Don't like the sound of that word.'

'Somewhere quiet.'

Can't trust these fucking quiet places. Makes you say things you regrets when once again you finds yourself in a

tribe

crowd. But Ann insisting and I'll go with her because she's nice to know and she loves me in her own way and I loves her in a way which is as close as I can get to the Gorgio she wants me to be.

'Not too fucking expensive though ...'

'My treat.'

'What's the catch?'

'Oh, I want paying back.'

'When?'

'Later tonight.'

'With interest?'

'Lots.'

Star and Garter Steak House up in a street off the city centre. Never been near the kip before. Only place would take us at such short notice. Bit on the pretentiously fucking posh side for me. And the cunts can somehow tell I'm a Tinker. See them whispering behind their hands and shaking their heads and pointing at Ann as if to say what's a respectable young woman doing with a dirty diesel-head like him. Considering whether to let me stay or not and Ann's superior demeanour saving the day. Looking down on the manager who comes across with a septic smile and enquiring after our requirements. And I hates this kind of cryptic discrimination. Come out with it straight and keep the fucking opinions where they should be. In the open. So that we all knows where we stands. Otherwise slide off and say fuck-all.

Manager speaking American with a Liverpool accent and the waiter cunt saying your table will be ready in a few minutes — sir. Would you like to have a drink at the bar while you wait? Of course we fucking would and what will you have my little loppet?

'Dubonnet and lemonade, with a cherry please.'

'You heard that barkeep ... and a pint of Guinness with a pickled onion.'

'No Guinness, sir.'

'Why the fuck not?'

'Not much call for it here, sir.'

'What sort of a fucking pub is this?'

'Its a restaurant ... sir.'

'He'll have a whisky.'

'What kind of whisky, madam?'

'Famous fucking Grouse.'

'Dubonnet and lemonade and a whisky ... madam.'

'Thank you.'

'And don't forget the cherry, you cunt!'

Barman sneering. Dicky-bow round his neck and half the fucking till in his pocket. Hesitates before getting the drinks. Places the glasses on the counter with a well-practised flourish.

'Dubonnet with lemonade and cherry for madam. Whisky for sir. Six pounds please.'

'How much?'

'And that doesn't include the service.'

Cunt would milk fucking pigeons! Count out my change on the counter. Five pounds seventy ... eighty ... ninety. Took me a fucking hour to earn this today. Ann saying in a low voice she'll pay. But the higgler already sniggering and I'm not starting all over again.

'Thank you, sir. That didn't include the service.'

What the fuck is he on about now? Why doesn't he piss off with his frown and his inflated fucking prices? Ann kicking me in the shin.

'What was that for?'

Ann with another kick and the ponce-faced cunt still standing there. Waiting for his wages. A whisper.

'You're supposed to give him a tip.'

'I'll give him a tip on the fucking ear ...'

Cunt quickly withdrawing to the other end of the bar with his face frenzied. That didn't include a tip he says back at us — louder than he needs. Everybody in the place looking. I'll crack open the bastard's scull and dance on his small fucking mind.

'Don't make trouble, Owen.'

'Listen to him shouting ...'

The waiter returning in the nick of time. Cloth over his arm and a walk that could be used to follow funerals.

'Your table is ready now, sir.'

'He doesn't tip!'

Another roar from the glibby shite behind the bar. I'm going to pull out the cunt's teeth with his arsebone. Ann

tribe

grabbing my arm and the waiter retreating with a double-
time quick march and a fearful frown.

'Don't show us up, Owen.'

'Its that fucking yawney ...'

'You should have tipped him.'

'Why? Will he come out to the clover field tomorrow and
pass me a pound?'

'Just leave it.'

All right Ann. Anything for a bit of peace and soft-pedal.
In we goes to the wooden tables and the light soft as a
sedative. Imitation log-cabin effect but with all the comforts
of cupidity. Big tank of tropical fish on one wall. Old
flintlock guns and assorted swords and daggers on all the
others. Trying hard for the American frontier look. With a
stuffed bison head behind the bar and other animals of
obscure origin on pedestals in crouched corners. Stars and
stripes forever and despite all the propaganda I knows well
the gunslingers and godfearers are just as bad as the
fucking Indians. Maybe even worse. Where will all the shite
end?

'It's nice in here, Owen.'

'Bit primitive for the fucking prices.'

'Stop being so grouchy.'

'Where's that waiter cunt got to?'

'Mind your language, Owen!'

'He's ignoring us.'

'Owen ...'

'Hey, you!'

'Yes, sir?'

'Can we have something to read while we're waiting?'

'Certainly, sir. Here's a menu.'

And one for madam. And see if you can keep that ignorant
escort of yours under control dear because we have some
sensitive people in tonight. Who tip us well for our trouble.

'What do you fancy my little flipput?'

'We'd get arrested.'

'Disgusting beor. Has you no morals?'

'Morals are for the mealy-mouths!'

'And there was me thinking it was something to do with
the law and order.'

Ann hugging my arm and a light kiss on the cheek. Feel the blood cooling down as the whisky warms my soul. Maybe this fucking place isn't so bad after all.

'I'll have the roast duck, with creamed cauliflower and croquettes.'

'Steak and chips for me.'

'Oh Owen ... where's your imagination?'

'With your morals.'

'What about a prawn cocktail to start with?'

'You knows I hates fucking fish.'

'It's not fish.'

'Yes it is.'

'What do you want then?'

'Chicken noodle soup.'

'Oh Owen!'

Green velvet curtains on the small-paned windows. Dark outside and the sound of rain on the bottle-bottom glass. Can't take you anywhere Owen. But you do Ann — you do. All along this primrose rackway that runs through the cosh of life and leads to the white marbled altar.

And where that path began I can't remember now. Somewhere back there is a marker on the turnpike between the open roads and my little flat. And I knows now there's no fucking going back. Heritage and history fades fast in the swirling mainstream of this gobbling grunting hog of a world. I knows that eventually I'll step finally over the line you've drawn on the ground. To the bright Gorgio grass on the other side.

'Hey, you ...'

Waiter avoiding my eyes. Cunt's ears closed to my call. The dummel-mop discriminating against itself. Awful fucking ignorance!

'How about some service here?'

'Don't shout, Owen.'

Must shout to be heard in this lousy life. Must push and shove and barrack and fucking bite. Those who don't or won't will have it fucking done to them.

'Would sir like to order now?'

'If you've got nothing else to do.'

'Very good, sir.'

tribe

Taking our order with a twitch and a snigger at the chicken noodle soup. Very interesting sir. And would sir like some wine? Madam will have a bottle of your best Beaujolais. If you're fucking quick about it. And then a slinking side-step away to his little kingdom of the kitchen.

'Could do with another drink.'

'He'll be back with the wine in a minute, Owen.'

'He thinks I'm low-life shite, Ann. Be lucky if he comes back at all.'

'Wait ...'

Bounce back up to the bar. See the ponce-face down the other end telling every cunt that I don't tip. Finger in the air to catch the fucker's eye. Bastard sees me but turns away. Just about to bang the fist down hard on the counter when I sees something that makes me hesitate. Sly looking cunt in a crombie dinking in and it's as if Lucifer himself had landed. Followed by four pavs with broken noses and 'blackguards' tattooed across their frowns.

Manager appearing nervously from his office and passing an envelope to the coat. Who nimbly counts a wad of notes and then quickly into an inside pocket. They whispers together with a lot of head nodding from the manager. Then turning they walks my way. As they approach it's as if the room grows darker and a distant rumbling noise comes nearer until it's not a noise at all but a hoarse voice saying. Savages! Time definitely to make myself fucking scarce. Ann scanning nervously round for the worried waiter as I returns to the table.

'No food yet?'

'It won't be long now, Owen.'

'That's what the man said when he cut the dog's tail.'

Wonder why some higglers decides to become skivvies and scullions. But then aren't we all — in one fucking way or another? That manager looks positively on the perverted side. Can imagine him standing in his raincoat. With trouser-legs tied with twine and climbing no further than his fucking knees and tie and shirt terminating under his armpits. Waiting for some beor to abuse him with her eyes.

No wonder the world's in such a fucking state. With politicians practising what they preach against and all the upper echelons of the civilised world thinking with their pricks. And the fucking clergy too! Maybe someone will create a party political penis to stuff up the holes of all hypocrites. Ten more minutes and still no sign of fucking dinner. In the meantime the maulers has been seated at a discreet table and served straight away.

'Prawn cocktail for madam.'

And a snigger for sir. Foot out and over the cunt goes. Slip sliding with the chicken noodles held high over his head. A stagger and then a sprawl across the next table. Arse in the air and face in the food. I'm looking all innocent and oh dear, how the fuck did that happen? Waiter what have you done with my soup?

Commotion at the next table. Frozen peas on the floor and look out you clumsy cunt. Waiter apologising and wiping and scraping and get the manager you dog's bollocks and what the fuck's that all down my wife's best dress? Chicken noodle soup sir. Manager mortified to the scene. If sir and madam will just wait a minute or send me the cleaning bill and don't worry — our fucking solicitor will. Manager's puss purple and screaming clean up that mess you little cunt. Cushti feeling returning as the last of the Scotch slides slowly down. Ready now for a taste of this wicked little wine.

'Wasn't that exciting siúcra?'

'Owen ...'

'Yes, Ann?'

'Why do they keep staring at us?'

'Who?'

'Those over there ... at that table in the corner.'

'Castes in the eye, I thinks.'

Slippery Sam finished now his mopping up and over at the kitchen door telling the manager that an object which felt very much like a foot was thrown deliberately into his path. With the definite intention of causing chaos. Roll a cigarette while I'm waiting for the main course. Forget altogether about the fucking soup. Now needed as evidence. Ann frowning down at the tobacco tin and also the black stains of tarmac and diesel oil and donkey shite in the wrinkled rolls of my knuckles. Which just won't be washed out with any amount of Swarfega.

'Couldn't you have bought some proper cigarettes?'

'These is proper cigarettes.'

'You know what I mean.'

'I doesn't.'

'It looks cheap.'

'I am cheap.'

'You're just looking for an argument, Owen ...'

'I'm looking for my fucking dinner.'

'You're ruining the evening.'

'Fuck the evening, for that matter.'

'I saw you trip the waiter.'

'You definitely did not!'

'I don't know what's wrong with you ...'

'It could be the old question.'

'What question?'

'Whether to fart now or hold it 'til I gets home.'

'Don't be so vulgar.'

'Don't be so fucking virtuous.'

'Can't you have just a little self-respect?'

'Why should I?'

'Don't shout!'

'Why shouldn't I?'

'I won't be shouted at!'

'I won't be sneered at!'

Manager cunt interrupting across my shoulder. Is something the matter madam? Grab him immediately by the bent down bow-tie. Only a fucking clip-on and coming away in my hand. A startled retreat with his black dickey-bow being flung after the cunt across the floor.

'Good-bye, Owen!'

Manager returning just as Ann makes her exit. Cunts from the corner table with him except for the crombie who sits there smiling. Done it this fucking time. Wait for me Ann. I'll behave in future and promise only to offend those gobshites who needs it — for their own fucking good. But she's gone!

Fist up quickly into the manager's face. Scream stifling in the cunt's throat as his teeth bite into my knuckles. Attack always the best form of defence — learnt that at a very early age. Rest of the bastards closing in and customers in all directions scampering for safety. Time I thinks to say my prayers. Grab an antique sabre from the wall and swing it round the head shouting. Get back you fucking gruntys! Then a crunch of glass breaking off the bone. Feel something warm running down the back of my neck. Beaujolais or blood?

Days can sometimes disappoint no matter how hard you tries. And people can turn like snarling dogs on the innocent bystander. See the mouthy grin of one of the maulers through the haze — as he tries to break my clutching fingers with a chair leg. A siren sounds somewhere in time and I slips easily out of the trap and into the dark gentleness.

6

Wobs uncommonly decent about it all. Seems they're used to trouble at the Star and fucking Garter Steak House. Not as reputable as it would like people to believe. Had my head patched up for me at the hospital and then starry for the rest of the night. For my own protection the wankers told me — but I can't seriously think why. Out on the mizzle morning with no charges pressed. Made me miss work with the Blackberry though. Which is certainly no way to create a good impression. Went down earlier onto the site to make amends. Dark scowl out from under the cunt's hat but saying he'll give me one more chance to turn up — on Monday.

No sign of Ann. Missing her usual Friday after-work visit to organise the weekend. Maybe she's finished with me for fucking good. Couldn't blame her for that. And if she has what can I find to fill out the little vacuum in my heart that's left behind? The clock striking seven and just can't wait any longer. Off down to the Rose and Crown to see that cunt O'Connell.

'Another Guinness there.'

'Make that two.'

'Owen — what happened to your head?'

'Had a meal that didn't fucking agree with me.'

'Where's Ann?'

'She's fell out with me for some reason.'

'Jaysus ... sure, in that case we better have a few drinks.'

'Not too much for me, Con.'

'Why the fuck not?'

'Yud ain't up to it.'

'Do your head a power of good man. Two large whiskies as well there!'

This is almost like the old days. When O'Connell and his crew first hit town. Fresh off the Holyhead ferry. A fiver between them and plenty of hard fucking neck. Determined to make their fortunes in this land of diminishing assets — and a demolition man's dream. Met him first when I was on the knock for scrap at some redundant factory and he was blowing down the chimneys. He took to me because my daddy was an Irishman. I liked him because it was still sometimes possible to see the gasúr-beag soul looking out from behind the big-man eyes.

O'Connell got on well. Because his uncles had taught him a few tricks with the fucking gelignite which some people said were definitely dubious and couldn't have been learned legally. Bought his own big house over in Lord Byron Square which he calls the Hilton and where he rents out rooms to men who are now as he once was. Strangers in the new world and homesick for the hornpipe and the huckster.

'Two more pints of Guinness there!'

'And the whisky Owen, don't forget the whisky.'

But I loves the man despite his obvious flaws. And I daresay he sees only too well the crooked little glimes in me. Friendship is a peculiar thing. We has nothing in common. Who could ask for more? So as this night nudges on I'll squander my hard-earned airgead and drink the health of various lost fucking causes. I mean you must above all else get your priorities right. Otherwise you're definitely fucking done for.

'Last orders now please!'

'Christ, is it that time already?'

'Drink up there, Owen, and let's go.'

'Where to, Con?'

'Downtown ... the Blue Bullet.'

O'Connell hopping from his stool. The great orange giant that other pavs moves aside for. Stern disapproval of my hesitation showing in the bunched brick-red brows.

tribe

'What the fuck's up?'

'Must be getting old, Con.'

'Well, I'd rather not join you, Owen. So ... I'll be off.'

'Wait!'

'That's more like it.'

Into the China Garden first for half a ton of egg fried rice. In a tin bath. Oh and a pair of fucking oars. Dainty little Chinese girl behind the counter. Looking anything but inscrutable and wondering about these two half-drunk half-mad occidental idiots.

'Crispy pancakes Owen, must have the crispy pancakes.'

'And a hod-full of chicken chopsuey.'

Sitting at the green checked table cloth and feeling cushti. O'Connell laughing like a disordered bull through a cloud of cigarette smoke. At least they don't look for fucking tips in here. Food coming quickly and O'Connell clapping his hands like a big spoilt chavvy. Never mind them chopsticks and just give me a coke shovel because Owen I'm so hungry me belly thinks me fucking throat is cut. Sweet and sour sauce staining his whiskers and the rice spilling over onto the tiled floor. Horse into it there Owen! Horse into it! Don't mind if I does Con. And later out belching again into the evening and across to the Blue Bullet.

'How much to get in these days, lads?'

No immediate reply from the bouncer bastards looking us up and down. These cunts ain't the new-look fully licensed 'door supervisors' you have down London at the Hippodrome and the Higoshiter. These is just the old-fashioned skin-and-hair-flying fuckers. Stand up straight O'Connell. Show them you're a respectable Irish gentleman out for a pleasant evening on the town. Seven pounds apiece says the biggest and ugliest cunt in his black suit and bow tie.

Iron behind the velvet! In we goes and down the dark stairs. Lights low and blood red and a topless hoor taking coats at the bottom. Look but don't touch and is that a crombie hanging in the cloakroom? Blast of smoky air as we swings in through the doors. Pushing past the hot sweaty crowd to the bar. Voices all around. Indecipherable like Babel. You can tip 'em here if you wants — but they don't ask.

'Two pints of Guinness, pal.'

'No Guinness.'

'Not again!'

'What about lager, lads?'

'Fucking piss.'

'Have that if you want.'

'I can't believe this cuntin' place ... not even bottled Guinness?'

'Might be a few somewhere. Cost you though.'

'Find 'em and give us four.'

'And a couple of whiskies.'

O'Connell sending me to scout round for a table. And some talent as well Owen while you're at it. Comedian up on the small stage. Telling dirty jokes to the few listeners at his feet. Rest of the cunts telling their own. Talent in this place charges cash. Here comes the drinks.

'Twelve quid!'

'How much?'

'Told you the bottles cost more.'

'We don't want to keep 'em. You can have the fuckers back when we've drunk the beer.'

'Comedian's on the fucking stage, mate.'

'Bloody catch-penny kip.'

Barman with a shrug of the shoulders hopping up to the hidden till. Seven pounds for the club and a fiver for himself. O'Connell passing the booze back to me and wiping the beer off the wet bar top with the sleeve of his jacket as he goes.

'Well?'

'Well what?'

'See anything?'

'Not yet ...'

'Wait a minute ...'

'What is it, Con?'

'Jaysus fucking Christ, Owen — it's Patsy!'

'Patsy who?'

'Keenan. You don't know him. Met the cunt coming over here all them years ago. He went on down to London because he had a bit of business there and I never seen the fucker since. Oh, a quare hawk Owen. Knew his way around all right.'

'How can you tell it's him, after that length of time?'

'Never forget a forehead. It's him all right.'

'Wonder what he's doing in this dive?'

'I intend to find that out, Owen.'

O'Connell disappearing across the dancefloor. Guinness in one hand and whisky in the other. Swallowed up by the coalescing crowd. Let him fuck off. Comedian finished his turn in the limelight and the band now playing a few soft songs. People dancing. There's a chair. Get the arse down onto it quick before some other slag.

'Hi there, Owen.'

'Peggy ...'

'It's been such a long time, Owen. Who's with you?'

'Nobody. What about you?'

'Just a couple of girlfriends, but they won't be back for a while.'

'No?'

'Dancing.'

'Oh!'

'What happened to your head?'

'Had a nightmare and fell out of bed.'

'Don't tell me then.'

Little girl laugh. Come and get me. All right pretty Peggy who I hasn't seen since Collins left town. Works now at the Marks and Spencer shop. Ladies lingerie last time I heard. We went once to the same primary school. Delicate walker. Tantalising talker. Always the prettiest angel in the Christmas play. Finger with a dainty flick and fag ash falling. Eyes smiling across at me.

'I'll get you a drink ...'

'That's very nice of you, Owen ... a Malibu and pineapple please.'

How very chic altogether! Not really. Never heard of that one before. Where have you been Owen? Outside the mainstream of society by the sound of things. Back up to the counter and barman a large tijuana and applejack. With ice and lemon and all the trimmings and none of the fucking sarcasm. Put some butter on my tongue that even the passion won't melt. Then grow me a pair of wings to fly back with.

'That all right?'

'Tastes wonderful. Thank you, Owen.'

'Any sign of the girls?'

'Not yet.'

'Maybe they've run away and left you.'

'Ha ha. How's Ann?'

'Ann who?'

'I heard you were getting married.'

'Who told you that?'

'Nobody in particular.'

'He's a fucking liar!'

'Who?'

'Nobody in particular.'

So here you are again Peggy. Sitting beside me after all the long time no see. I'd almost forgotten your face and we never was lovers — before.

'Still living in Collins' flat, Owen?'

'It's my flat now.'

'How's he doing down under?'

'Never hears from him. Don't you?'

'What do you think? Probably afraid I'd follow him out there.'

'And would you?'

'I might.'

'Not all its fucking cracked up to be.'

'How would you know?'

'See how many of them cunts is over here.'

'You sure you've heard nothing from him, Owen?'

'Not a frash. Why didn't he take you with him?'

'Bastard didn't even tell me he was going. One day he was here, the next ... he was fucking gone.'

'Always a bit on the impulsive side.'

The band being good to me and playing now a slow dance for convenience. Baby baby. Honey honey. Sugar sugar. And all the rest.

'Like to dance?'

'I'd love to, Owen.'

'Collins won't mind.'

'Who's worried?'

Out onto the dancefloor. Coloured lights spinning overhead like fireflies. Kaleidoscope of kismet. Arms all

tribe

around Peggy's perfume. Hers lightly on my shoulders. Squeeze a little just to test the temperature. She squeezes back. Smell her hair like sugar — tastes like candy. Her thigh easing in between my legs. Gentle pressure causing a titupping in the fucking trousers. Growing bigger all the time. Stop it Peggy or we'll have to stay like this all fucking night. Dance dying and the lights going up again. Walks in front of me back to the chairs. Now borrowed by some other besoms. Have to fucking stand.

'I'd better find out where the girls are.'

'What for?'

'I need a lift home.'

'I'll get you home, Peggy.'

'Will you, Owen?'

'And another acapulco and crabapple?'

'That would be delightful.'

'Like yourself.'

Band finished its turn and a stripper now on the stage. Bending over in front of me I can see right up her hole. Can't get rid of this fucking horn and somebody pushing from behind. Bullrushing the crowd at the bar and the willy-jill directly in front wondering what the fuck's this thing sticking in his leg.

'Hey! What's going on?'

'Sorry ...'

'You a fucking shirtlifter or something?'

'Got the horn looking at the stripper.'

'Well, stick it somewhere else.'

'I surely hopes to.'

7

'I thought you meant *my* home, Owen.'
'And look where the thought left you.'
'This place hasn't changed much.'
'Be a crime to alter the ambience.'
'Curtains could do with a wash.'
'Collins would cry at the very idea ...'
'What would Ann say?'
'Not bothered too much. Calls it poky.'
'I meant about me.'
'She's very broadminded.'

Poke some life into the fire first. Coax a little warmth into this room. Then poke Peggy. At least that's the plan. Can't get this fucking horn to go away. Must be the Guinness. Only one way to get rid of it. Peggy I will kiss your adorable arse if you let me ease away this bodolula between your lovely legs.

'I'd like a cup of coffee, Owen.'
'At this hour?'
'Warm me up.'
'I can do that.'
'And get me in a good mood.'
'Black or white?'

Bang about in this kitchen looking for kettles and cups and spoons and sugar and shite. Never be able to come to terms with a woman's way of thinking. Thank God tomorrow's Saturday. Or is it Sunday? Long as it's not fucking Monday.

When I comes back the fire's ablaze and Peggy stretching in front of it on the mat. She pats the place beside her and says come Collins and make me feel at home. After a sip of the coffee slipping off her shoes. The buttons of her blouse opening by themselves. and the skirt zipper sliding down noiselessly and unaided. Moving to me — with warm hands from the coffee cup inside my shirt. Down onto the mat and her pink lips on my eyes and ears and my head full of Christmas angels and the fire turning to rainbow. Did she call me Collins? Not caring as her breasts caresses my chest and she whispers something indecipherable in my ear. Then turns her body to take hold of my hummeler with her candyfloss hands and guide it through the lucious lips and white teeth onto the licking tongue. Another delicate twist and her legs are around my neck. Urging my face up into the secrets of her woman's body. Satin holster for my gun and God save the King of Ireland and the Queen of England.

Pretty Peggy. There's dozens of cunts in the alleys and Collins is at the other side of the world not knowing what he's missing. And I'm here at the centre of the Earth and the street corner of the Universe.

Her thighs glisten and cover my ears so that the silent noise of passion becomes deafening and I gulps in mouthfuls of air and hair and the juice of Genesis. Feel myself coming already. Muscles in the prick pulsing and ready to pump the seed skywards. She knows it too. Can feel it in her felines. Releasing me and rolling over onto her back. Now my lovely little man! Don't need to be told twice.

Up into her. Pushing hard. Arms supporting underneath and the breath in short spasms. Groaning and moaning. Faces pressed together and tongues buried. Savage animals outside the window howling to get in. Birds screeching in the trees. Warning shot across her bows then the hot semen shooting. Fire! Fire!

Candy-coloured nails in my back drawing the blood. Angels we have heard on high sweetly singing. Muscles tensed into knots as the blue bombs blows up in my swirling brain. Then relax slowly. Slowly! Heavy heaving of the lungs and mouths snatching at the steamy air. Slower! Calmness

tribe

creeping and sanity slipping back slow. Slow! Lie together in the firelight room.

'Cigarette please, Owen.'

'Roll-up do, dear?'

'And a kiss ... for kindness.'

Roll off Peggy and roll up the tobacco. Light two cigarettes and watch her sucking in the smoke. Hope she got what she came for.

'Thinking about Collins?'

Little startled look in her eye. But then she turns away and drags hard on the cigarette. She smiles and the fire flames dances on her glowing face.

'Thinking about you.'

'Two-timer.'

'Call me a taxi-cab, Owen.'

'You're a taxi-cab.'

Hitting me a hard clout on the back of the head. And what's your hurry honey? She lies back and allows the blue smoke to curl up into the conscienceless room.

'Then how about a blanket?'

Beors is such complicated fucking things. O'Connell has gone off after Patsy Keenan and Ann's out there in the puke world systemising and synchronising. Tom Lee and Tolui and the rest of the Travellers is praying to their horse-god for Monday to come round quickly and deliver them from the civilised man's weekend. Collins is underneath the known world standing on his fucking head. Or maybe stone dead. And pretty Peggy lies here wrapped in a blanket in front of the fire. Still — don't think I'm complaining.

Daylight striking the outside of the glass. Key turning in the front-door lock. Who the fuck can it be at this hour? Wasn't expecting no company on this poggered Saturday morning. Look up from the floor to see Ann's ankles next to my nose.

'Why are you lying there?'

'It was cold in the bedroom.'

'And lonely, I hope.'

'What time is it?'

'Nine o'clock ... and where were you last night?'

What an unkind fucking question. Brain cells fighting for survival and she asks me things like that. Think carefully you cunt! Where was I last night? And sweet saviour of the Christian world tell me this. Where the fuck is Peggy?

'I went out with O'Connell.'

'I might have known. Put some clothes on, Owen, I could have been anybody.'

Maybe she nipped off home during the night. Or crept away blowing back a kiss before the dawn broke. And why oh why didn't I put the fucking bolt on the door? Not that it would have mattered much anyway. Maybe gave me time to hide — or pretend to be poodling.

'I'll make the coffee. You look as if you could do with some.'

Hope you're not in the kitchen Peggy. Or it was nice fucking knowing you. Stand up with this blanket wrapped all around me and oh God no! Women's clothes falling to the ground. Tights and other tiny things. She's still here.

The toilet flushing and it's too fucking late now to try to mummer it. Peggy standing in the bathroom doorway. Naked silhouette framed against the frosted glass and a husky voice saying Owen — we overslept! Sound of coffee cups smashing in the kitchen. Ann storming past and knocking me sideways into the cinders of the fire grate. I jumps back up with the arse covered in grey ash and tries to grab her arm.

'Ann ... wait ...'

'Get away from me.'

'I had a few drinks and it's certainly nothing like what it looks ...'

Out through the front door onto the morning street. Running after her still wrapped in the blanket. She won't listen to a fucking word I say.

'Ann ...'

'I said, keep away from me, Owen!'

'It's not a serious thing ...'

'You two-timing insect.'

'She's not a bad lackeen ... you'd like her ...'

'Keep your Tinker talk for her. Is that where you found her ... on the site?'

'No. Look, come back and I'll introduce ...'

Turning on her toes and bringing a hard knee up full fucking force into my bigamist balls. Whole life flashing before my eyes. Blanket falling to the ground. She kicks it away with contempt — down the street in front of her fury. Can't straighten up to follow her — or the blanket. Crowd beginning to gather. Cunts staring and stone the fucking crows. Litchups laughing and pointing at my privates. Got to get back quick. Hobble up the street towards the flat. What was that fucking flash? Just in time to see Peggy sliding out through the front door.

'Peggy ...'

'Got to go, Owen!'

'Wait ...'

'Don't need all this publicity.'

Pushing her way into the crowd. Siren sounding. No fucking police please. Wide grin on the face of the chinless wob and what's going on here? I can explain everything officer.

'I certainly hope so, sir. Where do you live?'

'Just here.'

'Shall we go inside and get some clothes on?'

And let me see if I can straighten up first before you cunts beat me back down into a bent-over position.

'If youse can only escort me through the crowd ...'

Wobs not really interested in the whole truth of the matter. Only concern is to make an arrest and an example of some poor fucking suspect. Accuse me of being a New Age raver and any cunt can see I'm not. Try to reason with them but they won't listen to my lies. And finger wet finger dry cut my throat before I die!

8

Another wasted fucking day at the wob station — trying to explain. This time charged with obscene and indecent behaviour in a public place. Cunts tried to make out I was some sort of mugger or molester and asked me to let them take forty-two other offences into account in exchange for a more lenient sentence.

Told them I belonged to a sacred sect and was performing a religious ritual. Let me out after five hours of careful cross-examination. On the strength of my own surety and on account of me having a permanent address. Must get fast down to the Rose and Crown. Heart all a-flutter and a drink or two badly fucking needed to steady the nerves. Into the saloon bar and every cunt staring at me. What's the matter? Have I got two fucking heads?

'Owen!'

O'Connell up at the dart board — reading the late edition of the local liar which Ann's drotchel of a daddy owns. That's what's waiting for me if I gives in to her — flogging advertising space to all them cunts wanting to sell second-hand furniture and motors with fixed mileage clocks and redundant computers and dogs and cats and all sorts of other shite. Maybe she thinks I'd be good at it on account of being a dealer in the old days. A brandy please barman — as quick as you possibly can. Owen! And Jesus Christ O'Connell — don't shout! Fibres in a most sensitive state.

'You're a fucking celebrity, boy!'

'What's that?'

'See here ...'

God in his holy heaven! Some bastard had a camera and there's a picture of me on the front page. Ash all over the cheeks of my arse. Hands clutching battered balls and face twisted.

MAN EXPOSES HIMSELF ON ANCHORAGE QUAY!
POLICE RESPOND QUICKLY!

'You'll be famous Owen. They'll be round from the Sunday Sport to get the full and intimate fucking story. And if it's not interesting enough they'll invent their own colourful details.'

'Fuck off, Con! This is serious ...'

'It's hilarious.'

'I won't be able to show my face ...'

'Or your arse.'

'It's all your fault.'

'My fault? Listen, Owen, come over here into the corner ... where they can't all be gawking at you.'

'If you hadn't left me alone in the Blue Bullet, I wouldn't be in this predicament.'

'Oh now ... that's another story, Owen. But tell me yours first.'

Rat-eyes all around. Trying to look inside my soul. Shameless sniggers and evil excitement. Barman thinking of putting up a sign —

PHANTOM FLASHER DRINKS HERE!

Have the cunts coming from miles around to see. The dirty bastard!

'Reckon that's put the kybosh on you and Ann for good then.'

'You has a way with the understatement, Con.'

'Always said it's an ill wind ...'

Repressed laughter all along the bouncing bar. Hee-hees behind hands and sniggers and smirks and the odd horse laugh. Hey up there Owen! See your picture in the paper Owen! How's your bollocks Owen? Sod off you crowd of fucking cunts!

'Let's get away out of here, Con.'

Cheering as we gets to our feet. Some joker clapping. Give the cunt a hard clout. The rest of the shite-bags joining in with whistles and shouts.

'Ignore them all, Owen.'

And how am I supposed to do that? But it's dark outside now — thanks be to the good Lord. Turn the collar up just in case. Have to grow a moustache and a fucking beard. Shave my head to be on the safe side.

'Where do you want to go?'

'Home!'

'But it's Saturday night, Owen ...'

'Exactly!'

'I haven't told you yet what happened to me last night.'

'Will it cheer me up, Con?'

'It might. Let's go to the Leather Bottle.'

O'Connell can be a real fucking diplomat when he wants. Lights low in the Leather Bottle — not that it matters much. The place is so full of perverts and peculiar pimmocks that no one would even blink at what's happened to me. Most of them never seen a fucking newspaper in their lives. Except to wipe their arse with. Get me a brandy O'Connell — and tell me your sordid little story.

'Anyway, Owen ... Patsy remembered me. He took me into the back room.'

'Sounds right cosy.'

'Don't be a cunt. The back room at the Bullet's for friends — of the management.'

'Go on.'

'Well ... I'm sitting there with him, talking about the trip over all them years ago, when the next thing, a bottle of Scotch is plonked down on the table in front of us.'

'By who, Con?'

'Somebody behind me. Smelled like a woman.'

'That's no indication these days.'

'I don't like your insinuations, Owen ...'

'Sorry.'

'Anyway, we starts to horse into the Scotch ...'

'Just the two of you?'

'No, no. There's the manager and a few other lads there as well, all talking among themselves ... business and things.'

'What sort of business?'

'Business is business, Owen. Will you stop interrupting!'

'Just trying to get the picture.'

'Oh, you got the fucking picture all right.'

'Thank you!'

'"What are you into, Con?" says Patsy. "Oh, a bit of demolition and excavation and stuff like that," says I. "Really?" says he. "That's very interesting." It turns out anyway that Patsy is quite a big-fucking-shot up in London. Y'know, with the boys and all that.'

'What boys?'

'The *boys*, Owen. Them that runs things.'

'Jesus Con, don't go getting mixed up with them fucking cunts!'

'What are you talking about? I was just having a drink with a friend.'

'You only met him once ... years ago, on a boat on the Irish Sea.'

'Owen, will you listen — this lad's into everything. The whole lot. "Con," he says to me, "you got a woman with you?" "No, Patsy," says I. "Have one on the house," says he. The manager sends one of his boys out of the room and back he comes after a minute with three hoors — *three* Owen! And they were all nice, *very* nice. "Take your pick Con," says Patsy, "or maybe you'd like two?" "Christ almighty, Patsy!" says I, "Can I have one for my friend Owen?" "Owen who?" says he. "You wouldn't know him, Patsy," says I. "He's an Englishman. But he's all right. I'll go and get him." "Don't be long," says he, "I have to be off in a minute. If I'm not here when you get back, see Lionel" — that's the manager's name, Owen. "Lionel," says Patsy, "you look after my friend Con here — anything he wants, any time."'

'You're a fucking ruillefein!'

'Why?'

'You don't take presents from these fuckers.'

'Why not?'

'Are you a complete lederim altogether? You ends up owing them, that's why not!'

'It wasn't like that at all, Owen. Anyway, listen ... I couldn't find you. Searched everywhere. So I'm coming back across the dancefloor when I bumps into this cunt who's a bit pissed. He spills his pint and then gets lippy ... shouting and swearing like.'

'So, you hits him.'

'Not at all, Owen. I try to console him. The next thing I know, the pair of us are being hauled upstairs by the fucking bouncers and slung out onto the street. I try to explain that I'm a friend of the management's, but the cunts wouldn't listen.'

'They did you a favour, Con.'

'Owen, we missed out there. And you said yourself, you wouldn't be in such a mess now if you'd waited for me.'

'Probably be in a worse fucking mess!'

'Next time I go down to the Bullet, I'm going to see that lad Lionel and take advantage of Patsy's offer. You can suit yourself.'

'I will.'

'You've no right to cast aspersions on me, and you hanging around with them fucking Tinkers all the time.'

'I told you, I *am* a Tinker, Con.'

'Is that right? These days you don't know the fuck what you are, Owen.'

'They pays me honest money. That's all I needs to know!'

'But listen here for a minute ... they says these prostitutes are good, Owen.'

'They says that God's a black woman.'

'You're a miserable cunt!'

'You're a fucking fool!'

'Be a miserable cunt on your own. I'm away.'

'Slán leat!'

O'Connell downing his drink and away — with the door swinging in his wake.

He's right. I am a miserable cunt. Go home and get into bed. Bury my fucking head. Where I can hide from the shite-swagger of this wanker-world. Moon pulling the tide over me. O'Connell will die violently and I'll be a careless callous

I-told-you-so and snigger at his funeral when they throw the gun into the grave after him — and a picture of me in the nude.

Still only half past eight. So fucking early! Maybe Ann will come round tonight. Turn the key lightly in the lock and smother me with a pillow as I lie asleep and dreaming of Peggy's pretty legs. Tomorrow's Sunday — day of rest. Badly fucking needed!

9

Sinister kind of silence all around and demon photographers lurking in amongst the shadows. Ready to leap out with their fucking flash bulbs and pop my picture.

Sunday was so refreshing! Staying mostly in bed. Nobody calling to see if I'm alive or dead. Watched some old films beamed all the way by the satellites across the oceans and allowed the thoughts to silently twipper inside my head. Finally coming to no concrete conclusions and falling into a frantic sleep.

See now the lantern of the paper shop with the shadowy creatures coming hump-backed out of the darkness for the news and fags and a packet of polo mints. Society is a mad dog snapping at my heels. Yesterday I locked it out. And although I was safe in my cloudaway it still snarled outside and scratched its summons on my door.

'Hey there, Owen!'

'Oh no!'

'Where the fuck did you get to on Friday, man?'

'Woolgoolgafuckingland!'

'Saw your picture in the paper.'

But couldn't read the caption underneath. Something I'm sure about sexual perversions. Go away Duck you cunt. Take your cant and your convictions and bury them half a mile up a horse's hole. I'm in no mood for the glad suffering.

'Did the Blackberry pass any comments?'

'Just turned his eyes up to heaven and said it didn't surprise him.'

Tyres screeching to a halt beside me and a head sticking out through the rolled-down window. Don't tell me it's the fucking press again. Now I knows what Princess Diana must have felt like. The Duck pulling at my arm as I turns my head away so's not to be recognised.

'Get in the back, you pair of fucking hug-a-days. We're late!'

Big Bill with his ears a-flapping and Jake with his eye blinking and Myles all smiles in the cab. Louis with a bright yellow hat in the back saying I sees Owen you're becoming a bit of a celebrity.

'Am I?'

'What was all that in the rocker rag?'

'A misunderstanding!'

'I'll fucking say.'

Change the subject quickly as we skims across the land to where the Blackberry is already waiting with foot tapping and thumbs a-twiddling.

'What kept youse?'

'Owen and The Duck.'

'Not me, Tom — only Owen.'

'You dog's bollocks wob-nark, Duck!'

At the clover field Tolui emerges from the tack-shed dressed in a red silk *deel* edged with gold filigree and tied at the waist by an orange *buus* which hangs down to the gleaming black leather Mongol *gutals*. He wears a blue silk *khada* round his neck and a pointed *janjin malgal* on his head and a haughty look on his face. Louis' eyes are green with envy as we boxes the pacer and loads the cart and harness onto the back of the pick-up.

Climbing with the Mongolian and Tom Lee into the Land Rover we all sets off again for the straight stretch of road near the town of Chelford. And as we covers the miles I feels as if I'm becoming part of something again. To be on the inside with my own kind must be better than being on the outside with the natchy strangers. Head full of confusions and contradictions and everything will all be irrelevant in the fucking end.

tribe

Tolui beside me on the back seat full of his finery and a grin breaking over his big teeth. Telling me he went to school under the Russian system back in Mongolia and can read and write the English which is more than most of these *mamlüks* can do. Agreed to come to this adopted country to make a fortune but so far seeing only heartbreak and homesickness. And is it true that the capital of your country is called Ukulele? Certainly not! Its called Ulaan Baatar which means red hero and I come from the Bulnaayn mountains to the north of Üliastay.

And it is a lucky country with gold and copper and cashmere and camels and many horses. And in the mountains are wild boars and wolves and snow leopards and elk and deer that see humans so seldom they are almost tame. And is it very warm there? Yes — in summer. But cold in winter. Worse than here? Much! Well I must say! You certainly learns something new every day. And the trees are eternal Owen, and the high hills are the axis of the world and the bridge between heaven and earth and the spirits of the mountains and the forests provide the people with everything they need.

And what Tolui does you think about these Travellers? They have lost their way and are no longer nomads — like my people. But they pay me well for my skills of horsemanship and soon I will be going back to my *yürt* and my herds and my small sons. And tell me this Owen *aanda* — what are you? I'm not sure.

The fields at the side of the road already half-full when we arrives. With vans and lorries and carts of all kinds. Some with portable tents set up and a bit of duckering going on alongside the bargaining and bantering and the shouts of bad cess to you and be-the-holy-man and a few fetichs being put on the heads of old enemies and wishing rings and fawnies bought and sold. Children running about with honey balls and potato cakes in their hands. Chased by crossbred lurchers and mad Manchester terriers. Myles saying Owen there's all sorts here.

Romanies trading with Tinkers and Pikies and Didecois dancing and Gypsies cursing in Gamon and a few of these New Age nuisances and others we can't even tell the origins

tribe

of — maybe Carpathians or the Kalderash or even some of the old Troglodyte Spanish. Cooking up clangers and hoddydods and some sipping jugs of shakles and jipper. All waiting for the racing to begin.

Tolui unloading Tom Lee's black horse and the rest of us taking the two-wheeled cart and harness from the back of the pick-up. Its light tubular frame and white-spoked wheels no weight or effort at all. Tom checking it over while Tolui shabbs the grai up and down the road for the spectators and bet-takers to see. Three other horses also trotting out along the carriageway.

Four goes in the first race and another four in the second and the best two out of both goes through to the final. Tom calls Tolui back and the horse is shut into the shafts and the trap harnessed up. Two moulders pulls across the road to stop any early-morning traffic and two more a mile or so further down at the finish.

'Have you put your bet on, Owen?'

'No ... where?'

'Over there. You'll get three to one on Tolui.'

'How much should I stake?'

'All you've got boy! All you've got!'

Taking out my last fucking twenty-pound note and looking at it before saying well. Easy come easy go. Tolui lowers himself expertly into the trap and takes up the whip and reins. His feet fixed in the wide stirrups and holding back the headstrong horse. The four pacer-carts lines up across the road and faces down the long straight mile to the finish.

A starting pistol fires and they pulls away fast. Neck and neck for five furlongs and followed by shouting cheering cursing hordes and the drivers lashing out at each other with their whips and trying to run each other off the road. A quarter-mile out and Tolui takes a slender lead. Our pick-up close behind and roars and shrieks from the cunts standing up in the back. Tom Lee already at the finish and leaping in the air with his hat flying into the nearest field as his horse crosses the line first. Followed close behind by a spotted Appaloosa.

The second race already started and heading fast in our direction. A palomino winning it by a short head from a piebald saddle-horse. The lorries at the start withdrawing into the field and allowing the light timorous traffic to pass once more. Same thing happening at the finish and soon the road is open again as if nothing has taken place. Except for the fucking and blinding of the bookmakers and the wailing of the losers and no attention whatsoever being paid to the objections of the unsuccessful owners and calls for stewards' enquiries and threats and shaking of fists. The four finalists taken away for a few minutes' rest and a little water.

Drivers limbering up and lashing down glasses of fáiche-fíon and the book-makers calling the odds for the final. Eighty fucking pound in my pocket already and this might be a good day after all. Them who thinks they knows about these things picking the palomino for favourite at a price of five-to-two on. Next Tom Lee's horse at even money and a little longer odds on the other two.

'What d'you think, Myles?'

'Put it all on, Owen.'

'All?'

'All!'

The trucks pulling back out across the road as the four grais line up for the final time. Pistol shot and away they flies with hearts in mouths and big money being bet and vehicles at high speed following the racer-pacers. Tolui taking up last position at four furlongs and Myles and the others screaming for him to move up. The Appaloosa getting entangled with the saddle-horse and its cart overturning — sending both drivers sky-diving down an embankment into the ditch below.

Tolui and Tom's black passing the driverless piebald after this unfortunate accident and only now the palomino to beat. Which is two lengths ahead and the same number of furlongs to the finish. Tolui leaning forward in the stirrups and saying something into the horse's ear. Animal immediately quickening its pace and pulling level with the leader. And for a brief moment Tolui becomes the horse and the horse becomes Tolui. They are one in time and space.

Half a furlong out and they're neck and neck with the crowds at the finish and those following as well going wild. Then with the lightest flick of his whip Tolui drives the black pacer on and the horse crosses the line with little more than the steam from his nostrils in front. And when the curses and swears and rows and ructions eventually die down — I pockets a hundred and sixty easy pounds after rising this merry morning with only twenty between myself and starvation.

'Not too bad a day after all, eh Owen.'

'Certainly not complaining, Myles.'

The Blackberry more than a little pleased with himself and paying out a fistful of fifty-pound notes to Tolui. The ebony pacer patted and kissed and packed away in its box for the journey home. Suddenly the sound of fucking sirens in the distance and a far-off flashing of blue lights in the cold morning air.

All bedlam immediately breaking loose. As if things weren't fucking bad enough before. Lorries cutting each other up and jeeps and cars and caravans and carts all crashing and colliding in their panic to get away from the wobs. Horses rearing and complete fucking chaos reigning all around me. And where the blue fuck has the other cunts got to? See the tail-end of Tom Lee's horsebox disappearing into the distance and no sign at all of the pick-up. Vehicles driving away at top speed and spraying gudgell and grai shite everywhere.

Suddenly I'm left alone — hands in pockets holding on tight to my bollocks and my hundred and sixty pounds. Standing in the middle of the road and scanning the horizon for a sign of the blue pick-up and the fucking gavvers about to grab me. Big bottle-green four-wheeler pulling up beside me and an urgent voice shouting. Prastie! No need to be told a second time and I looks now across from the speeding passenger seat to see Felix the Yella Lad Cashin and behind on the back seat his three little girls and Litzy, his lovely twilight wife. Soon we're too far away down the road for the wobs to catch and Felix relaxes his foot on the accelerator pedal.

'Well ... Owen, is it?'

'Aye.'

'How did you manage to get yourself left?'

'I don't know.'

'It's every man for himself when the wobs come. You got to be quick.'

'I knows that now.'

'Lucky for you we was late away. Couldn't find the youngest, she was playing with some of them Doran girls ... from down Wexford way.'

'Thanks.'

'What's it like living in a caer?'

'I lives in a flat.'

'Same thing.'

'Not exactly.'

All along the way home the fighting man loosening up a little and telling me he wants to get away from the road — for the sake of his girls. And he's matched soon in a bare-knuckle bout against the Irish King of the Tinkers. A man called Glasheen from Crossmaglen in the County of Armagh. And if I wins this Owen I'll make enough money to buy a bungalow and a bit of land and settle down somewhere near Manchester and send the girls to a good school. It has to be an already built house because even though the authorities is encouraging Travellers to buy their own land it's almost impossible to get any kind of planning permission and the cunts will confiscate your caravan now for a parking offence.

He says he's also trying to break into the legitimate fight business and hopes soon to meet with some men who knows the ropes. All the time his lovely *lózeczko* wife Litzy nods her silk head in agreement and Felix tells me she's a true Romany and he met her in a settlement on the river Siret in the Carpathians when he was over there in Eastern Europe doing a bit of dealing and travelling on the tarmac. And it's rare for them to marry out of their race. Because he's an Irish Tinker — born on the side of a Longford road and left because of the persecution and poltroonisms and anyways Owen all Travellers is one. There's really no difference between us.

'Why does you want to settle, Felix?'

'I told you Owen, for the chavvies.'

'But what about you ... and Litzy?'

'We'll adapt. Anyway, we're fed up with the harassment from the Gorgios.'

'They're not all bad.'

'Most. You knows yourself ... they puts us onto sites and then expects the place to look like a holiday camp. But it's not a holiday camp ... we're not on holiday. Trading and tarmacing is our way of life. I sees some caers so full of filth they ain't fit for a dog to live in. My trailer's fit for the Prime Minister to come stay. Just because we looks dirty sometimes we's classed as dirty. You knows well, Owen, that we believes if a thing or a man is clean on the inside, there's no need to worry too much about the outside.'

'I knows that ...'

'Does you still, boy? You can't put a sign up saying no black people, or you'll be done good and fucking proper. But you can put a sign up saying no Travellers.'

Felix with a frown talking like my dead daddy about the old days when it was worse. With the cunt-bag vigilantes saying all Travellers had polio and we was cannibals and child-stealers and the swede-gnawers and candle-eaters coming down at night with their guns and fucking petrol bombs. And people Owen don't mind Gypsies if they looks pretty with horses and vardas — not with trailers and tarmac and scrap. But we've always been treated like bloody beggars and killed and kicked around. That's mostly because Owen we've never had no leaders. So its every man to look after his own little family.

A silence falls in the four-wheeler for the rest of the road home. Felix looking straight ahead and concentrating on his driving. The girls asleep in each other's arms on the back seat. And me occasionally gliming in the rear-view mirror. The dark eyes of the Romany woman.

10

Fairy lights flickering as I walks up through the gaytime town. And a giant Christmas tree in Ordsall Park all covered in tinsel. Worrying worm of conscience chewing away at the back of my mind — telling me I must go see my little mother sometime over the holiday. But first get this final working day out of the way.

The whole hatchintan swimming in seasonal spirit by the time I gets there. Every cunt larking about and looking forward to the sweet yule-tide yogs and some getting ready to move out and visit other parts of the world for Christmas. The Blackberry already taken off for a place called Pencarreg in the coshes of the Welsh hills with his wife and his trailer and taking also a few horses for the trading.

So today we must work with the Cashin boys on the tarmac. Big double driveway which has already been dug out and now needs only the base of hard-core and skelpings to be whacked down and then the hot tarmac spread and rolled. Felix out in front leading the way and Myles driving a Leyland lorry in his wake with the spreaders and shovels and barrows and rollers and red diesel. Sense of security getting stronger all the time in me. Maybe my mother was wrong after all.

Maybe I belongs here with these misunderstood pavs. Airgead ain't too bad and the familiarity of the past few weeks keeping my spirits up and breeding a kind of congruity. But deep in my heart there's an uneasy feeling that one day I'll wake up and the cunts will have disappeared. Fucked off somewhere. Leaving me alone in the Gorgio world with no one but Ann and O'Connell to keep me company.

Still — lately I've been trying to keep out of trouble and at present there's only one dirty drop in the bucket. Been sent up for trial in April on account of pleading not guilty to the charge of gross indecency. A nice fucking present for the coming year. Haven't seen Ann since the incident. Nor Peggy!

My father was an Irish Tinker-man who found English towns threatening and who never all his life rode in a taxi. Too stubborn to settle on these filthy foreign council sites and too proud to admit to the defeat that time has in store for us all. Dragging his small woman of a wife away from her roots along the Galway seaboard after bearing him his first and oldest son. Then siring two more fucking Sassenachs to ensure for her the burning of all boats and a broken heart.

'What's that, Louis?'

'Rum, Owen.'

'No whisky?'

'Got some blood.'

You ungrateful fucking natchy. Pass the bottle round the lorry cab and lash this dark spirit of the sea into the cold wambs. A good swig for me. Even if I does have a preference for the malt.

'Not too much boys. Felix will go ruille.'

'Fuck Felix!'

'Tell him that to his face, Jake.'

Rum quickly running out as Black Jake takes the bottle and won't give the cunt back. A wrestling match between himself and Louis in the cab of the moulder. Making Myles swerve and almost crash on a couple of occasions.

'Stop 'em, Owen!'

I gets in the middle and finally manages to pull the cunts apart. Myles screaming that the Yella Lad will break their fucking heads and this fetich finally bringing them back to their senses.

At this ould lad's driveway at last and we unloads in the now drizzling rain and begins to pound down the mixed base of hard-core and skelpings. Three whacker plates on this job. Louis and Black Jake having a duel with two of them and Big Bill vibrating on the third. Myles Cashin supervising and shouting and Felix saying come along with me Owen. To the tarmac yard.

We takes the empty moulder and travels down to the láithreán where we needs to have loaded twenty ton of the tarramhacadam.

Daddy died suddenly. Some said it was a stroke. Others had their doubts and said he had his head broken in a brawl outside a public house. I was too young to remember much about it. Fucking priests wouldn't let us bury him around his homeland area near Lough Key in the county of Roscommon — so mother had to put his body in this gudgell English ground. To poison all the fucking maggots. Felix handing me a half-bottle of Scotch.

'Take a deoch, Owen. Keep out the could.'

Daren't tell him about the rum. Slug down the hard stuff and hand the bottle back. He takes a deep drink himself before we finds ourselves inside the yard office full of men and malt liquor.

'What's all this?'

'Christmas, Owen boy.'

A mankey man merry and playing a mouth organ. Good King Wenceslas looked out. On the feast of stealing. Grab us a couple of them cans Owen. And how much do you need today Felix? Twenty ton. Be the holy man — a big job? Big enough. Today of all fucking days. And I hope you don't mind waiting for a short spell? Don't mind at all. Does we Owen? What about the others? Sure haven't they to whack down the hard-core. And anyway — let the cunts wait.

A little dance going on in the middle of the room. Hey there — givvus an ould song. Something we can all sing along with. But keep it seasonal. And get them empty beer cans up off the floor because we don't want the bosses to walk in and think. We're as uncivilised as we fucking look! Watched a film on television the other night which was a sort of saga about the ignorance and cruelty and hardship of some century long ago. Looked familiar and I'm sure I'd seen the fucking thing somewhere before.

tribe

Driving eventually back to the job half dibby and finding Big Bill kicking Louis up the hole with his steel toecaps and Myles trying to pry them apart and Jake standing back smiling and smoking a cigarette and shouting stash him on the fucking nook Bill! The Yella Lad jumping down from the lorry with me not so fast to get involved.

'Let him be, Bill.'

'He called me big ears.'

'You'll hurt him.'

'I'll kill the little cunt.'

'The ould man'll call the wobs. You'll end up in starry all over Christmas.'

'I don't give a shite!'

Taking the three of us to haul the big cunt away from the howling Louis. Shaking a shovel-like fist back over our heads as the little litchup picks himself up off the ground holding his yud.

'I think the big bastard broke something ...'

'Your fucking neck, I hope.'

'It was his own fault, Felix ...'

'That's the last time you're coming out with me, Louis.'

'What was it all about?'

'He can't stop fucking harlickin', Owen — that fucking Louis. He'll get himself well and truly poggered one of these days.'

And have you fucking cunts finished whacking down the hard-core? Of course we have. What about the skelpings? Ages ago. And what kept youse two? A queue at the tarmac yard Myles. I'm fucking sure. On me old mammy's life. She's dead! And if you'd come back on time this wouldn't have happened and we'd be finished the job. Well — we're back now so get the barrows and spreaders before the black stuff goes off on the back of the moulder.

Weather conditions taking a turn for the worse and the sleet beginning to sheet down. Hard to work in these cunting conditions. But the job must be finished now and Black Jake helping me to barrow the twenty ton from the small sluice gates at the rear of the tipped-up truck. Felix and Myles spreading the hot tarmac while Louis and Big Bill pushes the heavy rollers and washes down the wheels with red diesel and Louis with a smirk mouthing the word DUMBO every time the big man's back is turned. Felix letting us have a little sip of whisky every now and then to keep the blood flowing and the bastard weather at bay.

And afterwards when it's finished we wipes away the sleet and sweat from our eyes and the Yella Lad says well done you crowd of litchups and youse definitely deserve a bit of a bonus — as a Christmas box. So let's go get some grub and afterwards the wallop's all on me. Whoops and hollers and a clapping of hands as we falls into this cosy roadside café.

A race for the counter and see what's on the menu there. Turkey and all the fucking trimmings. Sprouts and roast spuds and big mugs of thick tea.

Sober the cunts up I suppose — if nothing else. Rain easing off outside the steamed-up windows. A timid little sun trying to cast its fretful shadows across the countryside.

And no matter how hard I try to hush it away the docity of dinking back with these cony-catchers looming up in my mind. Should I really become a part of their little community again and learn all over to expect nothing from the outside world and to act on the moment rather than make pathetic plans? Spit on the Gorgio cunts with their fucking caers and their court-houses and their awful fucking conceit? And everyone will know me from my silver and gold — and class me by what I carry. Back to the future? A new identity in the old amorphous brood — the doorstep third-world tribe? A plastic pav? Playing a little part in the economics of a hostile society — yet keeping apart from it? And houses is all right the old woman said. But they've got them terrible walls!

Halfway through the Christmas dinner a black Jaguar pulling up outside in the street. Two large cunts coming into the café followed by a crombie coat and calling Felix across. The rest of us watches in silence through the sinister whispers and shoulder clapping and arms raised and final handshakes. On the way out one of the cunts stops and stares down at me and I feels the room growing dark and a sound of screeching filling my ears as the redneck storcher says —

tribe

'Haven't we met somewhere before, mate?'

'I don't think so.'

But the cunt continues to stare down at me saying I never forget a face and I sees his mouthy grin once more through a haze of blood and broken fingers and the smell of fucking chicken noodle soup.

'Come on, Bernard!'

The grunty finally growling away. Looking back at me from the door. And Felix tells us the crombie coat is a local big-shite by the name of Lionel who has connections with the legitimate fight game. The Yella Lad badly wanting his chance in the regular ring and the big money bouts. And this fairyman Lionel is just the cunt to fix it all up. I hears O'Connell's voice calling across the crowded dancefloor. You're a fucking fool Owen — and a miserable no good Tinker. And a sudden shiver runs down my spine.

11

Christmas Eve at last and all the catchpenny cliphouses open late. Bright lights inviting you in to buy armfuls of beer and good cheer. And a present for your old mammy. Gangs of loud litchup louts pissing and sicking up public house walls. Fucked up in the afternoon on cocktails of smack and speed and strong lager. God rest ye merry gentlemen let nothing you this way. Pass by the girls giggling and throwing tinsel. Scatter some on me please. Get me in the mood to see what else is happening on this nippy little night. Besides the birth of the small Saviour. Walk across town under the cold stars. Feeck a look through the laughing windows of the pubs. Don't feel like going in just yet. Don't want either to be left outside.

'Owen!'

O'Connell's great horny fucking hand landing on my shoulder as I stands near the bright door of this unfamiliar establishment and gazes at the gaiety inside.

'What the fuck are you up to?'

'You frightened the fucking shite out of me, Con.'

'What's the idea ... standing here gawking in through that door?'

'Just thinking.'

'Bad for the bladder! Let's go inside.'

Coloured lights and warm heartedness. Boughs of holly over the optics and a kaleidoscope of expensive decorations dangling from the smoke-cloud ceiling. Mistletoe discreetly above the kissing couples and the whole place full of laughing yawneys. All talking with high-pitched unnatural voices.

'Had your Christmas drink yet, Owen?'

'Not in here ...'

'Neither have I. Barman! What about our Christmas drinks?'

'Haven't seen you two before.'

'Get your eyes tested then. I'm a fucking regular ... know the manager personally. Go and get him if you want, but you know what he's like when he's disturbed for nothing.'

'I'll take your word for it. What'll you have?'

'Brandy ... and make it a double. The same for my friend here.'

'He a regular too?'

'He's the manager's brother-in-law.'

'You're fucking joking ...'

'Sure, can't you see the resemblance?'

'Now that you mention it ...'

'And for your scepticism ... make them trebles.'

'You'll get me fucking sacked.'

'Very fucking likely.'

O'Connell with a wink and then away from the bar quickly with the brandy glasses swirling. A table in the corner well away from the prying eyes. A little island for just us two — in the laughing jostling spending sea.

'What's on the agenda then, Owen?'

'What fucking agenda?'

'It's Christmas Eve, man!'

'You decide, Con.'

'I'm for the Blue Bullet, after a few here first. That barman thinks I own the place.'

'Not keen on the Bullet, Con.'

'Not keen on anything lately, are you?'

'I'm all fucking right.'

'So is Jack.'

'Fair enough then ... the Blue Bullet it is!'

'Good man yourself!'

I promised my mother when I was six years old that I wouldn't drink as much as my daddy. And that I'd join the pioneers and become a tee-totaller for the rest of my natural life. But it's difficult to later keep the promises we makes when young and ignorant.

The manager of this strange little pub propelling himself with a great deal of drunken dexterity to our table. Beer trickling from the corners of the cunt's dibby mouth and all apologies for not being there to meet us when we came in. Hoping that bollocks of a barman treated us two gentlemen with the civility we deserve. Not too good with the names — especially on Christmas Eve. But then — it's been such a long time. And the dear wife? Oh most certainly in the pink of her prime. Extremely unfortunate that she's gone out for the last-minute items of shopping. And of course the cow will be annoyed beyond all control if her little brother can't at least stay until her return. And when might that be? Nine or nine-thirty at the very latest. Pressing social engagement at eight-forty five. Peripheral connection with royalty. Can't say too much. I understand. But give the silly mare our love. I will — and what about another couple of brandies? That's very nice of you. Manager hoisting an inebriate arm in the air and the barman running with a bottle of Hennessey's best — for the special guests. Drink up men and be of good cheer. Christ is born in Bethlehem. And two more pints of beer.

Wifey returning at ten past eight. Arms laden with presents — but none for her little brother because surprise surprise the ould drotchel doesn't have one and who are these two strange men? Quick stagger through the bewildered crowd and out into the night — where the carol-singers haunt somewhere in the distance.

Down the hill at full speed with the manager screaming obscenities after us and the barman hysterical. Mind that sharp fucking bend at the bottom. Too late! O'Connell bull-rushing through the hedge and across the garden. Smashing the gnomes to smithereens and sailing through the back door and into some cunt's kitchen. Chased out again by a fucking Alsatian and a clob-head wielding a crowbar. Go away you carol-singers — trying to creep into my subconscience. Leave me alone to grow up in my own time. Take your naïve little joy and lie to all the small boys who

tribe

can't wait for Father Christmas to come. Maybe get stuck climbing down the fucking chimney so that they can keep the whole stash of toys and laugh in the morning at all the other little cunts who'll be screaming. Blue fucking murder! With nothing there when they wake beside the bed. I seen him once in his red suit. Smelled the whisky on his breath.

Blue Bullet full of seasonal swingers. Stripper on stage with tinsel on her twat and a sprig of holly up her hole. O'Connell bouncing up to the crowded bar — pushing punters out of his way. Who let all these fucking wankers in? Should be reported to the priests.

'Two small brandies, my man.'

'Hang on there, Con. You'll have to sell the Hilton to buy brandy in this place.'

O'Connell opening his coat just a fraction. Neck of the Hennessey bottle protruding from an inside pocket. He winks.

'We just want the glasses, Owen.'

'Thought that got left in the rush.'

'Never been known to leave anything behind me in a bar.'

'I don't think they likes you to bring your own booze in here.'

'You're forgetting something, Owen ...'

'What's that, Con ?'

'I'm a friend of the management.'

All the tables already taken so we leans up against a pillar by the dancefloor. O'Connell filling the glasses from his bottle and then placing it carefully on the ground between his feet.

'Happy Christmas, Owen!'

'Many happy returns to you, Con!'

Stripper doing things with the tinsel. Hope Father Christmas isn't watching. Maybe the cunt's in the audience — warming up his blood while he has some left. A whisky, a wank and then away. See you all next yule-tide. And what would you like little man? The stripper please! She's coming with me — to keep me warm at the North Pole. Dwarfs drunk on the picket line. Make the cunts redundant — until next November. If they haven't emigrated to County fucking Cork by then.

tribe

Master of ceremonies coming on stage and give the stripper a big hand. Certainly! The band will shortly be back after their interval at the bar.

'Any spare in tonight, Owen?'

'You don't need spare, Con.'

'Why not?'

'I thought that Patsy cunt said you could take your pick?'

'No need for the fucking sarcasm.'

'Have three or four if you wants he said.'

'You'll see.'

Wonder what Ann's doing right at this minute. Has she found herself some other cunt who'll save up with her for a mortgage and fuck her on the mat in front of the fire? A man with etiquette and a certain style. And a bow-tie on his bollocks.

Dancefloor swirling with colour and creaking with swingers, shufflers and *pas seuls*-ers. All ankles and shins. Knocking knees and trembling thighs. Shoes, shifts and spotted socks. Jumping and bumping to the beat and sweating to the sounds. O'Connell's face even redder than usual. Fingers of one hand clicking while the other fills up the brandy glasses again from his bottle.

'Could be a good night, Owen.'

'Someone looking at you, Con ...'

'Where?'

'Over there.'

O'Connell turning to face into a pair of big and ugly dicky-bowed bouncers. One of the cunts snatching the brandy bottle from his hand.

'All drinks must be purchased at the bar, sir.'

'Says who?'

'Says me — sir.'

The other cunt rubbing his fists together. Two more of the fuckers over by the door — watching. Like giant spiders ready to fly across the web. O'Connell smiling.

'Now listen, lads, I'm a friend of the manager's.'

'Really, sir?'

'Aye, really. His name's Lionel and I know him personally. Go and ask him. Tell him O'Connell's here ... Patsy's friend.'

The bottle snatcher glancing with a sly eye at the fist rubber — who grins back with a wink and a wanking gesture with his hand.

'That won't be possible, sir.'

'Why not?'

'Lionel's not in tonight.'

'Well ... there must be somebody in the back room who'll remember me.'

O'Connell attempting to push his way through. Fist rubber throwing him back against the pillar. That's fucking well enough of that! Bottle snatcher spitting teeth. Brandy and broken glass on the dancefloor. Screams from the swingers. Bouncers coming like bears out of the wood-work and the bastards surrounding us. Fist rubber trying to kick O'Connell's kidneys out through his back. A chair across the forehead to teach the cunt a long-overdue lesson.

Blood spilling onto those nearest in the crowd. O'Connell sinking under a hail of head-butts and rabbit punches and various other foul fucking blows. Hands grabbing at me amidst hysterical cries of get that bastard and he hit Charlie with the chair. Kick the balls off the slag. Dragging us both to the stairs. Up one step — then two. Heads banging off each as we ascend. More kicks to the side and back — then out through the door with a bloody thud onto the cold Christmas Eve pavement. Carol-singers across the street. Peace on earth to men of goodwill.

'Con ...'

'Aye, Owen?'

'I can't get up.'

'Hang on there a minute.'

O'Connell crawling over on all fours. Face bleeding and a bunch of hair missing from the side of his head.

'Try again, Owen.'

'Its no good, Con ...'

O'Connell up onto his knees and lifting me to a sitting position. Fire in my side burning like a blizzy. People hurrying past with a wide berth in the middle of this season of giving. O'Connell dragging himself to his feet with a heroic effort. You can't keep a dibby man down. Hauling me up after him and mind my fucking ribs. Feels as if I've been trampled on by a herd of stampeding swizzle swiggers. God fucking help me!

'Let's go Owen.'

'Where to?'

'The hospital.'

'Just get us a fucking taxi, Con.'

'Be a tall order tonight, Owen ...'

'Help me across to that fucking wall ...'

O'Connell dragging me limp-legged up the street and propping me in a standing position by the doorway of a Sainsbury's supermarket.

'Stay here. I won't be long.'

Disappearing then into the painful darkness around the corner. Stars bright and cold overhead and the smell of snow. Huddle back into this doorway to avoid the eyes peering past. Salvation Army singing 'Adeste Fidelis'. Money jingling in their tins. Crowd coming out from the cinema. Hot dogs and hamburgers to be had from the van vendors along the road. Or a pizza if you prefer or a quick kebab and all the other fast-food establishments represented in a row like tarts teasing. Otherwise it's vindaloo for you. And chopsuey for me.

'Away in a manger ... no crib for a bed ...'

Why am I singing? Jesus save me — it's a bad fucking sign. Heralding the termination of my young and wasted life. The fucking pictures will begin to flash in a minute before my wild eyes and I won't need no more clean shirts after that.

'The little lord Jesus ... lay down ... his sweet head ...'

Drunk staggering stocious across with a fifty pence piece clutched in his horizontal hand.

'Where's your tin?'

'What?'

'Where's your fucking tin?'

Christ — I'm being robbed of my fucking roll-ups. Too scurfed to resist. Knuckles of the hand hurting into the pocket while there's still some feeling left. Out with the tobacco tin. Drunk swaying to and fro and spitting as he speaks.

'Is that it?'

'That's it.'

Takes it from my feeble grip. Empties the contents out onto the gudgell street and places the lidless tin on the ground by my feet. Clink of the fifty pence piece hitting the target.

'There ... that's how you fucking do it.'

He sways away and a big tall besom coming up behind throws in another twenty pence or two.

'Silent night ... holy night ...'

Good Lord God — was that a pound coin? And a few more pennies from the pav behind. Money mounting up in the mêlée of booze and blood and I must surely look like nothing on fucking earth. More cash clinking in the tin and I takes it all back. Human nature has something to be said for it after all. Lights flashing now in my head as the trauma of it all begins to tell. Sinking slowly to the ground and falling over face down by the passing feet. Where the fuck is O'Connell? Try to crawl along the pavement — but can't. Is he building the fucking taxi or what? Sudden engine at the kerb with its horn beep-beeping. That must be him now. Come and get me Con because I can't make it across. Sound of a lady's shoe clicking on the concrete. Peggy's voice.

'Christ, Owen ...'

'You're not Con.'

'Get into the taxi.'

'Help me ... Peggy?'

'It's me.'

'You're my monyafetich.'

'I was in the Bullet. I saw what happened.'

'Where's O'Connell?'

'How should I know?'

'I has to wait for him.'

'Get in the taxi, Owen. The police will pick you up soon if you don't.'

'Something's wrong with my side ...'

'I'll see to it.'

'And what's this coming from my nose?'

'Blood, you bugger.'

Numbness spreading upwards to my brain. Hark the

herald angels sing. Glory to the Christmas fling. Taxi driver with a worried look — but Peggy saying you'll get paid. You bloody mercenary! Watch the back of the cunt's head turn to liquid and swim all over the windscreen. Peggy's pretty hand on my brow as this motor car speeds through the seedy streets. To God knows where.

tribe

12

In bygone years we threw grass at a crossroads to let other Travellers know the way we went. A tribe of dirty-faced chavvies with boxy-cakes in their hands and the old women wearing plaid shawls — begging from house to house and at all the farms along the road. The men would go hawking or picking potatoes and we would poove down where we could. And Travellers have always tried to support each other, despite and against all the fucking odds and evictions and other various vexations.

And vague memories of my father being towed out in the middle of the night with his trailer and his all-weather cans and his jacks. And the chavvies crying their eyes out and the beors blating their heads off and the whole world screaming at us from all sides.

Head floating on an ocean of soft scented soap suds. Steamy haze making tiny trickles down the pink and white tiles. Must have been dreaming. Otherwise I'm dead and gone against all the odds to fucking heaven. And can anyone tell me what became of my tobacco tin?

'Keep still, Owen ...'

Focus gradually on Peggy's face through the enveloping warmth. Remembering only bits and pieces of this fragmented shite-bag night.

'Where are we?'

'My house. I share it with two other girls.'

'The ones you were with at the Bullet ... the first night?'

'That's right.'

'Where are they?'

'Away, with their families ... for Christmas.'

'My head hurts. Jesus ... my fucking side ...'

'I tried to take you to casualty.'

'I can see you didn't succeed.'

Peggy telling me I went a bit crazy. Kept shouting that I didn't want to be a burden on the already overstretched Health Service. Told her to take me to a private clinic because I wanted to open an account. Medics has enough on their plates without cunts like me who won't lead nor fucking drive. What with the computers doing all this delicate laser surgery and deadly fucking drug-resistant bacteria and anti-impotence drugs being dispensed nilly-willy all over the world. Aren't we overcrowded enough?

'Taxi driver didn't want to wait. So I had a doctor come out and look you over in the back of the cab.'

'What did he diagnose?'

'Drunkenness! Said to take you home and sober you up.'

'Can't beat British medicine.'

'I was afraid you might have broken a rib or something.'

'Strong bones. Runs in some families ... like wooden legs. How did I get into this bath?'

'The taxi driver helped me get you inside. He didn't want to. Said he was running a cab, not a mobile clinic. I told him you were well connected ... and as well as that, I wouldn't pay him if he didn't lend a hand.'

'You little fairy tale teller.'

'It was all true.'

'Toodle-oo.'

Submerged and sober. Good girl Peggy. I loves you. Head under the water and try to stay down there. Peggy's hands gently harassing. Finding my flute. Back up for air and feeling much better already. Catch hold of her arm and drag her over the side into the splashing water — clothes and all. Mind my sore side. And my yawney yud.

'Owen! You rat!'

'Water rat.'

'My clothes are soaked!'

'And what have you done with mine?'

'In the washing machine.'

Peggy's smile sending me sailing. Peel the thin blouse off her breasts and the lemon skirt clinging between her lovely legs. Pubic mound pouting at my evil glime-eye.

Slide the cloth quickly off the contours. All her clothes on the bathroom floor in a watery pool. Then down to lie alongside me. Making little waves wash up over us. Splish-splashing out over the side of the bath. Covering me with her body caress. Senses floating on the bathroom smells and Peggy's kisses forcing my head underwater again — and making the pain run away like sand in an hourglass. Her gently thrusting arse rising and submerging — rising and submerging. Like a peach island in a soapy sea.

And after we're all clean again she runs and gets for me one of her girlfriends' dressing gowns — and her blue-bunny bedroom slippers. And pours me as well just the merest hint of Scotch.

'I likes this house, Peggy.'

'I hate it. Not the house ... sharing with the girls.'

'Don't you three have fun?'

'There's no privacy. I'd like a little flat of my own.'

'Not so easy on your own.'

'I wouldn't mind sharing ... with a man.'

'Be tougher than you think, siúcra.'

'You seem to manage, Owen.'

'I'm really only looking after the place ...'

'Collins won't come back.'

Sit down here on the sofa Peggy. Put such simple little thoughts out of your mind. Pour another drop of that mellow malt and then rest your head on my shoulder. Leave all these immature ideas in the bottom drawer with the raggy doll and the pig-tails and the navy-blue knickers and the long lost violated virgin.

'You seems to spend a lot of time in the Blue Bullet, Peggy.'

'Lucky for you, Owen.'

'You're definitely a lifesaver.'

tribe

'I should have left you. Only seem to see you when you're pissed.'

'Sorry about that. You knows ... before.'

'I'm not bothered. I know you love her.'

'Does you?'

'And don't drink too much of that whisky ...'

'Will the girls notice?'

'No, but I don't want you drunk again.'

'What time is it?'

'Bed time!'

Lights out in this long room. Gas fire fading. Up the stairs unassisted now with hands holding on tight to the white banister rail. One step at a time please. Into Peggy's pink room and her cosy leaf-covered childbed.

'I'm stiff as a board ...'

'Good man.'

'My side, you dirty little druvass!'

'Don't worry, Owen. Lie back and let nurse Peggy look after you.'

I'll buy you a belated present Peggy — when the shops open again. I'll buy you a woman's smell to replace the one now flying in my brain. And I'll write to you often from Australia. Maybe get Collins to drop a line as well. Lights red in my head as she kneels astride my thighs. Lithe and low down over the groin. Her blond-coloured curls covering my swelling smurlán. Taking it first in her hands and humming it a little tune that sends vibrations along every vertebra in the spine and down to the trembling toes. Then guiding it back and forth across the parting lips of the waiting womanhood. Breasts rising and falling heavily above my head. Electric excitement running through her and into me. All her entire body a pliable contortionate thing. Convulsing and contracting until the short spiritual spasms come — and then pushing me deep inside her and drawing the starbright light down out of my head and up into hers.

I hears a scrabbling from the chimney and sees a sack of nice things in the dead grate. Pretty Peggy. I don't want to ask where you learned these tricks. Not from Collins — who was basically a non-believer. Perhaps from books or from your mother's memoirs. I'm just glad that you did! Time now to wrap ourselves in each other's warmth and drift off to bye-byes. Two wandering Jews. Two babes in the wood. Bring a blanket of hope to cover us with and a pillow of popular dreams to keep at bay the dreadful nightmare that seems to stalk us. Holy shite! I forgot about O'Connell.

13

Christmas morning creeping in through Peggy's lace curtains. Clock on the wall claiming it's ten-thirty and church bells donging in the distance that a new Christ is born. Soprano sounds from the kitchen downstairs of some boy's choir singing seasonal carols on the radio — and a smell of sizzling bacon. My side still hurts like fucking hell and a sledge-hammer in my head. Must try to prise open the mouth and take an aspirin or two. Peggy when I descends dressed only in an apron. Eyes and body shining to spite the sanctity of the day. She smiles and I notices the neat pile of my clothes by the ironing board.

'When did you do that?'

'This morning.'

'Must have been up early?'

'I'm a light sleeper.'

Place my hands on the cheeks of her arse and pull her close. Look in through the little blue windows at her soul. She's older than Ann — though you'd never know it. A kind of animal thing looking back at me from inside. Nervous and vulnerable. Then gone as down come the steel shutters and the eyes become ice.

'The bacon, Owen ...'

'Never mind the bacon ...'

'You must get dressed.'

'Why?'

'I've got to go out.'

'Where?'

'I'm expected home ... for Christmas dinner.'

Pulling herself away and returning to the frying pan. Popping the bacon onto a plate and plastering thick slices of bread with butter. Hop into these freshly ironed clothes and sit down at the table. She seems a little distant this morning. Maybe it's got something to do with my flat refusal. Or maybe she's trying to tease. Women has all these strange little fucking ways about them. Nice and then ice. It's enough to drive you fucking demented. Never know the fuck where you are! Eat up Owen she says as she leaves the room with my eyes after her. Church-going cunts outside the window all rushing to offer their thanks. And to pray for the souls of those still in bed. Fornicating!

Whole town virtually deserted on this clear air morning as I walks eastwards across the ship canal bridge towards Cornbrook. Take my time and saunter along to Dinton Street and the red-brick number forty-nine where my little mother still lives. Clothes feeling nice and new. A few blood stains on the trousers that just couldn't be got rid of. Job for Sketchleys.

Now and then the excited cry of a Christmas Day kid with a new psychosis from the bullying consumer cunts with their gifts of greed and gimme and gollop to stand them in good stead for all their future years. And the neon hearts of poodling parents with small it's-nothing-much presents trying to steal back a little piece of the child's candour. Maybe I'll have a son myself some day. Carry my name and keep me alive long after I'm dead. Pass me down like an heirloom. Blood into blood. For ever and ever. Wob wagon pulling up sharply ahead of me in the street. O'Connell's battered face poking out of the back window.

'Let me out of here! McBride, you fucking cunt!'

Oh God — not now please! O'Connell struggling out onto the street through the back door. Wob wagon pulling away.

'What's up, Con?'

'Jaysus ... I don't believe it! Where the fuck did you get to?'

'I met a good Samaritan.'

'You should have waited, Owen. I searched every-fucking-where ...'

'Thought you'd forgot about me, Con.'

'What?'

'When you didn't come back.'

'It was Christmas fucking Eve, Owen! Do you have any idea how hard it is to find a taxi on Christmas fucking Eve?'

'I dare say it's difficult.'

'I thought you'd been picked up, that's what I thought ... so I went round to the fucking station.'

'Hope you was polite?'

'The fucking desk sergeant wasn't ...'

'Don't tell me ...'

'So I swung a scurf at him.'

'Jesus Christ, Con ...'

'They threw me in a cell for the night ... after a few wallops first.'

'Typical intolerance.'

'Let me out just now. Offered me a lift home, that's where they were taking me.'

'No hard feelings then?'

'I'll hard fucking feelings you! Where did you get to, Owen?'

'Salvation Army. Took me back to the citadel. I was too drunk to resist.'

'Look at you, all washed and clean. Even your clothes ...'

'It's great what they does for the down and out ...'

'Look at the state of me!'

'I suggests you go round there.'

'I'm going fucking home, that's where I'm going.'

'Maybe I'll see you later?'

'Not if I see you fucking first.'

O'Connell storming away up the street. Big bundle of blood and balls. Turning at the corner to look back and shake a frustrated fist in my direction. Surely — if Christmas is about anything it's about tolerance and give and take? Passing along by the old deserted shoe factories and the lines of red-brick houses all facing westwards into the setting sun.

Around me the ghosts of Christmases past. And the shrill death-cries of the years gone by me. Schizoid sounds of the mongrel children in the mobile schools with the dysentery and impetigo and hepatitis taking their toll. Along with the rashes and burns and breaks and poisonings and rampant runovers. Clapered chavvies in the caravan schools with discrimination and segregation from the Gorgios and the stillbirths and infant mortality and malnutrition.

And Travellers always afraid to camp near to a drawn well because it was bad luck and some dilling cunt might fall down it and die. Spectres playing hide and seek along the canal. Small ghostly hands touching me with cold fingers. Turn to see them run away with faces wide-eyed and white in the morning light. Sleep my darlings! Smell the disappointment and hear the poltergeists rattling away amongst the rubble. Sleep while the wind blows! Pawn your souls for a silver spoon to jam between your teeth. For fear you might never again be able — to unlock your jaw.

'We've all been to mass.'

'I'm glad, mother.'

'You knows I'd like you to go, Owen, at least once a year ... at least at Christmas.'

'I went to nine o'clock mass at St Luke's.'

'We was at nine o'clock mass at St Luke's. We didn't see you.'

'Must have been last year.'

'You're such a schemer, Owen.'

'Memory's been playing tricks on me lately.'

'May God forgive you.'

'I'm sure, mother, in his infinite mercy, he will.'

House full of Christmas aromas. Cakes and little sweets on the table for the grandchildren. Red lemonade bubbling in tall tumblers. And a sixteen-pound turkey browning over in the oven. Cut me a slice this very minute to stick in my face. Sees young Tim through the back window. Outside with his pigeons. Desmond in the kitchen drinking Guinness with his foot to the back door to stop his three English chavvies from coming in out of the bird shite. He's good to his mother though. Better than me.

'Desmond ... let those children come in!'

His New Age second wife Willow like a brown clucking hen sighing and supervising the goings on. While the dinner cooks away — with the help of a little drop from the gin bottle at every hand's turn. Willow gets on well with my mother. Although the ould woman wants them to come off the tramp — like me. For the sake of the chavvies.

'Sees you got your arse in the paper then, Owen.'

'Desmond!'

'Always said he'd be fucking famous.'

'Open the beer, brother ... and shut that swinging skipping-rope you calls a fucking gob.'

'No swearing in this house, the two of youse!'

Kids screaming blue fucking murder out in the yard. Let us come in daddy. We promises to be good and not get in your way.

'Go and fucking play!'

'Let them in, Desmond!'

'Oh, for Christ's sake ...'

'I said no swearing on Christmas Day!'

'Fuck Christmas Day!'

Desmond keeps to the old ways. Although Willow isn't a real Tinker she stays on the drom and never complains about the hardship and harruping. Maybe they're right! What's happening to the heritage in me? Or was there ever any at all? My daddy died too young — never had a chance to explain enough about the drom-days. Never said to me Owen don't compromise with none of these cunts because they'll all disappoint you in the end. There's a vacuum where my childhood ought to be. A black fucking hole of doubt and indecision and an impending future in this Gorgio universe full of unscrupulous cunts and serial killers and sinister economic entrepreneurs casting dark shadows all over the whole fucking world.

Maybe Desmond's kids will conform and their children will have their own poltergeists. Down in the cider-subways with henry and his daughter or the future frightened streets or the polluted parlours. Maybe they'll also ask themselves in quieter moments — why not some other world? Why this particular one? Why not his — or hers? Or the suffering and starving's? Or the pampered pop star's? Or the beautiful's — or the diseased? Why here? And now.

'Are you staying for a bit of dinner, Owen?'

'That's why I'm anseo, a stór.'

'I never knows with you. We're serving up nice and early, so no snaking off to the pub, or places like that.'

'Wouldn't dream of it, a mháthair dhílis.'

'That goes for you too, Desmond.'

'I'm a grown-fucking-man, mother!'

'Thank you for telling me. And what was all that in the paper, Owen?'

'A misunderstanding!'

'I suppose, the less said the better.'

'I'm sure God would agree.'

Step out into the long back yard with isolated islands of gaunt grass fighting for survival in the desolation of sand and gravel and pigeon shite. Lofts down the end that were kennels in my teenage years — full of mangy mongrels for racing on hundred-yard grass tracks in remote unlicensed fields. Standing in the rain amongst the puck-fices with cold hands and two pounds for a punt on anything you fancy now a bhuachaill? Mutton sandwiches with mustard. Toughs and touts and spivs shoving sticks up dogs' arses and some painted a different colour than they were at the fucking trial runs. Cans of beer and curses and a commotion of sounds, shrieks and snarls. All silent now.

'How're you doing, Tim?'

'OK, Owen.'

'Any work?'

'No. Not yet.'

'Should have stopped at school.'

'What for?'

'Got a few exams or something.'

'What for?'

'No future in pigeons.'

'Is there any in exams?'

'It's cold out here.'

'The birds don't mind.'

'How does you know that, Tim?'

'They told me.'

'You coming inside? Dinner's nearly done.'

'In a while, Owen. I'll come in now in a nóiméad.'

This is all out of time. This is ages fucking old — prehistoric! Uilleann pipes on a barren hillside and daddy turning in his English grave — unable to join his screaming ancestors. Sometimes I can feel the fucker in my blood. And in my ears the sound of him pounding through my veins. Trying to get out and evaporate into the air and fall again as red rain on an Irish field.

Tim and I is aliens in our own fucking country. We sees the Brit at the other side of the room. We looks him straight in the eye. But behind standing is another man. A faceless Celt who stays always in the shadows and who walks softly behind us on dark nights. Never catching up — but always there. Back inside now to the cushti comfort and the sweet smell of the roast turkey. And the warm oven heat driving the cold demons away.

'How's your love life, Owen?'

'Unmentionable, Willow. How's yours?'

'Ask Desmond.'

'Another Guinness?'

'Thank you, bráthair.'

Mother serving up the spuds and Willow worrying around the table and Desmond destroying the fucking turkey with a carving knife. Daddy didn't look dead. Even in the coffin. Except for the blackness down the side of his face that the cunts tried to cover up. Should have said something then — looking in over the lid. But what? Anything. Hello and why the fuck did you go? Sit down to this family dinner now and drink a drop of the port wine that mother's put on the table and isn't it nice you're getting some work Owen. We wishes young Tim could get himself a job and why is your face all marked like that? Have you been fighting? Again!

When every wanker in this world dies, the epic story of their life should be told in whatever fucking heaven or hell the cunts ends up in. In torrid technicolor on a silver fucking screen. The real intimate no-detail-spared shite-bag story. With all the seconds ticking so slowly. Every secret fucking ride and wank and lie and stab-in-the back each cunt ever committed.

In the audience would be all of mankind. Friends family and everyone else — past, present and future. And maybe the fucking animals as well. And everyone could see everything!

It's all too fucking easy this act of perfect contrition clats. Oh my God I am heartily sorry — don't even have to speak the words. Just manage to think them before you take your final fucking bow. I detest my sins above every other evil. And so here I am. At my fucking wits, end.

'Owen ...'

'What? Where am I?'

'Here's your tea.'

'Sorry, mother ... I must have dozed off.'

'You've been asleep in that chair since four o'clock.'

'What's the time now?'

'Half past seven.'

'Why didn't you wake me?'

'You looked worn out.'

'Where's everybody?'

'Desmond has taken his family away. Timmy's still out in the yard.'

'In the dark?'

'He has a light.'

'I don't think it's too healthy for him to be out there all the time.'

'Ah sure, they're his birds, Owen ...'

'You should have made him stay on at school.'

'He didn't like the teachers.'

Sip this small cup of weed in the big armchair. Fire bright and buoyant in the grate. Calm and cosy. Could I stay? Let me stay forever like this. Docile and half-dibby. Silent and sleepy. Never let the fire go out and never open the window to let the world in. And why mother did you make me go to school? I didn't like the teachers either. You was different Owen. Was I? Was I mother? How so? You was my little Gorgio boy. My little conishfein. Your father had his oldest son and I had you. Timmy's neither here nor there — he's a little bit ruille and not fit for neither code. Only maybe God. And you knows I was never a Tinker Owen.

Your father came to my family's farm in Connemara when I was a lackeen and his dark eyes and handsome face made me leave the land and follow him away on the drom. In them days there was nothing for a girl. The land went to the boys and we had to make do as best we could. Your father was good to me in his own way — not like some. He was a dacent man Owen. And you're a dacent boy buíochas le Dia!

'That nice girl called last night, Owen.'

'What nice girl, mother?'

'I think her name is Ann ...'

'What did she want?'

'Said she'd gone around to your flat, but you wasn't in. She thought you might be here.'

'Did she say what she wanted?'

'She wanted you.'

'What did you tell her?'

'You didn't tell me you was saving to get married, Owen?'

'What did you say to her, mother?'

'She has her head screwed on the right way. You could do worse.'

'Mother ...'

'I tould her you would probably be here today.'

'Christ!'

'Where are you flying off to now?'

'I said I'd meet Con ...'

'You should keep away from that O'Connell conya.'

'He's all right, mother.'

'He may be, but he won't take you anywhere ... except down.'

'Thank you for the dinner.'

'I'm thinking of going back to Ireland in the Summer, Owen.'

'You hasn't been to Ireland for thirty years.'

'It's time I went then.'

'Enjoy yourself ...'

'I want you to come with me.'

'I couldn't do that ...'

'I *want* you to come, Owen!'

'I has to be off. I'll go out the back way and say goodbye to Tim.'

Quick kiss on the forehead and away through the back door. Ireland! Jesus fucking wept! Timmy sitting in the pigeon loft with the birds shiteing all over him.

'I thinks you ought to go in now, Tim, mother's on her own.'

'In a little while, Owen ...'

'What?'

'Does you want a pigeon to take home with you?'

'I'm tempted, Tim. I'm tempted.'

Cold and dark in the back-alley and I can't get the rusty gate latch to fucking close fast enough behind me. What does she want me for now? Just when I was getting fucking right. Cats crying and clawing on the dustbin lids. Why the fuck am I running? I wants to not want to see her. I wants to sit in the pigeon loft with Tim. Birds shiteing on my shoulders and their coo-cooing holding up my heart and smothering my soul. Out into the light of the deserted street. Smug cunts in their armchairs in front of their everlasting fires. Tell them fucking cats it's Christmas! Turn quickly into Cornbrook Road and she's there. Right there in front of me. Smiling like the Blessed fucking Virgin!

'Hello, Owen. Merry Christmas.'

'Ann!'

Awkward silence as I tries to recover from the fright. Look away from her eyes as they scrutinise my secret thoughts. Shuffle the feet and smile.

'I went to the flat last night.'

'I was out with O'Connell. You knows what it's like ... Christmas Eve.'

'You didn't come home.'

'No?'

'I waited.'

'I was a bit worse for the wear, you knows. Spent the night ... at the Hilton.'

'I see.'

'It's cold.'

'Yes.'

'No use standing here ...'

'No.'

'Freeze to death ...'

'Owen ...'

'It's OK.'

'I saw your picture in father's paper.'

'Don't fucking laugh.'

'I'm not laughing.'

'Yes you are.'

'Sorry.'

'Let's go.'

Look up at the sniggering sky. Moon mocking down at me and the stars smirking. She puts her arm through mine and we walks away. Her head rests on my shoulder and the twipper of life in her lovely eyes. And my daddy always said that there was no bad men. Only bad women. Four pigeons aching overhead in the lamplight. Are they following me home? And did Tim send them? To warn me about the worly.

Christmas gone too quickly and none of the celebrating now like in the old days for Saint Stephen. When the pavs would go teelering for the wren and hang the little dead bird from a stick and go calling and carousing with a dance and a dingle and a song or two waving a bunch of bee-nettles and blind-eyes and creeping-jinny. And the robin's whistle-call to its little balchins in the snow and the wambs full of whisky and the warm feelings. All gone now except for the odd memory and melancholy.

But no use grizzling and a quick hop out of bed is the best thing on cold mornings like these. Ann still sleeping as I spies out the window at the last day in this year of our Yahweh. Third time she's stayed since Christmas night. Whatever will her flipput of a father think? The rest of the holiday evaporating so quickly now. Already New Year's Eve and only three days left before I'm back to the horse-shite and hot tarmac. But I'm a bit more optimistic and sure as any cunt can be that everything will turn out all right in the end. Keep the fingers crossed. And the toes too — for good measure.

A party round at O'Connell's tonight. The annual back-slapping floor-falling hooley. Wonder if I ought to go. The cunt might take a gun and blow my few remaining fucking brains out. Or worse still — set the moonlighters on me. Look down at Ann in her delicate and vulnerable little sleep. Can she see the future flashing past under her fluttering eyelids? All her dreams and plans coming true? I hope they do — whether I'm in them or not. I can feel the heat of her happiness and touch the almost smiling corners of her mouth. I knows her dreams so well — the unreality which is real and the fantasy that's fact. I knows where her small feet walks — but is there a ghost behind? Or is her dreams just the same as her nightmares?

Love is a word I've never really understood. But now and then I'm warmed by something other than the sun and I feels as if I could cry. Then — frightened by my own apprehension — I takes the sentiment by the throat and carries the cunt back to its cage and locks the door. But time now to get the breakfast going and maybe spend the rest of this day quietly indoors. Just me and her. Until of course it's time for the party.

'Didn't think you'd have the hard fucking neck, McBride!'

'Knew you'd be glad to see me.'

O'Connell silhouetted against the purple paint in the hall behind the half-open front door of the Lord Byron Square Hilton. Ann a little afraid and gripping my arm on this stone step. Then a smile spreading from the cunt's half-pissed eyes to the red whisky mouth. Flinging open the door.

'It's only because you're with him, Ann, a chroí. Otherwise he'd have felt the toe of me fucking boot.'

'Has a funny fancy for you, honey.'

'Oh Owen!'

'Since that night he barged in ...'

'You're embarrassing me ...'

'And you gave him a clout.'

O'Connell taking a swipe at my impertinence. Follow him through the door and down the long hall of the Hilton. Whole place split up and rented out to the Irish immigrants. Bunch of trainee barmen and cable-layers and sub-contractors of dubious credentials and a variety of other cunts. Fresh over from the back-of-beyond arseholes of Mayo and Kerry or the shirt-stealing side streets of Dublin and Dundalk. Six bedrooms with one kitchen between them all. And a saloon with a television the size of a cinema and a long wooden bar. Optics on the wall and barrels of draught beer under the counter.

tribe

A home away from home. Three beds to a room and O'Connell the only permanent fixture in the whole fucking place. Nice money spinner though — if you don't give a continental shite about the confusion.

'Fill up a couple of glasses there, Owen. And don't stand on fucking ceremony, both of you ... join in the celebrations.'

The New Year about to burst upon this band of silly cunts and casual acquaintances. Waiting for the chimes of the clock we forms a circle — arms linked and feet unsteady. Ann becoming a little dibby and still unsure about this strange purple place. Holding on to one of my arms and also one of O'Connell's — in the middle of this assortment of nosy neighbours and pricks from the local pub and general passers by. At least a dozen of the inverted immigrants in the kitchen — having their own private party. O'Connell shush-shushing until the hour strikes. Crowd in the kitchen carrying on with their sing-song. Not knowing what fucking year it is — or caring.

Clock chiming aloud at last. Arms swinging and voices singing. Should ould acquaintance be forgot. Louder! And never brought to mind. The year is dead. Long live An Bhliain Úr. Double delight and delirium fucking tremens. All a-hugging and a-kissing and three cheers for the Chinese.

'Fill your glasses, the lot of you. Owen, have you got a drink there?'

'Of course I have, Con.'

'I may go and sort out these cunts in the kitchen. I should have sent them all out somewhere for the night.'

'They're probably lonely, Con, so far away from home.'

'Why should that fucking bother them, Owen?'

'They might miss the religious aspect of this holiday.'

'I'll say fucking mass for them later.'

'And hear their confessions too?'

'Listen here now, Owen, on the serious side ... I'm expecting some special guests shortly. Call me immediately if you see them arrive.'

'What sort of special guests?'

'You'll know them when you see them.'

O'Connell away into his beer can of a kitchen to liaise with the wild lodgers. Some late arrivals with their arms full

— cunts all turned out of the pubs and turning up here. Nobody yet that could even be called remotely special. A crowd from the Rose and Crown darts team and a few others from the Salford Seafarers' Mission. Men rapidly out-numbering the few women. The odd dirty look and disgruntle. O'Connell returning to the party having failed completely to cut down the noise in the kitchen. Some cunt calling.

'Hey, O'Connell ...'

'What?'

'Where are these fucking women?'

'Don't worry, they'll be here.'

What fucking women? Only women O'Connell knows are barmaids or dressed in blue uniforms. What little scheme has the cunt solicited since I last saw him? Ann's arm around my waist and wanting to go home. But I knows it would be regarded as the height of rudeness to leave before at least half-past five in the morning. In any case I'm fearing for O'Connell's safety and what's more — I owes the cunt one.

'What women, Con?'

'The special guests, Owen. The special guests!'

'Who the fuck are they?'

'From the Blue Bullet!'

'Oh no!'

'It was all a fucking mistake.'

'You can bet your life on that.'

'No, Owen ... when we got heaved out that night. I was fucking raging about it. Rang up that lad Lionel and d'you know what, them bastard bouncers told us lies ... he was there all the time. He was mortified, in case I'd tell Patsy. Couldn't apologise enough. He said, "If there's any way I can make it up to you, Mister O'Connell, any way at all." So I says to him, "I'm having this party on New Year's Eve and I know there's going to be an embarrassing shortage of ladies." "Say no more," says he.'

'And did you, Con?'

'No need, Owen. He read the situation well enough. "They'll be a bit late," says he " ... after midnight. Have a few other venues to attend first."'

'You're soft in the fucking head ...'

Ding dong on the doorbell. Too late now for the second thoughts. O'Connell bouncing away down the hall. Giggling outside on the stone step. Come in come in and Lionel sent us. Good old fucking Lionel. Half-a-dozen hoors and strippers trooping into this awful abode. Still in their strumpeting suits and following them sideways to get in the door — the biggest black cunt ever to be seen north of fucking Nairobi.

'Who's the fuck's he?'

'He Edwin. You O'Connell?'

'That's me. What's he doing here?'

'He's our chauffeur. We brought some champagne, compliments of the Blue Bullet.'

They must really be frightened of that Patsy cunt down there. O'Connell leading the parade up the hall and into the saloon. And let's liven this party up a bit. If it gets much livelier they'll call the fucking gavvers. Booze flowing from the bar and onto the stain coloured-linoleum. Fog of cigarette smoke and the odd dart flying. Ann really ar meisce now with her eyes all aglow and her normally cautious nature oblivious to the danger. And Edwin standing alone in the corner full of wolf-whistles. Sizing up the clients.

'Lionel told them to put on a bit of a show for us.'

'It's worse than I fucking thought.'

'Don't be such a fucking spoilsport, Owen.'

'There'll be trouble.'

'There will not!'

'What about that lot in the kitchen?'

'I'll keep them cunts quiet.'

'And if you don't, Edwin will.'

'Its my fucking house, Owen!'

'So it is.'

O'Connell out in the middle of the room. Master of fucking ceremonies. And ladies, gentlemen, lord mayors and fellow shite-arsed peasants. We are fortunate to have in our midst some performing artistes who have kindly agreed to entertain us for a while. So if you'll all fuck up and sit down or move back to the walls — we'll get on with it.

Performing artistes handing O'Connell some CDs to play. Noise dying down and breaths bated. Lodgers still singing in the kitchen. In Dublin's fair city where the girls has green titties. Edwin watching like a fucking hawk. Mincing music blasting from the speakers and the first stripper out into the centre of the room. Red sequins shaking and black stockings beckoning the eyeballs out of the cunts' sockets. Two others joining in with her. Circling and teasing the tongues out of the tanked-up fucking heads. A good dart hand reaching out. Edwin fastening his fist round it with a hoarse black voice.

'No touching, man, unless the girls ask for it.'

'They *are* fucking asking for it!'

'Don't be foolish, friend.'

'Who are you?'

'The chauffeur.'

'Fuck off and chauff then!'

Edwin squeezing. Doing irreparable damage to an arm that will never throw a double-twenty again. Muffled scream and a lesson learned. Red stripper calling O'Connell out to join in the fun. Unbuttoning the cunt's shirt and trousers. Clothes all off including the underpants — right down to the red arse and the red pubic hair. Good clean fucking fun. One of the kitchen crew pissing down his leg as he passes the saloon door on his way to the lavatory. About turn to report immediately to the rest of the rawneys and come quick to see some dirty English doxies having great fucking sport in the next room. Thunder of hob-nailed boots charging through the door.

Frashed eyes that never before saw a naked female form — in the fucking flesh. Whole gang of them piling into the middle of the room and sending the rest of the so-called respectable cunts sprawling. Hands everywhere. Grabbing for the forbidden flesh and tugging at the off-limit tits. Strippers screaming. Crowd booing and Edwin up like a cheetah. First bottle whizzing past my ear. Time to fucking move! Grab Ann's bewildered arm and steer her quickly down the purple hall.

'Get a taxi.'

'Where?'

'There's a rank at the end of the road. Go ... now!'

'What about you, Owen?'

'I has to get Con out. I'll meet you back at the flat.'

A quick kiss then Ann unsteadily down the dark street. Looking back at me a bit bemused then running as bottles burst through the front windows and shatter on the street. Back up the hall to see Edwin breaking heads with a lead pipe. Lodgers lashing out at anything that moves and trying to poke the performing artistes at the same time.

O'Connell with a pissed expression on his face and a swaying attempt to get his trousers back on. Grab him by the scruff.

'Come on, you stupid cunt!'

'Me clothes ...'

'Fuck your clothes.'

Sirens outside in the street. People panicking and stampeding for the doors and windows. Punching and pushing. Out the back way just as the front door falls into the hall with a splintering of wood. O'Connell holding his trousers up at the waist.

Bare feet over the nettles and stones. Up quickly onto one of the garage roofs that lines the alley as the first fucking uniforms appear. Lie still and flat down on the cold corrugated sheets.

Pandemonium from inside the house. Edwin silhouetted in the shattered window. Six struggling wobs trying to saulk him. Footsteps running up and down the alley past our hiding place. Shouting and screaming coming from all directions. Men hurdling hedges and women wailing and wondering how the fuck they will ever be able to face the daylight again. Fists flattening neutral noses. Then a gradual return of sanity on its tiptoes as the worst offenders are dragged away to the waiting wob wagons. Sirens sleering off and the odd shout across the gardens from the brave cunts who ran away.

'They've gone, Owen.'

'Not completely. Look ...'

Two peeler-shites stationed at the back door. No doubt some others in the street out front.

'Let's get the fuck out of here, Con. But quietly.'

'Where to, Owen?'

'My place.'

'What about me clothes?'

'D'you want to go in and fucking get them?'

'What am I going to do?'

'I don't know. Come back tomorrow ... say you were with me all night. Must have been the lodgers, having a party without your permission.'

'What about them girls, Owen? They'll go fucking mad down at the Bullet ...'

'Have to keep your yud down for a bit, won't you.'

Climb quietly off the roof and gingerly away through the back lanes until we're out of the danger area. Hail a taxi who gives O'Connell a dirty look. Just come from a fancy-dress-party, driver. He went as a fucking lederim. In onto the back seat and speed off through the darkness to safety.

'Thanks for coming back, Owen. I'd have been banjaxed.'

'Evens now?'

'Aye.'

Here's my coat to cover your naked shoulders. And don't think you're out of the coshes yet. Be a price on your fucking head after this. Might turn you in myself.

O'Connell leaning back against the leather with a furtive look on his flushed Galway face. Orange lights turning red up ahead. Same colour as the rest of the painted town. Lost souls crossing the street even at this late hour. Sang the new year in and now stagger home to whatever waits by the fire or in the lonely bed. Could be worse? Could be dead.

January is the Monday of the fucking year and little flurries of snow falling through the streetlight outside the paper-shop window. See on the front page there's panic again on the Han Seng stock market and they're shiteing themselves on Wall Street and in the City of London. What the fuck are we all going to do? Find myself a ledge and fly off it with the rest of the fuckers.

All this financial bollocks is bad for the spirit of internationalism in this brand new *beau monde* millennium. Although sometimes I wishes I'd been born fucking rich instead of ridiriúil and could live all the year round in a warm climate. Cunt in the fag-shop being polite since I tried to scurf him.

'Sticking it well, Owen?'

'Sticking what?'

'You know ... with the pikeys.'

'Better in here, is it?'

'Jesus no! Open all hours, every single solitary fucking day. No furlough for us fag-and-paper men.'

'I'll swap with you.'

'What?'

'You carry on up to the hatch and I'll stay here.'

'Couldn't do that.'

'Course fucking not.'

Everyone wants to complain. A national fucking pastime in this country. Some bright cunt of an entrepreneur could earn a fortune. Sympathetic ears for hire. Fifty quid an hour. Pour all your troubles in one and watch them disappear out the other. Five minutes guarantee. Pull this coat collar up high round the back of the neck. Keep out the little cold pieces of manna that falls from the black barren sky. Wish it was summer. Wish I could make a mountain of money by simply singing a love-song. Wish my fucking life away in small pieces. There's The Duck.

'Shiteing snow, eh Owen?'

'Could be worse.'

'Aye ... could be wob-shite.'

'Or politicians' promises!'

Read here in the paper that several cunts have been arrested in connection with computer fraud. Isn't it all? And I hope Ann's not one of them. A week or so now since O'Connell's doomed party. I gave him some of my clothes that were too small for him and he wandered away the next day. A forlorn figure. Haven't seen the cunt since. Maybe he's gone to join Collins in the antipodes. The Duck waddling along beside me. Disguised in his donkey jacket as a gentile but unable to hide the purple nose from the secret spirits in the safe armchair at night.

The snow-covered clover fields soon looming ahead of us. Most of the horses inside the sheds and stables and some even in the tack-room with Tolui. Just the odd hardy donkey braying defiance against the aggressive climate.

'Must be an easier fucking way of making money.'

'What would that be, Louis?'

'Don't know. But plenty of them cunts is doing it.'

'I'd just like to be financially independent.'

'Of what, Owen?'

'Work!'

'The jackpot on the fucking lottery would do me.'

'Is that all?'

'Kill yourself in a fucking fortnight, Myles.'

'Not me, Owen.'

'What would you do if you won?'

'I'd buy Felix a bungalow so he could get off the drom like he wants to and wouldn't have to fight no more. Then I'd go to Ireland and buy a stud farm.'

'I knows what I'd do ...'

'And what would that be, Duck?'

'I'd rent myself a Rolls Royce car and park it here outside the clover fields and I'd sit there until you cunts came out, then I'd pull down my trousers and put my arse up to the window.'

'There's an evil streak in you, Duck.'

'My daddy used to say that.'

'How did he know?'

'And never mind the lottery ...'

'Why not?'

'Because we'll all get what we deserves when we dies!'

'When I dies I wants my skin tanned and turned into a lady's saddle. That way I'll rest between the two things I loves most in the world.'

This general and light-hearted banter breaking the darkness of the winter morning. No cunt all that eager to climb out of the pick-up and trudge across the weary fields to the waiting horseflesh. Tales of all the exploits over the holiday with exaggerated accounts of hunting and hooring and hangovers. The Duck examining his dick after Louis telling him the Gorgio woman he was with on New Year's night was one of them beors with bad habits. Myles singing a little song about Sullivan John and me lighting up a cigarette and warming my fingers on the match flame. Land Rover pulling suddenly up behind us and The Blackberry kibbling out. On his polio leg. Followed by this big cunt with a black moustache and a wide-brimmed hat. Louis saying very low the words. Oh no — Levesque is back.

'Come along you broomdashers, Christmas is over.'

'Fuck off, Tom!'

'Who said that?'

'The Duck.'

'I did fucking not!'

'I'm not paying you cunts to sit in that truck. Owen!'

'Aye?'

'Go with Levesque here. It's time you learned something serious.'

Don't like the fucking sound of that. Not one fucking little bit. And as for the rest of you lazy lackeens — you knows what to do. Bollocks! You will have when you're a man. Across the paddock in the wake of this tall cunt wearing cowboy boots towards Tolui who's waiting for us at the stables. The early morning taking on a strange sort of luminescence — reflected from the drifted snow. Out across the fields a vast expanse of pure whiteness. Overhead the sky clearing and still alive with stars and the dying moon gradually giving way to the day. The enchanted half-light sparkling off the snow like dancing fire-flies. Filling the place with an air of unreality — like some fairy tale.

I stops and stands transfixed. Head raised and arms outstretched. Suddenly I knows that all that matters is here — and now. Nothing has gone before. And nothing will follow. And I sees what Tolui says that Shambala ain't a place but lies hidden in the heart and the journey there is a spiritual one across doubts and fears and didges.

The big cunt ahead of me turns and beckons. Hasn't spoken yet nor greeted me in any way. Tolui comes forward with his contagious smile. He shakes my hand as if he was some long lost brother who hasn't seen me for many years. He also greets Levesque who speaks with a French accent and I can tell they knows each other well. Even Tolui seeming a little intimidated by this big fucker. But we've all got our own prejudices and I sometimes finds it difficult to come to terms with strangers. Cunts who comes and speaks with forked tongues and smuggles their way into every fucking facet of life.

Of course we envies the Asians their women and their easy way with money and our so-called fucking superiors wishing they could make us all wear caste marks. So they would know if we was. Untouchable! All be academic soon with DNA duplicating and genetic discrimination. Tolui telling me as we follows behind that this Levesque conya is a Cajun who comes from Calcasieu Lake in Louisiana and is married to Tom Lee's half-sister and is an expert with the mules and sometimes helps out with the horses. Tolui about to say more but Levesque calling us into the lunge ring and telling us that today we will break some young hunters for the Henley markets down in Warwickshire.

'What is your name?'

'Owen ... McBride.'

'An Irishman?'

'Grandfather was French.'

'Really? What region of *la belle France*?'

'He never said.'

'Tom tells me, Owen, that you are a little *nerveux* with the *chevaux*?'

'I'm getting better, thanks to Tolui.'

'I will cure you completely!'

Levesque telling Tolui to go get the black colt. And this Owen is a big strong mollypeart and definitely prepared to argue about anything he doesn't approve of. Obviously an animal which was brought up on a bottle by a weak woman. We must now come to a mutual agreement with him and teach him manners. His job is to be ridden. And he will do his job well. And so will you my little *irlandais* who comes to me like a lamb to the slaughter in an instant of tiny truth and a centering of the Universe.

And if you watch Tolui *mon enfant* you will see how he fits the cavesson over the headcollar because this is a haughty horse who carries his head high and always lunge off two reins. The top rein goes on the noseband and the bottom rein on the bit. We have a rule here *mon novice* that our horses when lunged wear brushing boots. Whether shod or not. You understand? No? You will. Now we are ready for the first lesson. And to avoid burning your hands always wear gloves when lunging or long reining. And never use nylon. Always leather!

Tolui takes up the two lunge reins and loops them together as if they were one. He holds the reins in his left hand and leads the stroppy young horse with his right into the wooden-fenced ring. All the time talking quietly to the animal in his own language and the grai seeming to understand every word the fucker says.

'Ask your grandfather what part of France he came from. Perhaps he knew *mon père*.'

'He's dead.'

'My father?'

'No ... my grandfather.'

'A shame. Now I will probably never know.'

tribe

Tolui starts to lunge the horse to the left and the tension on the bit rein Owen must be slacker than the one on the noseband at all times. The Mongolian moving easily on the offside just behind the grai's line of progress while the horse shabbs round in a widening circle along the wall. Tolui barely touches the young colt's gaskins with the lunge tape and soon the rooker's trotting hooves churn up a dark circular track in the snow.

And of course, my *irlandais imbécile*, you must avoid to get tangled up in the reins or the *cheval* will probably kick you and take a bit out of your brain. That is assuming you have one. Tolui makes the horse halt out on the circle and Levesque leans a hand on my shoulder and tells me to take notice as we are not *trot et halte* merchants here Owen and we must watch out for lameness and over-reaching as well as other things.

Tolui goes to the young horse and talks to him while leading him to the centre and turning him to walk off on the right rein. The colt finding the transition difficult but Tolui taking control and soon the animal is ready to roller.

'Do you think you can do that, young Owen?'

'Aye ...'

'*Bon garçon*! Show me.'

Tolui leads out the black colt and brings back a brown grai with white socks. Let me see now if I can remember everything I've been taught in such a short space of fucking time. Take up the reins and lunge the horse round to the left. Feel the power of this animal coming down along the noseband rein and I moves in a small circle while the young horse watches me all the time with his haughty eye. Levesque clapping his hands with Gallic glee and calling out very good *mon galant*.

Hard to stop the horse as Tolui did and I mistakenly turns him in and the cunt comes at me with the reins round his legs. I can't fucking gather up quickly enough and panics as Tolui just in time leaps over the wooden wall and grabs the grai by the bridle and stops him from trampling me into the fucking ground.

Levesque flinging his arms into the air and cursing with words which can only come from the Calcasieu Lake area of

Louisiana. So we starts again and Tolui saying talk to the horse Owen. What should I fucking say? That you are the man and therefore the master. And work together with him. When you work together you can do anything. And make round movements — not square. Read the horse's reactions or you'll get hurt.

Taking his advice I soon finds myself oblivious to all things around me. As if it's only myself and this colt. There is nothing else outside the lunge ring. He watches me and I talks softly to him and somewhere in the hazy distance Tolui and Levesque claps their hands and smiles at each other and say. There you are. I knew all along he was a *chevalier*.

At breakfast time we sits inside the tack-room with the others and sausages frying on a pan over a blazing yog. Tom Lee telling us it looks like being a blackthorn winter and Big Bill loppeting on a hay-bale and saying if you neglect your belly you'll soon be on your back. Louis suddenly grabbing hold of his ears and kissing him hard on the lips. The big man flailing to his feet. Kicking Louis away from him. Arse on the floor and a mug of hot weed spilling down into the little cunt's lap.

'I'm fucking roasted!'

'I warned him. Didn't I warn him ...?'

'You warned him, Bill.'

'I just wanted to give you a sweet kiss.'

'Fuck away from me you quare!'

'My balls are scalded now.'

'That's a sinful shame.'

Big Bill sitting back on the bale with a smirk on his face. Louis up onto his feet and taking a hot sausage from the pan he sticks it straight into a large left ear. Scream of outrage and a swiping about blindly of big fists. Bill grabbing hold of the glibby little cunt's scruff as he scampers for the door. A big bone-bending pogger in the solar-plexus.

Howls of pain as Louis crashes backwards into the makeshift table — spilling the weed and the sausages out of the pan. Mob of men fiercely up onto their feet. Shouting and swearing. Louis pushed and shoved and kicked shivering out into the snow. Grumbles and growls going round as the pan is picked up and the table reset on top of a saddle trestle.

tribe

Later as the day shabbs by I learns about rollering and rugging up and side reining and riding away. Being all the time on the lookout for them mollypearts who bucks and kicks and roots and grinds their teeth at you. And Owen you must ride a horse in a straight line for balance and the reins is not a safety belt — it is for control! And afterwards we settles the grais and cleans the sweat from them to avoid the galls and the scalds.

Some opens and shuts their mouths as if the rookers was trying to talk to me and Tolui says Owen *aanda*. They seem to have accepted you. At last!

We gets back to the site about six and Myles asking me Owen — has you ever had your fortune told? Plenty of times over the years but I'm still not fucking superstitious. Except maybe a little bit! Myles saying how The Duck's old daddy is a famous fortune-teller and they calls him The Duck because the Gypsy word for crystal-gazing is duckering and it's nothing at all to do with the way the cunt walks.

Inside the trailer this old Gypsy pav with a grey beard telling me to sit while he looks into his television — which is what young conya I calls my crystal ball and it's more than five hundred years old.

I'm still a little sceptical but he says we all wants to believe Owen — even though we says we don't. We wants to see what's in the stars. Especially us Gypsies. With our four-leafed clovers and our rabbits' feet and horseshoes and banshees' combs for good luck and never get knocked up on a Friday nor argue in the morning and a bird flying into the trailer is bad luck and so is the hawthorn blow and better never to have been born than cut your hair on a Sunday morn. Then there's one magpie for bad blood and two for good — three for a wedding and four for a death. Five for money and six for the story that will never be told. Who can say young yawney? Who can honestly say? And I'm not afraid of the dying Owen — only of the coming back again.

I gives him all the details I knows about my birth and he says them newspapers is all liars. They gives everyone born under a star sign the same horoscope. Gypsy horoscopes needs dates and times and even places of birth. Newspapers knows nothing about astrology. Astrology Owen was invented by three wise men — two shepherds and a Gypsy Chal. And he knows about my father and my mother and my two brothers and also that I am to marry soon and will have six sons of my own — from four different women. And I will live to be sixty-nine and never be ridiculously rich but will sometimes be happy and frequently content. Which is really all a man can reasonably ask for.

We talks and drinks strong tea and jipper and I remembers things from the past about some Gypsies who could hypnotise and others who could lay the fetich on you. And my daddy's words that travelling people believes that everyone has a good spirit and a bad spirit and that life is only a dream and reality begins when you're dead. When your spirit leaves your body. And some cunts like me dreams in black and white and others in colour and it's them ones who dreams in colour are the prophets and the peacemakers.

The old duckerer says he doesn't know his exact age but it's in the region of ninety-nine and his birth certificate is on a tree — somewhere in Spain. His words drift back to the old days when he'd be away on the tramp as soon as the blossom came and the thrush began to sing. And how he buried his old mammy outside Budapest with her pipe and her ounce of baccy to see her on her way and how when she was younger the yawn of her voice in song had a culture all its own. And Owen I thinks about it. At fresh of the morning and at balance of the day. I thinks about it.

tribe

16

January kicking and screaming its way out of the new year. February waiting in the wings and then a short month until spring. O'Connell's house in darkness across the street. Windows still shattered to this winter night. Glass all over the fucking ground. Bringing back memories for some strange reason of many years ago when I was very young — rising early every morning to fetch water from some roadside stream. On this day seeing a commotion and a flurry of tails by a nearby cosh. Dropping the bucket and running across I tried to get through the dogs but the mad fuckers just sent me sprawling. When I finally managed to kick a few of the curs out of the way I could see a small threadbare cat curled up in a ball of blood-sticky fur. The bastard dogs had torn a leg off between them and was savaging what was left in a milling snarling mass.

Edwin standing in the shadows down the street — watching the house and me as well. Cunt doesn't know I've seen him and doesn't seem to recognise me. Shive whistling away with hands in pockets and keeping cool as ice — as if I've come the wrong way and just remembered where I was going in the first place.

Told by my daddy to be always on the alert for the unexpected. I picked up a club from the bodgel by the side of the trailer and laid into them. Lashing out at the teeth-flashing snouts and sending the fuckers yelping in all directions. The mangled thing on the gore-soaked ground tried to crawl away — but couldn't. I crushed it with a rock.

Out of Edwin's sight now and duck down this alley glibby as a gooley-bug. Into the shadows and up onto the garage roofs keeping all the time down low. Nobody watching the back of the Hilton. Stupid thick-as-shite cunts. Down again into the gardens and without a sound over nettles and stones to the back door. Locked and still no lights. Climb through a broken window at the risk of being cut to ribbons by glass and begin a stealthy search from room to room. Keeping well crouched at the front of the house so as not to be seen. Little precautions can prevent calamities — like Badhu and Bhopal and Bosnia.

'Owen ...'

'Jesus Christ!'

'No, no ... it's me, O'Connell. In here ..'

O'Connell sitting on the beer-stained floor of the saloon. A whisky in one hand and a blanket round his fucking shoulders. Looking like the cunt just spent the past few days in a dosshouse. Frightened face. There in the dark.

'Did he see you?'

'Who?'

'The black cunt outside.'

'Aye, but he thinks I've buggered off. What happened?'

'A long story, Owen.'

'Tell me.'

'You were right, boy. I should never have had nothing to do with them fuckers.'

'How long have you been like this?'

'Since Sunday.'

'Have you had anything to eat?'

'Cold beans ... daren't light the fucking cooker.'

'Why didn't you come round to my place?'

'I don't want to get you involved in this, Owen.'

'I'm already involved.'

'It's worse than you think.'

'Any more whisky?'

'Here, but keep fucking down.'

'Talk to me, Con!'

'Came back New Year's Day, Owen. The police were still here, so I gave them your story ... about the lodgers. The boys backed me up of course, after they were released from the cells. Anyway, a couple of days later Patsy pays me a visit ... all smiles and friendly like at first, with that big black bastard out there and two other cunts as well. They ran all me boys off and told them not to come back if they valued their fucking lives.

'I tried to argue the point, but they broke two toes on me left foot with a hammer. "Been a bad boy, O'Connell," says Patsy. "Caused my friend Lionel a lot of bother. Lionel's not too pleased. Lost six of his best fucking girls, not to mention the hiding received by Edwin here. Edwin's not too pleased either." "I don't suppose he is," says I. "But," says Patsy, "there *is* a way you can make it up to us." "How's that?" says I." "A little job you can do for us," says he. "I've got a job," says I. "Oh ... this'll be weekend work," says he. "Look on it as overtime." "I never does overtime," says I, "... it's a promise I made to the priests at the same time as I took the pledge." So they broke two toes on me right foot.'

'The fucking bastards ...'

'Anyway, Owen ... I was persuaded after that. Arrangements were made for me to do this job last weekend ... down in London. Got in to Euston Station early Sunday morning, with me feet murdering me. This cockney cunt picks me up in a van, with two or three other fuckers in the back and takes me to a place in Wimbledon, next door to a Halifax Building Society.

'There's another gang of the cunts inside and I see that half the wall's already been knocked through and there's a great big safe on the other side. "Want you to blow open this steel door for us," says your man. "Where's Patsy?" says I. "Patsy doesn't get involved with the details," says the cunt "... he doesn't need to be here. We have all the gear ... plastic explosives and everything." "Can't do it," says I. "Why the fuck not?" "Don't know anything about that plastic stuff. I only works with the gelignite." "Same fucking thing," says your man. "By Christ, it's not," says I. "Well ... do the best you can," says he "... and make as little fucking noise as possible."'

'What did you do, Con?'

'Packed all the fucking explosives they had round this safe door and a long slow fuse back through the hole in the wall to the other building. All of a sudden I'm bursting for a piss, what with all the travelling and excitement and everything. "There's a lavatory out the back," says this thick-looking cunt with the cockney accent. "I won't be a minute," says I. "Is there anything we can do while you're gone?" says he. "Aye," says I, " ... light that fuse. I'll be back by the time it blows."'

'Jesus fucking wept ...'

'He did, Owen. He did! Sure, it wasn't a fuse at all, only that fucking detonator cord that travels at the rate of about six hundred yards a second. And there was more of a kick in that fucking plastic stuff than I reckoned for. The bang made me piss down me leg.

'Bejaysus, sure it blew down the front wall completely and the boys all crouched inside with surprised looks on their faces, on view to the whole street. The steel door went flying out into the main drag, taking the rest of the fucking room with it. From all accounts, there was fucking banknotes everywhere. Cunts murdering one another in the street to pick them up. I just put me head down and took off in the middle of all the confusion. When I got back these fuckers were outside the front door. They take it in shifts to watch. I just waited until dark and then struggled in the back way.'

'This is a stupid fucking place to hide, Con ...'

'Safest place, Owen. They don't know I'm in here and they're too fucking thick to search again. Can't run too good ... wouldn't last five minutes out on the street.'

'It's only a matter of time until the cunts suss you out ...'

'Only one thing for it, Owen. Must get to me van. Drive to the airport and then away to the ould country until this blows over.'

'I'll give you a hand. We'll get out the way we came in.'

'No! Sorry Owen, the ould fucking feet have swollen up and wouldn't make it over them rocks and stones again.'

'I'll carry you.'

'Owen ... I'm seventeen stone.'

tribe

'Give me another whisky, while I think.'

Black car drawing up outside. Peep carefully over the window-sill to spy Edwin getting into the back seat. Lights off and these cunts are definitely out to kill someone. Preferably O'Connell. Maybe break the rest of his fucking toes first — just for spite. Wish there was some religion left in the world. Could go out there and ask them to turn the other cheek. Or even look the other way while O'Connell makes a run for it. That's the fucking answer!

'Where's your top-coat, Con?'

'I'm wearing it.'

'Take it off. And I want that cap you wear to work.'

'What are you going to do, Owen?'

'Make a fucking run for it.'

'They're not after you.'

'They won't know it's me, you fucking yawney. Where's your van?'

'I've hid it close by.'

'Can you drive?'

'I'd say so ...'

'When they come after me, you clear out and get to the van. Drive straight to the airport and get on the next plane to Dublin.'

'Jesus, Owen ... if they catch you they'll give you an awful fucking hiding.'

'They won't catch me.'

'They have a fucking motor car!'

'Just get down the hall to the front door and be ready to go.'

O'Connell hobbling on the poor broken toes. Still protesting and Owen I can't allow you to do this. Fuck up! On with the top-coat and cap. Good job it's so dark.

'Owen ...'

'What the fuck now?'

'Take the keys.'

'What keys?'

'To this house. It's yours, to do what you like with 'til I come back.'

'You may not come back.'

'Then it's yours to keep.'

'Are you fucking ruille ...?'

'If you come over in the summer ... y'know, with your mammy ... look me up.'

'You got enough money?'

'Aye, Owen.'

'Let's fucking prastie then!'

Out through the front door and down the street like a bitch in heat being chased by seven sheepdogs. Headlights flashing on behind me. Engine roaring and a screech of tyres trying to tear up the road. Don't look back. Goodbye O'Connell. I'll miss you — you fucking lousy cunt.

Lights about to change up ahead. Fly quickly across. The motor car behind ignoring all legal restraints. A symphony of brakes screaming in protest. Curses and swears and you fucking stupid bloody lunatic. Down this one-way street. Take an optimistic peep over the shoulder to see the car doors flying open and feet following fast. Crowd of weirdo cunts in Howard Street. Up to no good for sure.

Zigzag through them and a bump in the solar plexus for an oul drochel with a moustache. Send the mare sprawling. Dirty knickers in the air and shouts of stop that man. He tried to molest me. Feet in fourth gear as the whole pack of perverts gives chase. Maniac on the loose. Mugging and murdering methylated spirit drinkers. Round the corner and down this dark alley with the heart trying to jump out of my fucking mouth and make its own escape. Off quick with O'Connell's coat and cap and stuff them into the nearest dustbin. Hear all the heels in hot pursuit. Out onto New Road at the other end of the alley and stop dead! Lean with feigned indifference up against the wall and nonchalantly roll a cigarette. A forest fire raging and roaring in my chest. Hope no fucker can hear it.

'There he goes!'

'Where?'

'Into the church. I seen him run into the church.'

Seeking sanctuary! Top of my voice sounding strange and sort of hysterical. Almost didn't recognise it myself. Pretend to take tut with the vanished bry and join in the hunt now with the slobbering hounds. Much better than being the fugitive fox. Edwin and his friends at the front being of fitter frame than the winos. Late service for all the faithful in progress as this odd-ball band bursts in howling and baying for blood. Being instantly subdued by the menacing voice of the vicar as he bellows out over their fucking heads. This is the house of God! In no uncertain terms. There *is* some religion left. For those who knows where to find it.

Grabbing just in time a sixty-nine bus back to Anchorage Quay. Legs fucking completely gone. Ann indoors waiting for me. Give us a cup of coffee a ghrá mo chroí.

And a loan of an oxygen mask.

'Where have you been?'

'Went to see O'Connell.'

'You said you were going to stay away ... after that dreadful party ...'

'He's gone.'

'Where?'

'To Ireland, on Concorde!'

'Thank goodness for that.'

'Amen!'

Collapse into a chair with the coffee. Let the life slowly return to the lacerated limbs. Be nice to me now Ann and we'll make plans together in this sane little room. And how long can you stay? All night if you want Owen. I want. This gentle girl to love me. Alone in our secret personal place in front of the friendly flames. And her small hands to run lightly over every inch of my trembling body. Only way to calm a troubled mind is with the balm of passion. Lower her down onto the fire-front rug and she rolls me over onto my back. Kneeling above me with her sly little smile which says I know your bell will go ding dong. If I ring it.

And despite everything else it's a comfort to know in my heart that at least one sweet soul would mourn my passing. O'Connell I hope is in the speeding van to the airport and from there to the open skies. A wild goose. And his keys in the pocket of my jeans that are now slung away across the floor. Making me a man of property and potential profit. Open Ann your lovely legs and let me climb up into your waiting womb. Be born again in another place. When the time is right!

tribe

There's a man in Texas been sentenced to death for shooting a used-car salesman. Is there any fucking justice? Peculiar also about these names like Whitehall and Whitehouse and Whitewash — with people behind the scenes pulling strings all over the whole world. And increasing evidence of phone tapping and letter opening and other kinds of fucking surveillance. What will it be like when the cunts invent telepathy?

But I've got my own problems. Welts on my hands from the leather long reins and bad feet from these fucking old bellus-brogues. Need badly a new pair of proper riding boots. Ann making noises about the amount of time I'm spending with the Travellers. Saying Owen you're beginning even to smell like a horse. The Blackberry saying March ain't out 'til the middle of April and a coolness still in the air although the birds can slowly be heard singing.

And Ann's little computer job proving to be a gold-mine of promotion prospects with all these tiny chips and bits and bytes and terminals and things. Twenty-first century technology running rampant with cyberspace and super highways and interactive internets and a computer soon to become essential in every home. Like a lavatory. Money rolling in and she wants us to marry just as soon as the proper arrangements can be made. A few minor repairs to O'Connell's windows and then move in before the squatters find out or the fugitive returns. From the land of saints and speculators. Make the cunt an offer he can't refuse. For his life! And here I am still standing round this glowing yog. Chance is a fine thing. Or would be!

'Wake up there, Owen.'

'Transcendental meditation, Jake. Dangerous to disturb me in this state.'

'Wha' is that, Owen?'

'Difficult for the self to get back into the body.'

'Och aye, a knows that fucking feeling.'

'You does?'

'Aye, laddie, and yer bones turns tae fucking jelly.'

'Well ...'

'Like being in two fucking places at the same time.'

'Didn't know it was such a common experience.'

'Och, well known in Glasgae ...'

'Is that right?'

'Especially on a Saturday fucking nicht.'

Time ticking and the hatchintan strangely quiet this morning as the brown and white voices starts to mingle with the March madness and another day begins to breathe.

'Are you still a virgin, Jake?'

'Don't be fucking ridiculous, ye cunt!'

'Does that mean you are or you're not?'

'Hold on there, Myles ... what goes on here this morning?'

'What d'you mean, Owen?'

'It's half-past seven already and no sign of anyone making a move.'

Myles comes closer and whispers in my ear that today is the King of the Tinkers fight. Why didn't you fucking tell me? We weren't sure Owen that Glasheen was going to show up. And as well as that them Gorgio walls has ears and we don't want the venue overrun with wobs and gavvers and muskra shites.

'Where *is* the venue?'

'The clover fields. Tom Lee talked to the farmer.'

Trailers and trucks arriving already outside the camp. Felix emerging from his caravan with Litzy behind him smiling through her sorrow and cheers and caps in the air.

We sets off in convoy for the clover fields where the crowds begin to congregate round the lunging ring. Horses frightened and flying away from these wild cunts and donkeys braying and mules being their obstinate fucking selves. Wish I'd been born on a South Pacific island several hundred years ago. Stare up at the high bright palm leaves from the warm sand. With a black-eyed native girl to fetch the fruit for me from the rain forest. Because I'm afraid. Of spiders. Often contemplated joining a religious order. Or becoming a Buddhist. If it wasn't for the fucking celibacy. Feel the warmer weather on the way. Be very welcome. And the Yella Lad enters the lunging ring sparring with the morning air in his blue track suit and bandaged hands. Cheering and calling out and commotion all around and book-makers taking their bets with two to one against the Yella Lad and two to one on Kevin Glasheen. And why the fuck should that be?

Suddenly a silence falling over the crowd as a white Mercedes pulls up outside the main gate. Followed by an entourage of other vehicles and the Irish is here boys! Crowd of mad cunts from these latecoming cars spilling over the fences and onto the field. And we're here to sort out the men from the girls today me-boys. Glasheen emerging slowly from the back of the white Mercedes in gold track suit and a jacket with a big lion's head on the back — the undisputed King of the Tinkers. Crowd going fucking mad and I sees from his size that he's a natural heavyweight. At least seventeen stones. Felix being no more than a middleweight. That explains the betting odds! And Myles saying don't worry Owen. Things like weight and size means fuck-all in a bare-knuckle bout. And Felix will be all right as long as he can stay away from the big grunty. And they've discovered three new galaxies ten thousand million light years away and revised the criteria for brain death.

So there is hope. For some of us cunts at least.

'Put your money on Felix, Owen.'

'Are you sure about that, Myles? That Glasheen's a big bastard.'

'Trust me.'

'I knows I fucking shouldn't ...'

But I still feecks the two to one against my hundred pounds and hopes that Myles is right. Glasheen enters the wooden ring and parades round for the admiration of the crowd before making a feinting lunge at Felix and then laughing. The line is drawn and the serious stuff begins. Glasheen lumbering round like a crazed ox in pursuit of the elusive Yella Lad. I sees what Myles means as Felix picks him off with stinging blows to the solar-plexus and the kidneys and the small of the back. Then darting out of danger before the bigger pav can connect with a killing fist.

Shouts of keep out Felix and flatten the cunt Kevin coming from the hysterical crowd round the perimeter. Then the Yella Lad taking a frash swipe from the King which sends him staggering back against the wooden wall. Glasheen sensing blood and stumbling after the dazed Felix. Another brutal pogger to the side of the face and Felix falls down. Fever pitch screams of get up you cunt from outside the ring as Glasheen stands over the Yella Lad and my fucking money now seems definitely lost.

But the cunt ain't corbed yet. He stirs and I sees him wink up from the ground at Myles who claps me on the shoulder and says. We're still in business boy! The Yella Lad scrambling quickly out from under the King and back to his feet. Circling Glasheen again like a snapping hound round an enraged bear. Fast fists flying into the sides and stomach and the big cunt beginning to break down. Dropping his guard to protect his hurting body and Felix launches a both-feet-in-the-air blow to the chin which sends the King crashing against the ring wall — knocking seven or eight spectators off their perches. Standing for a brief moment — his eyes looking past us into oblivion. Then the cunt falls like a felled tree onto his face. The crowd invades the ring and Felix is carried out — his head swollen and bleeding.

The Irish supporters taking tut and other fights breaking out amongst the crowd and get your money quick Owen before the book-makers disappears in the pandemonium. And I don't suppose there'll be any work done today now. Back to town and park the pick-up for safety at the camp. Walk the rest of the way to the pub with these pavs. Great to be away at this early time of day. Spring grass under our feet and the whole world smiling. Don't look back now but forward across the common to that little man walking his wolfhound. Not knowing the slightest thing about us as we passes him by. Giving the dog-brute a wide berth in case of the unexpected bite.

April soon be on its way now and if I'm still at liberty the later spectre of the stone fields of a homeland never seen and an ancestry never understood. With O'Connell smiling at me through the growing darkness and asking how are things across the water and is my fucking house still standing? Fear sliding an icicle along my heart. Trying to extinguish the cushti feeling on this immaculate morning. But I shrugs it easily away and the fucker lies unbroken behind me on the grass where it will wait with silent patience. For my return.

Swing in smartly to the Rose and Crown at opening time and what'll it be boys? God bless you Felix. Rounds of beer becoming brandies and whiskies and all kinds of other fucking top shelf shorts. And lash up the same again there barman and while you're at it stop the fucking clock exactly where it is so that we have no further to go along the road of this or any other fucking life.

By six o'clock only Myles and Louis and myself left standing. And what about some fucking grub but Louis feeling a little sick and unable to proceed. So we escorts him back to the hatch — hoping someone there will have a pot over the fire and any sort of edible shite sounding great to our deluged brain cells. And on the way we trip into Tesco's for a few take-aways. Ought maybe to let Ann know where I am. Ring up and say can I speak to the computer please. I don't care which one. Well then ask it from me if logically speaking God would have to be hermaphrodite. What? It says that God's merely morphine for the moribund. Must be some malfunction in the machine.

Fall through the swing doors of the supermarket and wheel Louis round in a wire mesh trolley. Tell this big tall mare by the bean tins that the cunt's on special offer. But only for today and she wants to know which shelf these colourful little men is on because she can't remember seeing any. Up to the checkout with a bottle of Bells and a dozen each of the Guinness and Greenacres ale. Louis doing all the talking and how much is all this missy? Forty-four pounds and ten pence exactly. That's a drooge because all I has is a fiver. You could put something back sir. Under no circumstances.

Louis at the till with a wink back to us and the worried face of the young cashier at these half-drunk Gypsy cunts holding up the queue. I'm a respectable member of the community miss and gives you my solemn word as a Freemason that I'll be back with the balance before you can say Sir John Sainsbury. Manager called and the pimply faced cunt eyeing us up and down before deciding not to send for the wobs and cause a fillyhoo in front of all these impressionable young mothers. Bad publicity like that could get back to head office. But you'll have to leave a name and address you understand. Of course. It's Behan. William. Big Bill to my friends and to those of closer acquaintance — taxi-with-the-doors-open. And certainly that's my address. Ask any of these honest men who knows me intimately.

We staggers back to our hide-away from the raw edge of ruefulness. Laden down with this booze that brings its own mists to lay in the hollows of our heads. Smell of jogray from the pot in Myles' trailer and his mammy dishing up the shackles and tandra-cake while we slugs down bolgams of Louis' beer and whisky. Whole world standing still because us Travellers has a cultural contempt for time and clocks and all that codology. And after the food a pretend game of poker for pennies until oblivion in the end calls all the bluffs.

Had to spend the night up at the camp due to the taking of too much fucking booze. And woken the next morning by Myles screaming his head off at seven.

'Lord save us ... look at the fucking time!'

'Woah there!'

'Wake up! Wake fucking up!'

'Myles ... what the fuck are you doing here?'

'I lives here, Owen. Where's Louis?'

'Who?'

'Find Louis for fuck's sake ...'

'Where is the little cunt?'

'How the fuck should I know? Get your fucking head out from under that calf-hide cover, Owen ...'

'Don't shout, Myles. I wants a cup of weed.'

'Fuck the weed. Tom Lee will go mad.'

'I'll go mad if I don't get a cup of weed!'

'Boil the fucking kettle then.'

'Where is it?'

'How should I fucking know?'

'Stop panicking, Myles. Tell Tom we was hijacked.'

'What?'

'Threatened with a fucking temperance badge.'

'What's going on in here ...?'

'Where the fuck have you been, Louis?'

'In the lavatory. What were we drinking?'

'I can't remember.'

'Whatever the cunt was, I could shite through the eye of a needle.'

'I could sleep on a fucking clothesline.'

'Shut the fuck up!'

Myles' mammy finally making us some tea. And a few clangers to eat while we're driving. Myles behaving like a frashed akhal-teite and Louis running back to the toilet as soon as the hot liquid hits his stomach. Tom Lee standing in the clover field with a furious look over his blackberry face.

'Where have youse three yawneys been? Half a day's work should be done by now.'

'Traffic problems, Tom.'

'What are you blating about?'

'Treacle tanker overturned in the road.'

'You people is still fucking dibby.'

'One pav stuck fast. Couldn't get him out no matter what.'

'I don't want to hear your harlicking. Don't give it to me!'

'Wobs had to shoot him in the end.'

'Galune!'

'Save the litchup from starving to death.'

'Enough! Get to fucking work ... right now!'

Levesque and Tolui with a bay colt ready for the breaking roller and breastplate. And the Cajun saying it's nice of you to join us *mon paresseux*. And how would you like to lunge this horse for a little while and mind your eyes from that flying *caillou* — to make sure you are still tomorrow. Able to cry. Tolui after a while shortening the reins to control the colt when he feels the roller. Telling me to stand to the near side and be prepared to hang on as you let out the reins Owen. Careful not to get in front of the horse or I'll end up flat on my fucking back.

Tolui now talking gently to the grai as he places the roller pad on his back. Letting the girth hang loose over the horse for a while so he knows it's not going to hurt. He gradually tightens up — using a crupper and making sure the girth and surcingle can't slip back around the belly to become a bucking strap. I'm in bad enough fucking shape without a dangerous fucking animal on my hands. This colt watching me with a wild eye as I tries to keep his attention away from Tolui and the roller — until I'm ready to let him go. And because a horse's eyes is on the side of his head he can see behind as well as side and front.

Then the Mongolian takes up the tape in his right hand and I lets the horse move off. Stepping back I begins to lengthen the reins while Tolui makes sure that the grai keeps going forward. Now the horse feeling the roller round his chest and going off in a series of natchy bucks and jumps to try and get rid of this new and needling restriction.

We works as a team to prevent the colt from turning in and coming at us. Tolui flicking the tape behind him as he roars and neighs and jumps with all four feet off the fucking ground. I holds onto the reins and keeps him moving forward round the outside of the lunging circle. Sweat beginning to form on my forehead despite the coolness of the day. Who the fuck invented drink? Whoever it was I wish the cunt eternal wind. And a septic arsehole.

Eventually the colt settles down and picks up the rhythm of the trot again. Tolui talking to him with words of praise. Telling him he's done well. Then I slows him to a walk and finally makes him halt out on the boards. We both goes to him and praises him with circular stroking before we tighten the roller even more. Once again the fucker bucks and kicks as he moves off and feels the tighter girth and once again I holds on until he settles back to a good rhythm of trot. I leads him back to his box and takes off the boots and cavesson — leaving him wearing his headcollar and the roller which will stay on until we're sure he no longer notices that it's there.

Levesque leaning back and lecturing us while we work about how horses should not be broken until at least three years old and never do serious work until they're four. And Owen *mon coquin irlandais* the two-year-old bones have not yet formed and their skeleton growth plates are still open. They do not fuse until three and a half years. And although thoroughbreds are raced at two this is definitely *injuste*. Racehorses are expendable and the veterinary fraternity will not criticise the racing men because of mutual financial interests. And telling us how in Canada they use pregnant mares' piss to produce hormone replacement therapy drugs for peevish women. Fifty thousand mares deliberately put in

tribe

foal each year to make the raw material and also boys the by-product of unwanted foals. *Les juments* kept permanently thirsty so the piss is more potent and tethered in tiny stalls and ending up with oedemas and swollen legs and serious psychological problems. Foals taken from the *mères* at birth and sent to feed lots for fattening before being slaughtered with the shagged-out mares.

And please Levesque could you fuck up. Because although I sympathise with your sentiments it's hard enough to get through this morning without listening to your fucking sermons as well.

Will the day ever come when fucking robots can do this kind of stuff? And rumours going round that the computers is already thinking about it. Only a matter of time they say until men becomes obsolete and most women too. More leisure time for the masses. Have to go back to school to learn how to live. Do all kinds of running and jumping and stepping and lifting to pass the time and lengthen the life. And hang on by the fingernails to the final few hours of heartbreaking humdrum.

After the breakfast we does a bit of grooming and Tolui telling me to go get Hercules the big jack Poitou who stands thirteen hands with his black cross and leg rings and throat markings that makes him look more like a zebra than a donkey and who brays and backs away as I tries to pull the hoor's-ghost along. Whole crowd of cunts laughing at my fruitless efforts and Hercules hee-hawing and me fucking and blinding and Tolui rolling round on the grass with glee and shouting push him from the shoulder Owen.

I finally lets the fucker go and trudges back over to the grooming shed. Head splitting and hearing the laughter of the other litchups following my ears. Scowling at Tolui as he tells me all new men Owen are eventually sent to bring in Hercules. And nobody has yet succeeded. I drops down between the buckets and brushes and holds onto my aching yud.

Of course it all depends on whether they decides to divide up the profits of this new world and give us all a little share. Or will they tell us that it's been swallowed up by invisible overheads and unmentionable expenses. Ann will probably be all right. Need the likes of her for a while yet. Until the machines can figure it out for themselves and I wouldn't put it past them. Cunning fucking calculators.

Someone sending out for more food. I'll have a horseburger and don't be cheap with the chips. And if they're available ask the St John's Ambulance Service to stand by at the gate. In case there's need for a transfusion of blood. Rhesus positive for me. I seen this cunt in the street once wearing steel-toecapped bedroom slippers. Purple plaid socks with an ankle-length gabardine trenchcoat and a bright red woollen scarf. He had a little dog on a lead who wore brown boots. I thought he was a tramp at first or from a different age. Some dismal depressed era long ago. It turned out we were related. In some strange way.

The Duck telling us on the way home that he's getting married in a month's time. To Louis' sister. God help the poor fucking girl. And of course we're all invited to the wedding which will be a proper Gypsy affair and no expense stinted. Only slawm being the fact that he'll have to move out from his mammy because two beors in one trailer is like two dogs with one bone.

Do tell! Ann won't be happy about the last couple of days. And this news of The Duck's reminding me of my own predicament and that I'll soon be heading in the same fucking direction. But every now and then Peggy's fingers touch my imagination and her pink perfume floats a little raft of coconut shells up onto the beach for my escape. And why is your dog wearing brown boots? Because his black ones is at the menders!

The back of the pick-up unusually comfortable as we travels the dark road home. Louis already asleep on some sacks and Myles sucking at the remainder of a cigarette. And me with dreams darting in my hungover skull. All the world is dead now and in amongst the trees the wild wind searches for signs of life. Tuck me in to my torpor and leave the light on outside my slightly open door. Because I'm sure I hears a tap-tapping on the window and a bumping under the bed. When I wake I will be free. And when I was a small boy. Me could fly!

tribe

19

Always wear something new for Easter — which makes a sudden entrance with smells of saffron from the fields and a blanket of bluebells halfway across the whole country. Then out again just as quickly with an unseasonal fall of snow — trying to trick mother nature and making things bad for the hedge-poker and the hay-bird.

They says the blood of integrity and fair play has brought the world along to the state it's in today. Was there a drop wasted? Or are we still as savage as when we first fell from the tertiary tree — with a hatchet in our hand? Waiting here in this codified corridor with an assortment of fallen angels. Shoulder rubbing with the pickpockets and pushers. Shoplifters and shysters and no your honour there are no witnesses. Too petrified to appear. What of? Picture in the newspapers. Next case.

Who? McBride your honour. A foreigner? Sometimes. I see. Indecent exposure in a public place. And really sergeant — this man doesn't look the type. Appearances can cause clerical errors your honour. Quite. And yes that's right — answered a call from a lady who was hysterical. Was it from fright or fascination?

'Mister McBride ...'

'That's me, your worship.'

'How do you plead?'

'Not guilty!'

'Are you saying you were not naked on Anchorage Quay?'

'No, your lordship ...'

'What then?'

'I was sleepwalking.'

'At nine o'clock in the morning?'

'It comes in sudden spasms.'

'Are you represented by Counsel?'

'Certainly not, your eminence.'

'Your situation is serious, Mister McBride.'

'Innocence needs no artillery.'

'I've a good mind to adjourn.'

Oh no your judgeship — don't do that. Because I couldn't stand the strain of coming again to this fucking court-house and seeing how so many of our citizens is committing crimes these days. And he told us your honour that he was a member of some silly sect — performing a religious rite. Is this true? Of course not. I was dreaming. And judge I wonder does you ever dream? Or does you in bed sit bolt upright wearing wig and gown and pass subjective judgements on yourself and your life? And what about your wife? Does the mare ever think of the poor cunts in the suicide cells — and the beors too? And does she sometimes feel the little worm of disgust creep crawling in her womb as you sentences her to a life of fucking intolerance?

'I find your attitude one of carelessness, Mister McBride.'

'Blame it on society, sir.'

'I blame it on you, sir. Guilty as charged.'

'Does this mean I'm now a criminal?'

'A petty criminal, Mister McBride.'

By that does you mean my crime was insignificant? And if so will my sentence also be small? As it is your first offence we shall show leniency and the fine will be the sum of five-hundred-and-fifty pounds. Nothing petty about that you fucking wigged cunt. The police barrister asking for costs to be added to my debt to society and a little weakness in the legs as I stands down from the fucking dock. I suppose it could have been worse — because once you finds yourself in the clutches of these cunts you could end up doing life in a solitary straitjacket. And they says a hot-cross bun baked on a Good Friday is great for the gout.

tribe

A couple of minutes after midday as I walks down the court-house steps. Pop in for a pint to this winebar where I promised to meet Ann on her lunch-break. Offered to pay ten pounds per week as I have not your cuntship the means at present to fork out such a lump fucking sum. Having until recently been a redundant scrap-dealer and part-time gaff-lad with erratic and ever so ephemeral resources and currently saving hard for a wedding cake. Judge prepared to accept nothing less than twenty pounds per week — or risk the wrath of the spunk-sucking bailiffs. Take away all Collins' little comforts. Ann finding me sitting here in the shadows. Hope there were no rag-arsed reporters present.

'Well?'

'Water!'

'How did it go, Owen?'

Ordered in future to paint my arse with black polish before showing it to women of a hysterical nature. And can count myself fortunate to have a young lady like yourself who's willing to put up with my perversions. But they says the old religions are on the upsurge again. So it's not all good news. Is it?

'Five-hundred-and-fifty pounds!'

'Plus costs.'

'Oh Owen!'

'Don't fucking blame me.'

'I suppose it was *my* fault?'

'Well ... maybe not all.'

But certainly fucking some. Ann at this point changing the subject and what about this Hilton house Owen? It is the end of April and not a single word from across the water. Is O'Connell still alive? Or dead somewhere in a ditch?

'The place will rot away, Owen.'

'Let it.'

'Why don't you move in.'

'What about the flat?'

'Give it back.'

'To who?'

'The Council, of course.'

'Not mine to give.'

'Collins is in Australia. O'Connell is in Ireland. Isn't it time you started to think of yourself, Owen ... of us?'

'The Hilton is not mine either ...'

'He gave it to you.'

'Not in legal terms.'

'What if he doesn't come back?'

'I've just come out of court, Ann. I certainly don't want another fucking skirmish with the law.'

'Write to him then. Ask him what he intends to do.'

'Don't have his address.'

'He could be dead for all you know.'

Then I'm sunk, scuttled and fucking scuppered. But I'm looking out for the lodgers and if I can convince the cunts that the danger has passed they might come back and sleep safely again in their little fleabag beds and pay their rightful rent to me. To hold of course in a protected place until O'Connell returns from exile.

'I'll see him in July, when we go over.'

'I haven't decided about that yet.'

'Why not?'

'It's throwing money away, Owen. I don't know anyone ...'

'Neither do I.'

'Then why must you go?'

'Mother insists.'

And although you can be quite adamant in your own way Ann — mother was never the woman to be easily put off. So I must sail to see the old country and can offer no logical reason for your computer. Except maybe to see O'Connell and also because of a funny feeling — in my feet. Mother saying bring that little lackeen Owen who called on me at Christmas — because she seemed so sweet and you could certainly do a lot worse. You can see Ann that if the senile dementure is finally setting in I wouldn't want to unduly upset her little make-believe world.

Ann saying if I must then I must but that it's very doubtful if she'll be able to come with me. Somebody after all must keep a close eye on our finances — especially in the light of this day's expensive events. And what about this wedding on Saturday?

'What wedding?'

tribe

'I told you, Ann ... ages ago.'

'You did not, Owen!'

'Are you sure? The Duck ...'

'Who?'

'His old daddy is a duckerer ...'

'Oh Owen, you're not serious.'

'I certainly am.'

She says that wild horses wouldn't be able to drag her there. So I'll have to go alone. Might be good for me and take my mind off all this unpleasantness and slander. Ann asking for half a pint of lager shandy and one of those rolls that look so appetising under the glass. And barman put another pint in there — of porter.

'Will you be going to work today?'

'Not now.'

'Do they know where you are?'

'Whole fucking town knows where I am.'

'Don't be so neurotic, Owen.'

'God knows how I'm not fucking unhinged altogether.'

Like that fucking lettuce. Wiping away a touch of tomato from the corner of her mouth and telling me that she won't be round tonight because of all the pressing problems in this age of website perversion and paedophile surfing. And apprehension growing daily that anonymity will soon be as dead as the fucking dodo bird. So I'll see you tomorrow at our usual time and we'll maybe trip along to somewhere different — because we never want to get ourselves or our little relationship into a rut. She blows back a kiss from the door and then disappears out into the lunch-time rush and crush.

Through the window of this casually chic winery I sees the sun peep out at me from behind a dark cloud. With a little grin which says don't worry a mhic because there are other places and planets circulating up here that you don't even know about yet. And when you die you'll go there for a holiday. As well as that the ozonosphere is shrinking which is good news for those cunts living in the temperate zones — apart from the red-haired fairskins. Soon be able they say to grow grapes in the back garden. And somewhere in a silent room the changeling lives his sad small hours. And we other cunts all knows. That the blue skies is on their way.

'I'm going to fucking strangle you ...'

'It wasn't me, Bill ...'

'I knows it was you, you little dog's bollix.'

'How do you know that?'

'The man gave me a description.'

Louis with eyes full of panic rushing round the site. Trying to hide behind trailers and tarmac moulders and small hills of scrap. Terror on his trail in the form of Big Bill the míol-baolach — barging like a bull elephant after a butterfly.

'Owen ... save me! Save me!'

'What's the fuck's up now?'

'The supermarket! The drink!'

Big Bill with his hands round Louis' throat before another word can be uttered. The little man's face turning purple and the tongue out trying to lick in some air. Several pavs attempting to intervene and prise loose the big cunt's fingers from around the narrow neck.

'You're fucking killing him, Bill.'

'Tell me I am! Tell me I am!'

'He's going black in the fucking face ...'

'Get his fingers!'

'He won't let go ...'

'Galune!'

Swish of a shovel cracking down onto the back of Big Bill's head. No immediate reaction except for a slight glazing of the cunt's eyes and a little grin spreading on the mad face. Trying to turn and see what hit him and then slipping in slow motion over onto his side. Fingers still dug into the gurgling Louis' gullet.

'He's sunk into him.'

'Like a fucking ferret ...'

'Do something quick, for Jesus' sake!

Louis' legs kicking and his eyes beginning to fucking pop. Felix at last managing to force loose a crazed finger from around the windpipe. Let in a little air to the lacerated lungs. Steady now boys. There's another one off — and another. Until the pair of piteogs is parted. Louis dragging himself to a sitting position. Clutching at his throat and glug-glugging down gobfuls of air.

'He was going to fucking kill you that time for sure, Louis.'

'He's gone fucking mad.'

'A ruillefein!'

'What was it all over?'

'Something about a supermarket manager ...'

'Round his trailer with the wobs ...'

'Looking for thirty-nine pounds and ten pence ...'

'An unpaid fucking booze bill.'

'Louis told him there was sympathetic organisations he could contact.'

Like Alcoholics Anonymous. Big Bill stirring on the saliva stained ground around the campfire. Rubbing the back of his head and wondering where the fucking mule came from that kicked him. And hang on there Bill. Just had a nasty fucking accident a mhic. Have I? Oh aye indeed. Of what nature? Seems from all accounts that something heavy fell from a great height onto your unprotected head. How come? Who can say? They throws all sorts of things out of them aeroplanes these days. Advisable to go lie down in your trailer in case of the after effects. People has been known to hallucinate. See super-market managers demanding money.

'My ould woman was mortified ... she still doesn't believe me ...'

'The wives can be fucking whimsical.'

'Been searching the whole trailer since, for empty whisky bottles ...'

Go grab his other arm Myles. And Jake get behind him in case of the quick about turn. Then march this poor mad cunt still seeing things across the compound to his caravan. Wifey with arms akimbo in the doorway. And it was a very severe blow missus. Is that right? There's the bump to prove it. That's no bump — that's his fucking yud-bone. You don't say? Alcoholics is well known to have odd-shaped skulls. Really? Oh aye. It's a medical known fact. And don't worry Bill we was all witnesses and there's solid grounds for a substantial fucking claim against British Airways.

'You boys is so good to me ...'

'You're our big babby.'

'Lie down now and rest.'

'Take tomorrow off as well.'

'What about the supermarket manager?'

'Figment of the imagination.'

'Are you sure?'

'These bangs on the head is known for it.'

'He looked real enough to me ...'

And raging. Must all push off to work now. So think no more of it and we'll see you when you gets a bit better. But before we go one question — did you pay the gavver?

Weather warming despite the late snow and Litzy standing on her steps as we piles into the back of the pick-up. Black hair shining in the early morning sun. I'm sure I sees her glime my way and a small smile break across her beautiful face. But even though the Yella Lad's gradually becoming a good friend the other reason I must put all thoughts of a secret seduction out of my suicidal fucking mind is that the cunt would certainly kill me.

Levesque telling his tales of alligators and Indians and the nights of trapping around the Louisiana swamplands. And you think *mes amateurs* that you have hunted in this nice little *charmant* country of yours. I will tell you that you don't know danger and you have not lived until you have shot a rattlesnake.

Today we works with the mules which I knows to be the cross between a jack donkey and a mare horse and the other way round between a stallion and a jinnet is known as a hinney. Isn't life a wonderful thing altogether? Levesque tells me Owen a mule is stronger than a horse and longer lived and they are rarely sick or lame and can live anywhere in every condition. They have *mon vieux* great stamina and resilience and are exceptionally sure of foot. And if they are stubborn and *en grande colère* it means they have been badly brought up. Mules Owen are sensitive *bêtes* and have a distrustful nature. So it is up to the human being to behave like one. If not the mule is a fast and accurate kicker and if he misses *mon celte* it is because he intended to. They have superior willpower to most humans and superior intelligence to many. Mules are jealous *créatures mon ami* and although they are unwanted in this *stupide* country of yours we still use them in America. On the Bright Angel Trail in the Grand Canyon and for logging and trekking and showing and driving and West Point has a mule as its mascot.

After Levesque has made his speech and stopped swaggering I'm sent to see to the donkeys' feet. Tom Lee takes me with him in this area of his expertise. And the donkey's hoof Owen is the same thing as the nail on the centre finger of a man. His foot is the most complicated part of his anatomy and contains a very great number of moving parts. It must be minded with great care. When problems happen — like turkish sandal or quicked heel it's generally because of our ignorance and insistence that the donkey must live outside the Mediterranean and Arab countries which are his native home. The donkey's hoof Owen is softer and faster growing than that of a horse or pony. Most is unshod and their hooves grows quick and has to be trimmed regularly. You watch me this time but you'll have to do it yourself the next. Tom Lee saying softly that cutting a donkey's hoof correctly is not Owen a difficult job. But it still must be done with a trained and steady hand. Otherwise you could cut too deep to the quick and draw the blood.

He shows me how to use a hoofpick and a farrier's knife and a horse rasp and snips and pincers. Tom talking all the time to the little donkeys just as Tolui does to the horses and Levesque to the *mulassier* mules. While he picks and cuts and snips and rasps. And the donkeys don't need to be broken thank God and are only suitable for riding by children with a saddle and snaffle bridle. The Blackberry knows these little animals and keeps them from harm and also the parrot-mouth and seedy-toe and bog-itch. His beasts is healthy with no laminitis nor lungworm nor lice. Tom telling me that driving a donkey is a skilled art whether in singles or pairs or tandems. But no problem for a pav. And a travelling man Owen is a gifted man. He can do anything.

Later in the day Levesque drags me screaming back with him again despite my pleas and petitions and his French *bouche* never stops bragging. For one fucking minute! Tom Lee trades his mules all over the world and they're used in places like Pakistan and Putrachoique and South America and Spain. Still part of some armies and pack-mule units is more help in the jungles than any helicopter.

And I knows by now that mules is broken in the same way as horses but they matures slower and must not be worked hard until at least four years old. They must be handled continuous and can easily get out of order if turned away for a year or two.

Levesque smiles his affection for these animals and mules young Owen have a great sense of humour. They will put you to the test as much as you them and they'll refuse to do today what they happily done yesterday — just to frustrate you and get you going. They'll spook at any strange object so you got to be careful with them *garçon*. Patience is the answer. And a mule cannot be forced to do anything Owen. They have to be persuaded. Mind you I have known several *mesdames* like that as well. Many's the mule trainer has given up in despair. But not me Owen. I love the animals even more than the horses. And the beauties *m'aiment* and are *très gentilles avec moi*.

I stays that evening again at the camp for supper. And in the dark-time I goes out with Myles and some others coursing the hare with the lurchers. Bets being made by moonlight and the hares is turned in the long fields with always an ear open for the muskras and yoggers. Myles steering me in the right direction as far as these dogs is concerned and telling me which ones is cushti and which is crap and after a few courses I've made a few more easy pounds.

tribe

In the small hours we sits by the sheltered edge of a field and one of the older pavs cooks up a hotchi by killing him first and cutting the cunt off at the top of his head right the way around to his tail. Puts then the fingers slightly in underneath the belly and keeps pulling until the lot comes away. He leaves the feet on because he says he likes it that way. Although you can snip 'em off if you prefers. He rolls the animal up in a ball with good clay — digs a shallow hole with plenty of the dead leaf and teens a sweet little yog on top. And while the hotchi mozes away and hobhouchins twipper in the flame-glow the bransings from the fire-dogs sends sparks flying up into the night air like blizzy-flies. And they says the meat is very good for the baldness.

On the way home with light just breaking over the low hills and the taste of hedgehog and hare and jipper soup still in my mouth and the low growl of voices carrying across the stillness. Talk is of learning new ways and reading and writing and asking a Traveller to spell the words of his language is like asking a stone to speak. And how it's getting harder and harder to get a touch these days and a story about this beor who had a caer but had to get planning permission to park a trailer on her own land — simply because she was a Gypsy. And the farmers can give you twenty-eight days if you works for 'em but no longer and how the Children's Act can sometimes prevent evictions — but not always.

I knows that Ann will be going fucking frantic. Calling me all kinds of names from a great fucking height and threatening termination. But I can't help this. A cauldron of conflict and confusion inside my soul as I looks up at the infinite sky and wonder. Just what the fuck it is I thinks I'm doing.

Dancing can be a dangerous kind of diversion. Especially at Gypsy wedding ceremonies. With Janey Mac me shirt is black and what'll I do for Sunday? Go to bed and cover your head and don't get up 'til Monday. Dinking the chavvies and auntie Mary had a canary up the leg of her bluires. And when she farted down it darted lying dead on the floor. And cunts lashing out with intoxicated legs and ould ones displaying their drawers. Enough to drive any sane cunt psychotic. Wonder what it's like to be always sure of everything and never have to ask a question.

Sitting here in this hired-out community hall with Myles and Felix and Litzy and the three little girls out dancing in their bridesmaids' frocks. And I can tell even now that this kiss-me-arse event will liven up even more as the day goes by. The Duck all done up in a silver suit and a hat with coins sown onto the headband. His bride far too young and beautiful for a cunt like him and blushing as she's introduced to all these strangers.

'Owen, this is Lindra, my new wife.'

'She's lovely, Duck. Far too good for you.'

'And you knows of course these Cashin people, my love ...'

'Yes, Nathan.'

'Nathan?'

'That's The Duck's real name, Owen ... Nathan Navarre.'

'No wonder the cunt keeps it quiet.'

Louis dressed in light blue silk and sequins. Butting into the company with let me dance with my sister Duck you fuck. And before any objections can be raised the queer cunt whisks his mortified young deirfiúr away across the floor in a leg flying display of Gypsy flamenco. Daggers follow him from the eyes of his family and the sister looking round with an open mouth for some sort of rescue. Litzy drinking a sweet sherry and watching after her girls and giving me the odd glime. Felix and Myles engrossed in grunty gab about breaking into the legitimate boxing game and all around swirling bright colours and excited voices and songs and swinging music from the fiddle players in the group of musicians on the small stage.

Up to the bar with Myles and as the booze is free we'll have a couple of sizeable fucking Scotches to knock back while we're waiting for the pints to be pulled. Litzy wanting to dance and the Yella Lad trying to put her off at least until he's a little more fucking merry and doesn't care about looking like a complete yawney.

'Owen there will dance with you.'

'Oh be-god no ...'

'Why the fuck not?'

'Not really a dancing man ...'

'Go on ou'a that!'

No fucking choice now. Out onto the floor with this dark-skinned woman who smells of lavender and celandine and who looks away rather than into my lascivious súils. I tries some small talk but she's reluctant at first and then as we slides slowly round the floor she begins to sneak in the odd sideways glime and answers some of my questions about her family. The girls is called Omey and Ablina and Golia and her father was a Romany Rackley and her mother a *Gitana Española*. She wants to settle like Felix does and become a *nouveau* Gorgio. Because the shite-bag sites is not good for the chavvies. They're always near rubbish-tips or flyovers or sewage plants or dangerous railway lines. Places that's useless to anyone else. And no one's ever asked us Travellers what we wants in a site. Some council clerk's always done it. Now even they are going Owen and she's a little afraid as she knows that Gypsy children is

tribe

discriminated against and segregated and subject to racial harassment in Gorgio schools.

I says I knows all about it and can't see anything wrong with her present way of life. She laughs and calls me a foolish *forastero* and says it's all right for me because I've got out and can go back to my caer and my comfort and my Gorgio woman at any time I like. I finds myself whispering for some reason that if I had a woman like her I would never go back to any of it. She flashes a look into my face then abruptly leaves the dancefloor for the table where her husband sits. Fucking done it now!

No option but to brazen it out but before I can sit back down Myles drags me to the bar again. Three pints and a sweet sherry you there behind the makeshift counter. And while you're at it two large whiskies. Must go to the fucking lavatory Myles. Wait and I'll come with you. Outside in the toilet we sees Louis shiving about and pissing on his tie. Out again to the bar and what about the large whiskies? You drank them gentlemen before you adjourned. Well then we'll have two more. Are you sure you fucking-well should? Perfectly fucking positive!

Litzy says nothing about my indiscreet words and Louis joins us at our table where the talk is now about families and how us Travellers always looks after our old and don't put them away in homes like the thankless Gorgios. And the head of a Gypsy family is always respected. They're important for advice and they passes the history down through the generations. Felix saying how his father was illiterate and was afraid of schools in case they taught his children about sex and drugs and our people has always had strong traditions about morality and men and women's relationships.

Christ! I wonder why the cunt mentioned that? And you know we doesn't believe in divorce Owen. Litzy and me — we'd get out and hit each other before we'd divorce. That's the Traveller way. Louis butting in and slobbering about weddings not being what they was and there's no going off any more and they gets married in all sorts of colours these days the nupes. Once it was always white. Once there was no marrying out but now it's all fucking different. Louis

tribe

looking at me with his inebriated eyes and saying there's probably not a single pure-bred Gypsy left. It only takes one of your sort of people!

'Leave Owen alone, Louis. His blood-line's fucking longer than yours!'

'What did I say?'

'Look, they're taking pictures of the family ...'

'Are they?'

'Shouldn't you be in them?'

'So I fucking should.'

Litzy straightening the cunt's tie and pushing back his long hair across his forehead and thank you dear for that. Black sheep of the family being shunted to the back of the photo group so that only the top of his head and his shirt tail can be seen sticking out. Me and Myles helping ourselves to more of the free booze while all this shite is going on. Trying all the time to avoid the flashing cameras. And when the picture-taking session is over Louis stands at the very centre of the dancefloor trying to lead everyone in a sing-song while the musicians takes a break at the bar.

'Louis, come and sit down ...'

'What's that, my dears?'

'Sit down for fuck's sake.'

'Whatever for?'

'You're making an eejit of yourself.'

'No I'm not. Am I, Owen?'

'Listen to what Myles is saying.'

'They don't want to sing, at least not one of your fucking songs.'

'Why don't they?'

'They're not as pissed as you.'

'Why aren't they?'

'Give them a bit more time.'

The little man finally coaxed to a chair as the musicians resumes the evening's entertainment. Slowing the pace down. Catering a while for the old folks with a few evergreens. And a singer with a voice like a vexed fucking corncrake taking us through the old nostalgic numbers like 'Goodnight Irene' and 'Sequidilla' and 'Rêve Angelique'. Then the Romany fiddlers gradually livening things up with a few feet-flying hornpipes and whirling flamencos — then slowing things down again with a medley of slow waltzes and minuets.

'Regrets, I've had a few ...'

'Shut up, Louis!'

'But then again ...'

'They don't want to hear you.'

'Too few to mention ...'

Off across the swaying dancefloor. Tie twisted right round and hanging down the cunt's back. Shirt tail trailing. Flies undone. I did what I had to do and saw it through without contention. Dancers dividing to let this fucking lunatic through. Then up with a little leap onto the stage. Grabbing the microphone from the startled singer's grip. What is a man? What has he got?

'Get him down, Myles.'

'I'm not going fucking near him, Litzy.'

'Felix, you do it.'

'Not fucking likely.'

'Owen ...'

'Why me?'

'They won't do it, because of what he is.'

'Neither will I!'

'But they believes his condition is contagious.'

'What makes you think I don't?'

'You've lived with the Gorgios, you know it's not, Owen.'

'Some of the fucking Gorgios think it is too!'

'*S'il te plaît* Owen ... do it for his family ... or even for me?'

Can't refuse her eyes. Creep across to the front of the stage. The singer trying to wrestle the microphone back from the wailing Louis. Someone's foot kicking over the guitarist's chair with a string-twanging crash and one of the fiddle players sticking his bow up another cunt's nose. Grab Louis by the fucking leg and the dibby bollocks being awkward as a tup and not wanting to let go and screaming. If not himself then he has not!

'Get down out of there, Louis.'

'The right to say ...'

'Get down, you little cunt.'

'What he truly feels ...'

tribe

'Get the fuck down.'

'And not the words ...'

Lively pull at the leg and Louis flying off the stage and onto his arse. Still clutching the microphone and entangling the flex round the bodhrán player. Sliding him off his stool and bringing him bum-bouncing down to the dancefloor. Wire wound all around Louis' lashing legs and dragging several amplifiers across the stage and over the edge with a high frequency wallop. Everything in a clamorous cagmag! Untangle the cunt finally and haul him away to the bar. Where he stands with a silly smirk as the musicians tries to pick up the pieces. And while they unravels the hornpipes from the reels Louis whispers in my ear. Of one who kneels!

'What is the time, Owen?'

'Five to ten, Louis.'

'Fuck! The free booze is finishing.'

'Is it?'

'I should know. My papa is paying for it.'

'That's a bit sleery ...'

'He carves his meat so thin it tastes of the knife, Owen.'

'They should have named him after that Roman ...'

'What Roman?'

'Titus Arsus!'

Disappearing behind the counter to the barman and saying don't worry you glibby higgler because I'm family and it's all fucking paid for anyway. Out with a litre bottle of the best malt and looking round for spies before hiding the liquor behind a cistern in the lavatory.

'Every time we has a piss, Owen, we can take a swig.'

'Be in here all night. Why not bring it back to the table?'

'Every cunt'll want some.'

Money being spent on big rounds now as the bar becomes a paying concern and through the rest of the night me and Louis staggers with kidneys collapsing into the leithreas at every hand's turn for a slug out of the Scotch bottle. Booze having an increasingly adverse effect on Louis who begins a funny hopping little dance and stopping in the middle of the floor takes off his piss-soaked tie. Silk jacket next and then the sequinned shirt. Swinging it round his head and letting it fly at the crowd. Clapping and forming a circle for the

tribe

clown. Shoes and bright-coloured socks. Trousers and velvet trunks. All naked now with the hampton at half mast. Bride's father furious with his disgraceful son. Calling all the family together and bundling this caora dubh out through the door. Fling his fatigues after him and don't you ever dare to darken the door of my fucking trailer again. Louis lying in the road laughing. Get the Scotch Owen! Get the fucking Scotch!

'What the fuck will I do now, Myles?'

'You'll have to get him home, Owen.'

'Why me?'

'You got him into that fucking state ...'

'Drinking the whisky in the lavatory ...'

'Don't think we didn't see youse.'

Outside on the street I tries to get the little cunt to put his clothes back on. And hang on for fuck's sake! Is this an arm or a fucking leg?

'You're a bastard, Louis.'

'You just saw my father!'

There's enough violence in this shite-bag world. Without you and your fucking family adding to it all. What with left and right and black and white and all the in betweens and ups and fucking downs and didderers. They say on the streets of some pig-kretch countries across the sea the scalps of small children hang from the brutal belts of the intelligentsia. And screams of save me from the pornographers' pleasure palace. And the abused and tormented and tortured. So my little friend — resign yourself to the walking off of all this fucking imbecility.

'What about the whisky, Owen?'

'I have it.'

'Give it to me.'

'You've had enough.'

'How do you know?'

'I've been fucking trained.'

'What about a cigarette then?'

'OK.'

Set him down gingerly on this grass verge and pull the bottle from his greedy gob after a small reviver. Drink as much of the remainder as I can myself to stop the little bollocks getting his paws on it and killing himself altogether. Stick the almost empty bottle into the coat pocket as the lightning spirit finds its way even now to my own lost brain. Unsteadily roll a couple of fags and look for a light.

'No fucking matches ...'

'What'll we do?'

'Don't worry.'

Because we're bound to meet someone along this way back to the site who smokes the baccy. And while we walks Louis starting up his fucking song again. The record shows — I took the blows! No other sinners out on this silent night. To give us a light. And did it! My way! Echoes hollow down the street as we continues to dib at the last of the whisky. Louis banging on a late-night door. Muddled ould cunt in pale striped pyjamas looking out at us from the low light of his hall.

'Could you oblige us with a light please?'

'Are you mad?'

'Maybe.'

'It's two o'clock.'

'That early?'

'In the morning.'

'That late?'

Wifey calling down in her curlers from the landing. Who's that at the door dear? Two escaped lunatics love. Go back to bed. And what about our light? I don't smoke. Jesus Christ — you must have a gas fucking cooker. Of course. Well then?

Traipsing away to the pilot light on his second-last legs. Thinking to himself they must be simpletons and they say it's better to humour these people as they're favoured in the sight of God and you'd never fucking know. Coming back again with the crumpled roll-up. All alight and the frightened wifey peering from the bottom of the banister. Thin thread of smoke spiralling. Very kind. We'll have this house earmarked for salvation. Light the other fag from the glowing butt in this black night. Street lamps long since extinguished.

And the bottle at last empty as we wends our way in the general direction of the hatchintan.

'But now, as tears subside ...'

tribe

'I finds it all ...'

'Fuck up down there!'

'Who said that?'

'Obviously a music hater.'

'I'm trying to get some fucking sleep, you pair of bastards!'

'Come down here and say that.'

'You thick-as-shite slob!'

Window slamming shut on the second storey. Cheek of some fucking people. Continue our little arms round the shoulders walk along this alley. Frightening all the cats. Fling the empty whisky bottle away with a fetich and hear the glass shatter down the oncoming road. Scramble then across the common as some nosy fucking Gorgio lights go on in the nearby caers. The spirit taking its final toll and we falls to the ground on all fours. Must keep moving! Louis up ahead of me on his hands and knees. Follow the direction of his arse as we flies through the darkness clinging to this insignificant little comet and waits for the sudden stars to flash past. On their way to heaven. Or maybe hell.

Feel a hard kick in my kidneys and reluctantly turn over. Another boot brings me back to my senses. Louis totally unconscious beside me and standing over us a crowd of blue-shirted fucking wobs. Some holding back dangerous-looking dogs and others speaking into crackling radios. And what the fuck have we here? Couple of pikeys from that wedding sergeant. Intent on causing trouble. I struggles to my hunkers and tries to say something but immediately met with a knee into the face. Falling back to the ground and then pulled up again to my feet. This time the wrists forced behind my back and handcuffed. Louis being dragged along the ground by his hair and the pair of us flung into the back of a van with meshed windows. Then away down to the station and a box and a kick and a piss-covered cell for the rest of the night.

Laughter from the duty room and phrases like fucking pikeys and what about that gay gyppo and let the pair of dirty bastards stew there in their own shite 'til the morning.

Don't know which cell Louis is in. Bothered because a Traveller can't hold himself together in a small confined space. Then I hears a soft crying from down the hall and I whispers don't worry a chara. And don't let the fuckers see you in distress. Imagine you can see them stars above you in the sky and feel the free wind across your face. Sleep for a short while and we'll missly away out of this starry come early in the morning. And they says a little knowledge is a dangerous thing. But complete fucking ignorance is a crime!

Train from Manchester taking its time as we heads west towards the Mersey estuary. Couple from Cambridgeshire in the same carriage. With a brace of bull-mastiffs for showing in Ballsbridge. And an American girl with a knapsack on her back asking directions to Dingle. Sun hot and strong on the outside of this express. Glad to be away for a while from Ann and the usual routine and even the Travelling People.

Looking forward to the salt air and seagulls and the wild wind on my face. And the Irish Sea which some silly cunt once tried to cross in a converted oil-drum. Hasn't been heard from since. Radiation probably turned him into a tin of toasted fucking tripe. Ann saying we might take a little break together later — when the out-of-season prices are more prudent. And don't do anything over there that you can't tell me about when you come back. And miss me. I will. Mother in her best Sunday suit. Silent and staring out at the streets and fields as they fly past her window seat. Tim's head buried in a picture book about birds. Looking lost now without his pigeon loft.

'Oh aye, been to Dingle many times.'

'Say, that's really swell.'

And are you going there this trip? I wish I was. Then I could share your sleeping bag on the way down.

'Going to Galway ... Connemara, the home of my ancestors.'

'Some guys, I'll bet.'

'Kings of Connaught.'

'Wow!'

'Cú Chulainn was one of them.'

'Hot dog!'

Canine couple smiling. Keep those fucking dog-brutes from devouring my freshly polished shoes. And if you sits here beside me in your shorts and athletic looking legs and takes out your road map — I'll show you the shortest way to Dingle. Or even dissolution.

'My name's Karen. What's yours?'

'Owen.'

'Sounds kind of traditional.'

'Like a tickety-tope?'

'What's that?'

'A tiggley-bump.'

'You're a funny guy, Owen ...'

'You mean, like a yawney?'

'I mean, like interesting.'

'Why, thank you, Karen.'

'What's Galway, Owen?'

'It's a county. Like a state in your country.'

'I've heard about the Bay ...'

'We're going to a village called Barna, just outside the city ... on the coast.'

'Jeez ... sounds exquisite, Owen.'

'It's kind of quaint.'

'And you say your ancestors ...'

'Were the Fianna.'

Train through these black lies lumbering into Liverpool and on across the city to where the ferry sits bobbing out in the bay. Down onto the platform and a stretch of the legs for a bit before boarding the boat that will bring me back to the fatherland from the motherland for the first time. Tim holding his mammy's hand to help her up the incline to the deck. And me watching out all the time for a sign of Karen with her Cheshire cat eyes and the pure gold shining out from under her American skin. Maybe I can convince her to come for a short spell to Barna before slipping on down the Atlantic seaboard to Dingle.

tribe

'I sure as hell love the sea.'

'So do I.'

'You do, Owen?'

'Sailing man all my life. Mostly luggers out of Grimsby and the great Humber Mouth.'

'Say, that's extraordinary!'

'Herring, and hake. North Sea and around the Faeroes. Sometimes over the Circle.'

'What circle?'

'Arctic, of course.'

'My grandfather fished off the Nova Scotia coast.'

'You don't say?'

'Sure, Owen. I learned a lot from him.'

'So ... what do you know about horses?'

And tell me also why you're going down to Dingle. To meet some friends. American I hope. Why yes and we're all flying home together in a few weeks' time. And Karen — have you ever been to Barna? I only asks because it has attractions little known to the travelling tourist. Are you inviting me Owen? Aye!

No sign of land now. Sea smooth and shining. Helping me to hold onto my sea legs. Only other time I've tasted salt air was with the gaff-lads on a trip to Thornton Cleveleys not far from Fleetwood. Water too fucking cold even for wading — so we drank cider on the beach with the skippers. But this Irish Sea being kind to me now. As if it knows me from the last time I crossed. In my father's chromosomes.

Mother down below decks with her secret thoughts. Hasn't said hardly a word since we left. Seems to have some sadness hanging over her which won't be discussed. Tim running up and down the deck trying to catch seagulls with his bare hands. And this brown skin new world girl climbing ahead of me into one of the lifeboats. My helping hands on her green shorts and her brassièreless breasts squeezing against the wooden side as she slips over the top. Quickly up after her before being seen by some sharp-eyed sailor. Lie close together on the hot canvas cover and the slow swell of the sea acting like an irresistible aphrodisiac. The brand new smell of this girl breaking on my brain like a wave. Against my paler skin she could be almost coloured.

tribe

And I knows very well you yankee women are emancipated and likes to take control of the situation. But I've been around a bit myself and believes I knows what I'm doing. Slipping off the shorts her skin underneath a little lighter and tempting me all the more with its contrast to the rest of her brown body. My tongue and lips caress over her smoothness and she responds with a touch which is flawlessly mechanical. And as we bobs about on this infinite ocean and the fresh salt stings down inside me I finds this Karen surprisingly calm and taking the tightness from my overdue oysters with almost too perfect a precision. The memories of all my previous passions melt over my mind and I wants to take out my heart and fling the fucker overboard — she stays strangely aside. Milking the seed from me like some programmed robot for mercenary and professional masturbation. Her cool eyes without fire staring up into mine.

And when at last I empties my magazine and rolls over her hands slip gently down across her breasts to the beige triangle. I watches closely as she begins to slowly manipulate herself with a rhythmic motion and she says hoarsely it's nothing to do with you Owen. But I've never come to orgasm with a man. What about a woman? And Karen you still don't have to do that. No? Because I can do it for you. With my mouth organ.

At the North Wall near Dublin we takes a coach which brings us to Busáras in the city centre. From there a double-decker to Heuston railway station and a slow train across the scarred countryside and the flat plains of the Curragh — with its stacked turf and military miasma to the midland town of Athlone and the great Shannon River. On into the Province of Connaught with its low stone walls and little towns with names like Aughrim and Attymon and Athenry skimming past in the early evening. Then at last the city of Galway and we're almost at our final destination. This tall cunt with a blond head waiting for us outside the station. Saying he's my first cousin Phelim and how's it goin' there, boss?

Not too bad and how's yourself?

'Where is she going?'

'With us, mother.'

'Who asked her, Owen?'

'I did.'

'What about your fiancée?'

'I'm not fucking married yet.'

'It's not right.'

'Don't worry ... Phelim, can Karen come?'

'Oh, certainly ... to be sure.'

'There, Phelim says it's OK.'

'It would be, with him.'

Bags and baggage into the boot of a black Opel Vectra and all along the coast road past Salthill to Barna. Me up front with my new cousin and mother and Karen uncomfortable in the back with only Tim between them. Phelim looking in the rear-view mirror at this lovely American girl and whispering to me your fiancée is very beautiful Owen. Why no you silly cunt — you've got hold of the wrong hoor. I only just met her on the way over and she asked to stay a few days. See some of the local fucking colour. And this blond cunt's eyes lighting up and of course we'll be able to find a bed for her.

The village a mixture of ancient persecution and *nouveau* prosperity. None of the talked-about thatched roofs and definitely no pigs in the well-carpeted parlours. Buildings of grey Atlantic-washed stone mixing it with the modern bungalows which dots the harsh landscape and the narrow streets where every second shop is a public house that never closes. Except for the blackest hours of Good Friday. And even then the shadows can be seen inside the back room where sometimes the Garda gudgells comes after hours to play a few hands of poker with the fucking priests.

This is your Auntie Kathleen's house Owen where we'll be staying and isn't it nice and only new built because there's a lot of money to be made now from the European Community. For a bit of reclaimed bogland. And the Celtic Tiger making millionaires of militiamen and motor mechanics. Long as the boom-time bubble don't burst and send all the cyber-euros skedaddling. And we're sorely sorry Owen that you and young Timmy may share the same bed. But we thought the young lady wasn't coming. Isn't she lovely God bless her and such a strange accent. And if you'd told us we'd have made more suitable arrangements. What? Oh no! The priests would never allow Tim to have the bed to himself. And you and her only engaged. We may be a bit behind your English times here but we value our theological principles. And sure won't there be the consolation of getting blind drunk with your uncles and not a cross word said to you? And Phelim's sleery eyes not leaving Karen since the station.

On down after tea the short walk to a public house called Merrins. Mother installed by the fire with Auntie Kathleen and Tim outside looking seaward to see if any of his flock have followed him over. These four pavs walking with me who anyone would think were life-long fucking acquaintances. All said to be brothers of my mother. And giving me little sideways glimes because they knows my father was a travelling man who naifed away their sister when they weren't looking. And Phelim out in front. Holding Karen's hand.

'What'll you have there, Owen?'

'Pint of Guinness please.'

'And what about the young lady?'

'Ask her.'

'I'll have Guinness like everyone else.'

'A half?'

'A pint!'

'Ho-ho!'

And after an hour or so of chat and cordiality a fiddle playing in the public bar called in to entertain the foreigners. Bringing with it a squeezebox and a tin whistle. Landlord loaning down a bodhrán from the wall behind the bar and a reel of lively proportions resounding round the little room. Karen keeping up with the pints and having herself a little tap-dance to the music. In her well-watched shorts. A jug of dubious fucking content coming out from under the counter. And try a sup of this stuff Owen.

'What is it?'

'Poitín.'

'I've heard it's fucking firewater.'

'Oh, good stuff all right!'

To warm the cockles of an English heart. But none for the lady because it's said to make them forget their manners.

Phelim slipping some into Karen's drink when the others aren't looking. Not that the cunt needs to. Enough had by half past two in the morning and bejaysus Owen you'll be no good to her tonight. Long trip. Dead fucking tired. Tomorrow. Fair enough. And home in the spectre light from the sea and the night cries of this wild west coast.

23

'Sweet mother of the divine Jesus ...'

   'No ... listen ...'

   'Get out of my house!'

   'Mammy ...'

   'Out of my house this minute, the pair of you.'

   'Ouch!'

   'I'll throw a bucket of water on you ...'

   'Will you listen ...?'

   'What's Father Byrne going to say?'

Quietness of the cricket chirping morning broken by these cries of blue fucking murder from Phelim's room. Sound of breaking glass as the broom strikes a picture of the Sacred Heart and another sacrilege is committed. Phelim screaming and howling and the whole fucking house awake now. Let me get out of this hungover bed — holding onto my aching head. In case it falls off and rolls down the hall. There to be kicked like a football by the blating Auntie Kathleen.

Karen running naked from the room — clutching her clothes. Mother turning Tim's head away and Phelim in his leaba with the sheets up over the cunt's head and the auntie walloping indiscriminately with a sweeping brush and sending several hurling trophies flying to the far corners of the degenerate den.

   'Ouch! Ouch!'

   'You dirty little up-all-night.'

   'Ouch!'

'Owen ... Jesus, Mary and Joseph ... what must you be thinking?'

'Galune! Can you hold the commotion down, Auntie ... please. My head ...'

'What must you think of us?'

'I don't understand ...'

'Don't understand! You poor amadán. I come in here this morning to give this óinseach a call ... and I find him lying naked with that young woman of yours.'

'She's not my young woman, Auntie.'

'What?'

Phelim's hammered head taking a painful peep out over the edge of the blankets.

'I was trying to tell you that.'

'Who is she then?'

'A tourist.'

'How long have you known her?'

'Since yesterday.'

Holy water may now be sprinkled and at least ninety novenas recited to the Blessed Sacrament. Auntie Kathleen looking a little faint and mother's eyes saying I told you there would be trouble as an uncle arrives in the nick of time with a brandy and port — to save the situation and take Auntie away for a lie down. Karen deciding that things in this village of Barna are a little too small-minded for her Milwaukee ways. Wouldn't be persuaded to stay for the silent breakfast of scowls and saying goodbye with a promise in my ear to pick me up if ever she finds herself again in England. Don't leave it too long darling. For who's to say what might happen in the interim. And be careful not to dangle. In Dingle.

Phelim's face silent and sad as we wanders down for a hair of last night's fucking dog. All quiet in the public bar except for the click and clack of pool balls and the odd growl from one of the local midnight cowboys. Guinness sinking down slowly and Phelim saying how he's taken a few days off from his job at the cattle market to keep me company. You're a conishfein cousin. But because he's from my mother's blood and not a Tinkerman he doesn't know much about me and there's an awkwardness in the air as we try for cordiality and conversation and he asks me things about the drom that I don't really want to talk about like evictions and life expectancies and bould besoms and loppeting on the larch. Then at half past eleven a great roar from the open front door.

'Owen!'

Red shadow on the flagged stone floor and a face to frighten the hackles off a fucking hyena. One hand grabbing my shoulder and the other pumping the blood out of my arm.

'O'Connell!'

'Owen boy!'

'How's your feet?'

'Fine, and your arse?'

'No publicity lately.'

'Good man yourself.'

'How did you know I was here?'

'I've had scouts posted since April.'

'You looks fit.'

'Hard work. And the house ...?'

'Still standing.'

'What about the cunts from the Bullet?'

'Haven't heard a thing.'

'Safe to go back, d'you think?'

'Who knows?'

'Sure, we'll have a fucking drink and discuss it. Barman ... a bottle of Jameson and three small glasses.'

O'Connell then carrying in a suitcase from outside the door and shaking Phelim's hand as we adjourns to a table in the corner. And where do you think you're going with that? Why back to the land of fortune and frozen fucking assets of course. Because I've been a miserable bollix here Owen and was only waiting for the fucking word. And now that you've brought it at last — wild fucking horses won't hold me. Phelim here will tell you Owen that I knows your Auntie Kathleen well and also her reputation for hospitality. That way we can sail back together. Anyway — I've heard there's a vacant bed.

Tomorrow rapidly becoming today. And O'Connell reluctantly accepted into the new-built bungalow and sleeping now in Karen's room. But only after a signed statement

saying there would be no further fucking shenanigans in
this good Catholic household — that's always been
considered a credit to the community. Up very early this
morning and a strengthening sun over the Atlantic as I
walks alone along these ancient clifftops. To see a land that
should be in my blood — but strangely is not.

In the wind I think a cry of Tone or Emmet and the
hounding shrill of Cromwell's cowards as they follows their
foes to hell. But not to Connaught. And who are these cunts
still here today — after all the assassinations? Old faces of
fear still sceptical of this boom in stony fields and cherishing
their treasured isolation. Younger ones that once looked
westwards to America — or eastwards to the ferryboats
waiting to take them to a new kind of fucking poverty in a
sneering strutting ignorant island which offered only disgust
and dissolution. Now with the glint of Euro-gold and a new
fire of international identity holding them at home. And at
times like this I'm sometimes glad my father was a Tinker.

Here I stands then — on the edge of a continent.
Surrounded by the barren acres of wild will-o'-the-wisps and
hearing in my head the lonely keen of a pagan piper from
the side of some soulless hill. Looking up at the free sky and
wishing again that I could fly. Not this time to love but to
the face of the fucking sun. And from there laugh back down
at these poor cunts. Scuttling in their everlasting struggle to
be free. Just like me.

All of a sudden I finds myself part of the picture which
I've been watching for years on the wall. And I becomes
insubstantial like that pav there across the dunes who looks
at my eyes to see if there is inside me. A soul! Instead of a
half-imagined past I sees the present and following in a
dissolving mist — the future. Avoid his eyes you eejit! Avoid
his fucking eyes! I wants to run but as in a dream my
fucking legs are lead. He catches closer with arms
outstretched. But instead of an embrace there's a nail for
each of my hands and feet and a hammer to bang them
bleeding in. Cold chill in the bloodstream causing panic. Fly
away inland from this psychedelic sea. Falling in fright
along the lanes of blackthorn and bramble until I'm
completely lost and there's not a fucking sinner in sight to

ask the way home. Collapsing onto the roadside I tries to catch the breath which comes in short painful spasms.

Can't stay here! Get up on your feet you cunt and fuck as fast as you can up through this overgrown churchyard with its subsiding headstones and hope there's someone inside — to point me in the right fucking direction. Pass by old Celtic crosses with weather worn inscriptions to a heavy wooden door which creaks when I pushes it open and step stealthily into the gloom. Just a little light from the high stained-glass windows and a single candle which burns before a menacing crucifix.

'Jesus! You gave me the fright of my fucking life!'

'Did I?'

'Lost my way.'

'Did you?'

'I was expecting a priest ...'

'Not a woman?'

'No.'

'The priests have gone, to the new church in the village.'

'Did you light the candle?'

'Of course I did. Would you like a cigarette?'

'Is it allowed?'

'No longer consecrated.'

Just in case — I'm sure the cunts coming pissed out of the pubs on Saturday night might pull their winkles up against the wall. Or worse! And this strange looking hoor with the mad black eyes in front of me. Blowing smoke from her cigarette into the unconsecrated air. Who the fuck is she? Real at all or like the cunt on the clifftop. A vision from my long lost karmic past.

'Who are you?'

'I know who you are.'

'You do?'

'You're Owen McBride.'

So I am. And how does you know that — with your black hair and your big breasts and your laugh licking at me like streaks of lightning? Why are you here in this deserted fucking place? Lighting candles for some old-time lover? Or maybe to a dead life that won't desert the memory and orders this — a yearly pilgrimage to the scene. Of the fucking crime.

'None of your business who I am.'

'It is if you knows me.'

'I knew your mother. Long ago, before she ran off with your Tinker father.'

'Is that so?'

'I was just a girl.'

And now you're a fucking ghost. Come here to kill me with kindness. And did you also know my father? And did you ever ask him if he was going to die? And did he tell you no. Never! Because I drinks a small bottle of the porter every day and can higgle and harlick with the best of them.

'I'm a widow, Owen.'

'I was wondering about ...'

'Don't you want to know what happened to my husband?'

'No!'

'I killed him.'

'Jesus ...'

'Pushed him over the cliffs.'

'Christ!'

'Many years ago.'

Must be who the fucking candle's for. An anniversary. A macabre funeral rite or some sort of black fucking Mass. Maybe she's one of them fucking banshees I've heard about who comes back again and again to howl and roar for all eternity?

'You can call me Mary.'

'Mary who?'

'Just Mary. Do you believe in heaven?'

'No.'

But I'm not so sure about fucking hell. She seems to glide closer on a cushion of air. No movement except from her lips that now draws back across her teeth in a threatening smile. Under her light dress I feels no foundation garment as she rubs herself against me — as if her whole body was assaulting mine.

Catching my hand quickly and holding it with surprising strength she draws me reluctantly forward towards the top of the church where a small altar stands. The candle flame grows larger until it becomes a blizzy and they say that Judas hanged himself from an elder tree and burning the wood unleashes the devil. Up the steps in the chill twilight of this unholy fucking place I feels hypnotised with fear as she begins to strip me until I stands naked before her. Then she drapes her own dress across the altar and pushes me down like a sacrifice on the slab.

The candle flame blazing at me from her eyes and her lips blood-red and pouting at my panic. My mind is fucking moulting and I thinks I'm in some time machine which now begins to whirl. Slowly at first but with increasing speed. The woman mounts me and somewhere in the distance a door slams to lock out all logic from this strange and savage scene. Her voice like velvet asks me how old I thinks she is. I says sixteen in my confusion and she tells me she's forty-two. And I like you Englishmen. Why? You're so fucking soft. Like syrup. On this missing morning. And the woman in her prime of life sucking out my tongue from its stretching roots while her strong thighs squeezes and writhes above me. Clasping my coileach in a paroxysm of passion. Her hands tearing the fucking hair out of my head and her heavy breasts brushing across my chest. Then bending over she sinks her teeth into my shoulder and pushes down hard with her haunches. Eyes rolling in her head. She feels my frame under her tense and grow rigid and she laughs as the bisting erupts from my very soul and we come together in a rolling ball of soft sweat and sighs.

I'm too fucking haggled to think as she dismounts from the altar and lights up a cigarette. Her hair in a fury round her crazy face. On quick with the trousers and grabbing the shoes and shirt as I makes a stumbling run for the door. But the cunt's locked. Must have been the fucking wind! Won't open! I'm locked in a deserted church with a raving fucking madwoman. And why did you murder your husband? Because he wouldn't fuck me. Silly!

'You can't get out that way.'

'No?'

'I know where you can.'

She comes closer — leaving the dress draped over the altar and the candle flame flickering on her shining skin. What's that glinting behind her back? Could it be a fucking cockle-corber? Oh Jesus no! Or a double-sided dagger to do me in with. And if you kiss me I'll tell you. Otherwise I'll kill you. Help me mother! Her arms go back round my neck and I feels her hot breath blowing softly in my frightened ear.

I knows now I've seen too many Sundays and like a sailor buying the wind I offers her the silver from my soul. Laughing hysterically she pulls away and points to a little door behind the altar which leads to an old sacristy. Can't get fucking quick enough down along this low corridor and out onto the coast road. From there a signpost tells me the way to town and as I runs I hears the mad laughter ringing from behind. In my hair on end ears. And have I really just been raped?

'Do you know someone called Mary, Phelim?'

'Plenty of Marys, Owen.'

'Fortyish. Black hair and eyes.'

'You must mean the widow.'

'Where does she live?'

'Up past the old church, on the coast road.'

'That's her. Tell me, Phelim, is she mad?'

'For it, that's all.'

'Did she murder her husband?'

'I doubt it.'

'Why?'

'He left her. Ran away.'

'When was that?'

'Some years ago now. They say he sailed to America.'

'They *say*?'

'Left in the middle of the night. No-one's seen him since.'

And the tides is fucking strong. In these wild parts!

24

In this dibby month of July we courses the hare and shoots at the hedge-poker along with a bit of broomdashing with the ferrets hung down the legs of the trousers during the day and a little setting up of the peters and bands and bottoms in the coshes at night. Weeks soon gone between the gun and the greyhounds and now only one short lá left.

For a finale we takes a little trip into this sophisticated city of Galway. Just the three of us. With the weather warm as we drives and the wild clouds scudding on a gentle sky. Seen no sign of the madwoman since. Wonder was she real at all — or just a personification of my perfidious fucking past. Come to haunt and harass me. But feeling better about it now and time to put the memory behind me.

Stroll down the historic streets of this worn ancestral city with these two cunts who aren't much bothered about my pedigree and in whose company I feels secure. Don't want any more trouble or complication in my life as I already have enough fucking problems. And so have the currency pedlars and politicians and the wheelers and dealers and buyers and sellers. And not least of all yourself O'Connell if you thinks the fucking gangsters have forgotten your name so soon. I just prays to God to keep me away from all calamities.

'You sure you're not being a bit hasty, Con?'

'Do you think so, Owen?'

'Difficult to be certain.'

'I'll have to fucking chance it sometime.'

'I suppose so.'

'Maybe I ought to stop off in Liverpool for a day or so ...'

'Oh aye?'

'Give you a chance to suss things out.'

'How am I fucking supposed to do that?'

'Nose around. You know, Owen.'

'Jesus, Con ...'

'Good man yourself!'

I knows that this is going to lead me into more fucking mischief. But I can't be bothered to worry about it now and wants to spend this last little day in the good spirits. Phelim saying don't forget there's a bit of a do in the house tonight. For the fond farewells. But sure before then we'll have a few here. And what about a little tour? Oh aye. To be fucking sure. Heart full of good feelings while poodling through the crowds of tourists and bright colours everywhere and nupes pretty in their summer dresses.

Sudden thought of Ann flashing across the subconscious and O'Connell saying how he could chop straws with his fucking arse for ever allowing himself to be made such a cunt of. And young Phelim still in Karen's arms and wondering to himself if all them ones in America is so free with it. Or do they — like some spiders? Kill their mate after copulation.

Realising as we leaves the third public house that we'll be well and truly fucking dibby before we gets halfway up the fucking street. But none of us caring about such trivia on a bright day like this with the warm sun shining in at us through the windows of the pubs. And the ould cunts over from the bookies for a buckshee and a ball of malt and a gander at the gee-gees galloping on the colour television above the bar. Tiptoeing through the hours and gathering friends of Phelim's as we goes. Until we ends up at last in a place called Bolgers, seventeen strong and O'Connell roaring for a noble call. Each singer in turn firing out a hard-core rebel song remembering the bad old days and all shoving clenched fists in the air for the finale. Whole fucking pub resounding to the racket and then some shite-bag bastard shouting out my name.

'Owen McBride!'

'Fuck off!'

tribe

'You can't say that.'

'I can't fucking sing.'

'You must answer the call.'

Slow fucking hand-clap beginning to start. O'Connell nodding me to my feet. Saying you must fucking sing Owen — it's a noble call. You *must*! Fuck you! And these Celtic cunts with their customs and their cocksure fucking cluelessness.

'I don't know any songs.'

'Course you do.'

'Get on with it ou'a that.'

'Never knew a fucking Englishman who could hould a note.'

'All tone fucking deaf.'

'And a bit on the thick side as well.'

Forehead frowning now to find some familiar fucking tune. All the faces watching. Grins going round and the gifts of the gab. Early ears for the first false note.

And does you know this one?

'God save our gracious Queen ... God save our noble Queen ... God save our Queen ...'

'Jesus fucking Christ, Owen!'

'Send her victorious ...'

House fucking hushed. O'Connell with his hand over his eyes and a look of horror on the cunt's crimson chops. Phelim's mouth falling open to catch the speechless flies. Barman panic stricken and gathering up the glasses. Calling a boy from the other bar to help him down with the television set and hide it under the counter.

'Happy and glorious ...'

Stand to attention and salute now to make things even fucking worse. And look round at all the glazed faces gaping in anxious wonderment at the English imbecile who knows no fucking better.

'Long to reign over us ...'

O'Connell peeping through his petrified fingers and expecting a fucking explosion at any second.

'Go-od save our Queen!'

Sit down quickly in the corner with all the snake-eyes still on me and a deathly silence screaming. Even the fucking birds in the backyard have flown and who will be the first man to make a move?

'English cunt!'

'Who the fuck does he think he is?'

'I heard he's a fucking Tinker!'

'You're not serious ...'

'Got guts, I'll give him that.'

'Aye ... I suppose you could say that.'

'Phelim's fucking cousin.'

'Is he now?'

'Going back tomorrow.'

'If he's fucking lucky.'

Rumble of mixed feelings and black scowls and a few gormless grins going round. O'Connell keeping quiet and despite the best of intentions. Definite fucking enemies made now.

'Your call.'

'What?'

'You have the noble call.'

'Phelim!'

'Aww now, Owen ...'

'Come on ou're that, Phelim.'

And the situation suddenly relieved as the hands begin to clap once more and Phelim up lively and leaping round the floor. O'Connell leaning over with a whisper.

'Jesus Owen, what the fuck were you thinking of?'

'It's the only bloody song I know. Learned it at school.'

'You're lucky none of the quare fellas was in here. It might all be peace and politics at the moment, but there's still some things that won't be fucking tolerated. You could have told a fucking joke or something.'

'You didn't fucking tell me that was allowed, Con ...'

'They make special exceptions.'

For the senile and simple-minded! Who can quite easily become too fucking dangerous to be seen with. And after Phelim's little turn we leaves — with the rest of the cunts following us back to the bungalow where the party has already begun. All the neighbours invited and others too who'll talk about us tomorrow when we're gone. And ease their counterfeit consciences in the confessional.

Father Byrne standing by the fireplace with a big brandy in the cunt's hand and mother by his side with all the news from heathen England where the loose hoors live. The priest's eyes all alight and is it true missus that the whole place is heaving with homosexuality? Timmy out in the kitchen with a song thrush on his shoulder and a few people playing accordions and the small girls in their costumes céilidhing. We all bursts in and it's ahh there youse are and we were wondering what was keeping youse. And there now is that lad O'Connell who some say is a wanted man. And mammy is it all right — because we've brought back a few of the boys?

'You've had too much already, Phelim.'

'Nonsense, mammy, I'm not even merry.'

'Leave the buachaill alone, Kathleen.'

'I will if he'll stop that singing. We can't hear our ears.'

'Youth will have its swing.'

'And put that porter in the kitchen, lads ...'

Where it will be in easy reach. Right youse are. Over in a sudden corner sits Mary. Watching me with her hot eyes and cleaning her nails with a fucking carving knife. Who invited you here? The priest. Auntie Kathleen calling me across.

'Come here, Owen. I want you to meet Mary. She's been over to England.'

'Is that right?'

'To London.'

'Lovely.'

'That was in my younger days.'

'Before her husband left her.'

'Left her, did he?'

'The louser.'

Be a good boy now Owen and go to the kitchen and get Mary a drop of gin. Auntie being whisked away by the hoolie — swinging around like a whirlwind with whoops of skinnymalinksmelodeonlegs and cries of mind the dresser there Maggie and lift your fucking feet will you. Mary following me out. Frightening the bird away and Timmy out whistling after it. The madwoman picking up a small hatchet from the woodpile by the black range. Twisting it teasingly in her hand.

'How are you, Owen?'

'I'm fine.'

'I see you've kept our previous meeting to yourself.'

'Oh aye.'

'I thought maybe you'd be back to see me.'

'Don't know where you live.'

'Anyone could have told you.'

'Anyone?'

I stands by the wall well away from the fucking hatchet and hopes that the presence of the priest will prevent her from fucking maiming or even murdering me. Smiling she lays down the axe and says there's really no harm in me Owen. As long as the love lasts. Just then some of the drunken scowlers from the pub bursts in upon us waving their prejudice like a flag and sullen faces sneering and saying you shouldn't take liberties with us you Tinker cunt. And I can see that hatred ain't no national pastime but can cross seas and cultures and can sow its disease in the most infertile of soils.

'There he is.'

'Get the gobshite.'

'Mary's in here.'

'Get out of here, Mary.'

'We want him.'

'So do I!'

Hold my breath as she grabs up the fucking axe again. A wild swing missing the first cunt only by a whisker and the rest falling over themselves trying to get back through the fucking door. Another wicked swipe of the weapon and the shite-bags scatter out amongst the dancers in the parlour and pretend to be doing a fucking double-jig. For the benefit of all and clergy.

'There ... now you owe me your life.'

'I could have handled the cunts.'

'No you couldn't.'

'I don't like debts.'

'This one you'll pay.'

'When?'

'I'll let you know.'

She leaves the kitchen showing her shape with an accentuated swing of the hips. Am I the only conya here who knows she wears no brístín underneath her summer dress? Or are they all familiar with her favours? O'Connell blustering in.

---

tribe

'What's the fuck's going on?'

'Nothing ... now.'

'I seen that crowd of fucking eejits come in here after you, but I got caught up in a half set. What happened?'

'Just had my life saved.'

'Eh?'

'And put on the never never.'

Somewhere deep in my hidden heart I hopes you do collect some day Mary. Despite the fact that you're a killer my dented sense of self-respect demands a rematch. Maybe next time it might be different. Maybe I could even cool your flame and break your wild streak with my silver soul. Who knows? But now the singing and dancing reigns supreme and early in the morning I'll be off back across the sea. Never again to set foot on this fucking island. So I'll put an IOU in the post and address it to hell. When the time comes. To die!

Phelim waking me with a shake at five in the fucking morning and go away you bastard let me sleep. O'Connell up already with a bottle of milk to his mouth and a hairy hand dragging me out of the bed.

'Get up, you bollix. What's happened to you since I left England?'

'What time is it?'

'Five.'

'I didn't get to fucking bed 'til four.'

'See what I mean, Phelim.'

'I do indeed, Con.'

Drag myself awake and into the kitchen for a fucking mouth opener. Mother already there and Auntie Kathleen as well. No sign of Timmy yet. Be saying goodbye to the fucking birds. Quick cup of thick tea and then the best thing will be a fast getaway before the sentimental tears begins to flow and threaten to wash us all down to the sea.

'We're not going back, Owen.'

'Who ain't?'

'Tim and I.'

'Christ, mother ...'

'I knew you'd have something to say about it, Owen — that's why I didn't tell you.'

'I'm not against it ...'

'Can't be changed now anyway.'

'You decided this before we came?'

'Yes. Sold off everything. Handed the house over to the Gypsy Council, which is where it came from in the first place.'

'What will you do here?'

'Your uncles are building us a little bungalow, and giving Tim a job on the land.'

'That'll be good for him.'

'More than he'll ever get in England.'

'Why did you wait so long?'

'Didn't want to leave your father.'

In his rotting grave. But mother you've left him now. Never! I had him exhumed and cremated. What was left of him. Have him with me now in a little urn which I'll always keep close. For luck. Good or bad? And now Owen I can get back to what's left of the life he took me away from. Not that I regret a minute of it all — but it's time to come back. Before I die. You and Desmond will have to take care of yourselves but I know youse can. Desmond has his family and I've given you a taste of the settled life. You'll have to make your own choices in the end. If there's any choices left these days.

Seems quicker going home. Probably because of O'Connell's company. Auntie saying don't be a stranger to these shores for so long again. This house is always yours and the door is forever open. Even in winter when the wind blows hard on your heels.

Mother turning away without saying goodbye and walking slowly into her new world. Maybe not new but long lost and half-forgotten. Say Owen that you won't ever forget me in your exile and offer up a little prayer now and then to your pagan god.

Shaking Phelim's hand at the station. See you cousin and if I comes again which is fucking unlikely I'll bring you a black woman. Who'll maybe stay a little longer than Karen. On the boat a fine fresh wind and the sea a little choppy. After a couple of pints O'Connell sleeps below on the cushioned chairs and I stands up here on the drumming deck. Looking back at the wash and listening to the sharp cries of the carrion birds. No sign now of the land that has disappeared below the hyperbola of the horizon. The sad salt breeze blowing away all my recent memories. But Mary's mad laugh lingering and her black eyes looking at me. Out of this seagull's head.

Some people saying that the developing countries will eventually be the world's leading consumers of supershite. Just as soon as they get the hang of humming a catchy tune and make some money. Stop being so fucking hysterical over nothing and join the first world in an orgy of overindulgence. China could export antiques and Russia could have a Smolywood — and a Dysnaland and all the other cunts could wait in line for their time at the top of the futile heap.

Even Mongolia where Tolui comes from. With its sheep and its shamans. And Rigden Djapo could be called Mister President instead of Lord of Shambala and the blue city and the red sun would be a kind of downtown Dallas with forty-storey *yürts* like giant white beehives and all the people practising *cakrapuja* and sacred sex and supervised by the lords of the circle. To achieve a completely new perception of reality.

'Glad to hear you had a good time, Owen.'

'Good enough, but not great, Ann.'

'And what a surprise about your mother.'

'I wasn't surprised.'

'Weren't you?'

'Maybe, for a moment.'

'It's funny, I never really thought of her as a person ... I mean, other than your mother.'

Neither did I. Oh and yes siúcra the crossing was fine. But a little wrinkled on the way home. And I brought you back some glass for the cabinet and a little linen for the showing off with. And don't worry that you didn't come. Because you wouldn't have enjoyed yourself. Why not? All drinking porter in the pubs and singing songs and slobbering and you know what the fucking Irish are like. Not really. Think yourself lucky then. And certainly I saw O'Connell.

'Has he settled down over there?'

'No.'

And he never will now. How can I bring myself to tell her that the cunt's back — and living in fucking Liverpool. Just waiting for my phone call to come and reclaim his birthright. And Owen I have a surprise too. Your father's dead? Don't be ridiculous. He's bought me a motor car. What kind? A little pink Peugeot. Very pretty. And I think it was meant as a lure — to get me to leave you while you were away. The cunning cunt! But it didn't work and he let me have the car anyway and you can use it too Owen. Thank you. Thank father. For his sense of humour.

She busies herself with making a light lunch on this shining Sunday. Eyes all optimistic and I do love her so much. Truly wishing I could give her what she wants and eliminate all the odds of disappointment from the rest of her little life. She looks almost angelic with the light making golden strands of her hair and the sounds of Claude Debussy on the radio station in the background. But I must take a trip round to the Hilton this afternoon to see if there's any sign of surveillance. Although I don't suppose the gruntys will still be there after all this time. But you'd never know. Revenge can have a strange effect on the psyche and can turn yawneys into raving yobowchins. O'Connell will have his way but I can't help a feeling of fucking foreboding about all this.

She brings my mind back saying I don't think I'll holiday at all this year Owen. But Ann — why not? Because we're getting married soon. You did agree to *soon* Owen! I did? Owen! Sorry. Don't sulk. We'll need all the money we can get to do up and decorate your house. O'Connell's house! Of course.

'Shall we go for a spin this afternoon?'

tribe

'Got to go round to the Hilton.'

'What for, Owen?'

'See if it's still there.'

'I'll drive you.'

'Might not be safe.'

'I'll risk it.'

For a biscuit! In Lord Byron Square this sleepy sabbath there is no sign of life outside O'Connell's paint-peeling door. And inside things are still the same. Ann's eyes assessing everything. Programs running in her head for the pulling down of this wall and the putting up of that and the colour schemes and carpets and the overall and general reshaping of the kip to suit the tastes of the modern and career-minded married woman.

'We could really make something of this place.'

'It's not ours, Ann.'

'O'Connell will never come back.'

'He already has!'

Don't joke like that Owen. It's not so good for the heart — or any of the other vital organs either. And what's more it's not funny. Ann standing open-mouthed as I tells her the news she doesn't really want to hear. She could easily be sent sprawling now by the slightest tap of a fucking feather. Inside her I hears a shattering of dreams and a hurrying away of hope from her light eyes. And I feels like a proper fucking cunt altogether.

'Oh Owen ... when ...?'

'He's in Liverpool.'

'Then, what are we doing here?'

'Sussing the place out. Seeing if it's safe.'

'You should have told me, Owen.'

'I knew you'd be disappointed.'

'I am.'

'I knows that.'

'When is he coming home?'

'As soon as I rings him.'

'And tell him it's all right?'

'That's the idea.'

'You could tell him it's not ...'

'No!'

'You can't be sure, Owen — they might still be watching ...'

'It wouldn't matter. O'Connell will come anyway, he's already made up his mind.'

'Damn him!'

'This house is too big for us, Ann.'

'We could have made it fit.'

'For phoneys.'

'Fuck!'

Language honey please — it's all academic now anyway. May resign yourself to the poky little flat until our names come to the top of the Greater Manchester housing list. Which will probably be in the year before dot unless we have six quick chavvies. Or maybe wait 'til the interest rates is right and we can manage a mortgage and by then if we're not careful we could have grown used to each other.

Ann out of the house and furious to the car. Have to console her at times like these even though it's her own fucking fault. Can't always be a callous cunt and once in every while must try to look inside the skulls of others. See their little tocks ticking and all the fears and frustrations in a line like lemons. She won't wait and I hurries after her out onto the dusk-gathering pox-hole street.

Engine revving and I barely manages to jump into the moving motor. Lean over and kiss her. And a large brandy and port just as soon as we can get to the nearest hostelry. To soothe the hurt. While she sits and sips the spirit I'll place a coin into this public telephone box and ring a Liverpool number. To hear O'Connell's voice hoarse on the other end. With anticipation.

Eighty-five fucking degrees forecast today on the early morning radio. And that's only in the fucking shade. Some kind of record for this part of the country. Thank you God you cunt. Already I'm sweating just sitting here in the back of this fucking pick-up. Nothing has changed since I've been away and lots of questions about ould Ireland from those cunts who knows the country. And even from those who doesn't. No change either in the market for redundant metallurgists. So I suppose I may stay where I am for now. Whether Ann likes it or not.

The Blackberry conspicuous by his absence today and Myles saying he's gone off to a hairy ass fair in the west of Wales. Tolui and Levesque holding the horses on this hot morning and me lying across their sweating backs to test temperament. Hoping that the cunts have been properly broken and won't buck me bone-breaking off. Tolui legging me up and down quickly for the first few times. Then when he thinks it's safe he shouts stay up and leaves me leaning over the withers. All the time praising the grai and patting him on the neck so the fucker won't send me flying. Then when the cunts are used to the feel of a bit of weight on their back we tries them with a small saddle first and then the bigger stock saddle. Then we walks them into the lunge ring for mounting.

Surprising myself over the past few months and find that I'm quite a competent rider now. Even able to go upsides and keep the tight-lipped colts calm when in close proximity to the fillies. Not something I set out deliberately to do but the skills just sort of crept up on me in a natural kind of way. Can tell from this colt's eye whether he's ready or not. First a slow walk with a light rein and then a trot. And when the fucker's confident a canter. Horse must feel the positive vibrations from the rider on his back. Equine psychology as Levesque calls it. The capall must want to do what you asks of him — not feel he has to.

Trailer full of new thoroughbreds soon arriving. Grais that will never make the winner's enclosure at Epsom or fucking Ascot. Some with rain scars and others with tendons tightened by bar-firing. All looking neglected and nervous. Racehorses is like athletes — they has a short period at peak and over three thousand horses is dropped out of racing every year. A horse lives 'til thirty so they must go somewheres. Have to be re-educated for hacking or show-work or other kinds of things. Most sent on to smaller markets and fairs around the country to be bought by people who will mistreat them and eventually they'll all end up in abattoirs. These ones here is hot-blooded fucking time bombs that will have to be brought back to basics and taught new tricks to survive. See the tears in Tolui's eyes as he tries to console them.

But after breakfast we forgets all about misfortune and lies in the clover field with the asals grazing round our ears. And elder flowers laced in the bridles of the horses to keep the flies away and the bees buzzing and butterflies and gooley-bugs flitting across the clover flowers and eyelids heavy in the heady air. For a long time we just hazels in the sun with no cunt stirring and I doesn't ask why. Content just to lie here and making a hollow promise to God that if he won't ask me to get up and work again I'll be good in future and never try to find philosophical fault with blind faith. Or make a fucking savage of myself on Sunday.

Eventually Levesque makes a lazy movement in the long grass. And says *mes lambins* what do you think about calling this a day? Seeing my surprised look he adds Owen *garçon* — shouldn't you know that we Gypsies are not like your Gorgio friends? We work only to live — not live to work.

tribe

And on a day like this one when the world is bright and fragrant and warm, no man should have to toil. But only lie back in the long *pâturage* and dream. And they says in America there's a millionaire made every fucking minute. How?

Just before midday we says *adieu* to Levesque and *bayartai* to Tolui and heads together back towards town in the lazy heat of noon. Lunch-time drinkers in the Golden Cockerel. Smooth office cunts in the saloon ordering toasted sandwiches and chips and the slaggy secretaries with salads to clear up the complexion and keep the figure trim. Sexual suggestion in the glances going between the fast-laners and high-flyers. With halves of lager and lime and a Perrier and a port and fucking lemon. And the daring cross of a stockinged leg tells all.

Here in the public bar a different story. Of builders, Tinkers, yobs and yossers. Pimply punks at the pool table and smack pushers and ganja-heads nervously throwing darts and a crowd of hoors from the dry cleaners jammed up against the jukebox. The Duck saying his new wife will skin him alive and Louis not wanting to get involved in the round but Big Bill ending all the arguments and calling for quiet! I'll get the fuckers in! In that case make mine a Guinness. And a pint of mild for Myles. Jake will have a jock strap full of red-eye and a litre of Optrex. And get Louis a lover. And The Duck a dog. And barman write it all down on a piece of paper. Because we'll be back for more and might not be able to fucking remember.

Go sit round that table the whole set of you while Big Bill brings the beer and a deck of crumpled cards from under the counter to play for pennies. Because bigger stakes cause fucking trouble even between the best of friends. And anyhow the higher wagers is strictly banned in this esteemed establishment.

Louis dinking up to the cleaning women at the jukebox and asking for a dance. And are all you gyppos allowed to be in here? Of course. Because ladies we's won the football pools as a syndicate and just sold all our trailers for scrap and bought a whole block of new bungalows. Over on the financially correct side of town. Now we're just like you

tribe

fuckers. Jaded! And was the sum substantial? Certainly. But I can't tell you the exact amount. Why not? Because we put an X on the coupon. Too much publicity could cause problems — have all these Avon and Ann Summers ladies calling at my door.

'Leave the beors alone, Louis. Come and play cards.'

'Don't want to play cards. I wants to dance.'

'We'll be taking him back in a minute, girls.'

'Where to?'

'The sanatorium.'

'As soon as the fucking straitjacket arrives.'

Louis with a little dink and a giggling girl trying to jive to his jitterbug. Big Bill with a shovel fist round his beer glass and downing the whole fucking pint in one mouthful. Looking up with a frowning eye. Who the fuck's round is it?

'Not so fucking fast, Bill ...'

'You're like a bunch of ould fucking ladógs sipping milk stouts.'

'Hang on there a minute ...'

'Get over here, Louis, and finish this fucking beer.'

'It's your round.'

And get a fucking tray to take the empties back you little bastard. Louis with a bow to his dancing partner while her mates clap and chirp to themselves and wonder who this queer little cunt really is — maybe some eccentric millionaire. Like Salvadore Sackoshite. That's right barman — the same again. While The Duck deals the cards in this game of thrumps and twenty pence pieces in the middle of the table indicating the ante has already been upped and will rise again at a later stage when the serious games of poker and brag begins.

And the screams when the high kings is thrumped by the low deuces and the pleas for a dog's fucking chance and you bastard you never followed suit and yes I did you fucking liar I laid a spade last time and diamonds are it because it's my fucking call this time having had the highest number of fucking tricks. And if you can't play fair fuck off! Barman leaning over his counter and calling. If you can't play quiet fuck off! And hark to that fucking higgler. He's a horse of a man but he can't shite trotting.

'I'll have a large whisky this time, Jake.'
'Jest because a act the cunt, disn'ae mean a is one.'
'I've got three fucking pints in front of me already.'
'Drink the fuckers then.'
'Get me a Pernod.'
'What sort o' a wee fuckin ponce is you, Duck?'
'If Louis can have a short, so can I.'
'What's the time now, Bill?'
'There's a clock on the fucking wall.'
'Can't read it.'
'Who laid that fucking card?'
'I did.'
'You shite-arsed skunk.'
'Thank you!'

The pints all gradually turning to top-shelf shorts and the playing cards swimming all over the table and a good head on the ashtray. Tell me this much — ha'e youse heard the joke aboot the Pope? Drinking turpentine? Nae nae certainly fuckin not! Is this an Irish joke? Ha'e the fuckin hell can it be an Irish joke ay it's aboot the fuckin Pope? You never knows these days. Is it a Gypsy Pope? Galune! Jake won't be put off and starts to tell his joke about this punter cunt he once knew who'd bet apparently on anything. And yon punter wa'e abed on Freeda night. Last Friday Jake? Nae yeh muckle great fuckin twit. What Friday then? Any fuckin Freeda. And why Jake must it be Friday? It disn'ae ha'e tae be Freeda. A jest said Freeda. An whae dinna youse all whisht 'til a tells the friggin thing?

Aye. Anyway yon punter hae this dream. Wet? What bastard thrumped my fucking ace? Thit the Pope dies. I knew it was an Irish joke. Fuck up! Was he a Gorgio? Probably. That explains it all. Ye haven'ae fuckin heerd it yet. An whin he wakes up yon punter heads straight for the bookies and asks the wee jimmy behind the counter fir the odds agin the Pope dying by Monday.

'What day is it supposed to be now?'
'It's Monday, you fucking eejit.'
'Is the Pope dead then?'
'Nae nae, it's still Freeda.'
'It's bloody Monday, you Scots pav.'

tribe

'In the joke, ye cunt ... it's Freeda in the fuckin joke.'

'No it's not.'

'Whae is it then?'

'Saturday morning.'

'Sae it is.'

And for Christ's sake Jake. Will you get on with it. Och aye. Thin this wee jimmy goes awae tae the back room and rings up the Vatican. You can't just ring up the fucking Vatican — just like that. Why the fuck not? Hasn't they got a telephone? Ex-directory. It's jist a fuckin joke. It's nae a true story. You said it was. A didn'ae. And dae yis want tae hear the fuckin thing or no? No! Let him finish it now. All right. Get on with it for fuck's sake.

So the lad in the Vatican tells the wee bookie that the Pope never filt better in his life and he's as fit as a fuckin fiddle. Hold on there Myles — it's not your fucking lay. Of course it is! So the wee jimmy gives yon punter odds of a thousand tae one aginst.

'Who's fucking round is it?'

'The Duck's.'

'It is not!'

'Duck you cunt, they give you the right fucking name ...'

'How so?'

'You're as tight as a duck's arse, and that's water-tight!'

And Jake what about this fucking joke? A'm trying tae tell the bloody thing.

Where were you? At a thousand tae one. We're with you. Yon punter takes ten thousand poond oot o his pocket and planks it on the counter. A straight win? Aye. And the tax paid? Shut the fuck up! As he's leaving the shop he spies this little ould lad aw in tatters n rags and tearin up his bettin slips and swearin cause he's had nae luck at aw. Does the punter tell him about the Pope? Aye a course. That's part a the joke. An says it's a sure thing — and here's a pound for the stake.

'Where's my fucking whisky, Duck?'

'Bollocks to you, Louis.'

'Get him his whisky.'

'No!'

'Jake's telling a joke.'

'A long fucking joke.'

'Who poured their beer in the fucking ashtray?'

'Louis.'

'Liar!'

And I think Jake I've heard this fucking joke before. A fine time tae tell me. Well the rest of us haven't. So carry on. Righto! On Monday mornin the telephone rings and yon punter picks it up. Who is it Jake? The Pope. Nae it's noo — it's the betting shop. Ladbrokes? Hae should a know? Get your fucking facts right. I'm fed up wae tellin this and a wish a hadn'ae started. So do we. No. Keep going now. Will ah? Aye. Anyhow — apparently the Pope's died on Sunday night an the newspapers and television cameras are aw ootside the bookies and a wob cordon tae hold back the crowds. How much fucking longer does this go on?

Jake's eye bulging and his face black. If there's any mare interruptions. All fingers up to the lips and shush-shushing everyone in the pub. Except for Louis who's in a clinch with three of the dry cleaners and asking them how to get squirrel stains out of satin. An they send roond a limousine for yon punter tae pick him up and take him tae collect his ten million and all the cameras are a-flashin. Oh no not the flashing fucking cameras! An the money is aw there in several suitcases because he did pay the tax an it's handshakes aw roond except for the wee bookmaker who's crying behind the counter.

'Is that it?'

'Let me finish ... on the way oot the punter sees the little ould lad in tatters n rags tearin up his bettin slip.'

'Didn't he take the fucking tip?'

'Well, the punter says, "Whae aboot the pound a gae ye?" And, "Didn'ae ye take the bet at a thousand tae one agin the Pope dyin?" "Och aye a did," says the little ould lad. "But, sure didn't a put him in a double wi' the Archbishop o'Canterbury!"'

Jake laughing like a fucking lunatic and slapping his thighs at this joke he's heard a thousand times before. Barman eventually asking us to leave as he's not strictly allowed to serve Travellers in here. And why not? Brewery policy. Nothing to do with him. The cockeyed cunt! Big Bill having to be restrained from tearing his throat out and we resigns ourselves to the usual discrimination and makes our way like dogs to the door. The impressionable hoors leaving Louis with a thanks for the dance. Myles handing half the cards back to the barman. With the other half floating on the floor. And we must reluctantly evacuate now this oasis in a desert world and some wanting to head for other places that will accommodate us Travelling People.

But the majority vote is for back to the site with everyone a little rat-arsed and a whip round for some bottles and Big Bill trying to remember something which seems familiar and to do with the price of off-licence beer and why his wife no longer trusts him. Back in Myles' trailer we scoffs down the jogray and clangers dished up as the cure for drunkenness by his mammy and then plays poker for stakes as high sometimes as fifty pounds. Bottle opener passing round in this room full of silver and chrome and china and glass and turquoise beading.

The old beor away early to her bed at the back of the big trailer with a sweet evening to you conyas and don't keep the nupes waiting too long. And we bid cushti dreams to this fine old woman who has known motherhood in the mountains. And has prowled across the hostile concrete plains of many a cold cathair. And the gamey aromas of the food lifting our intoxicated spirits up to an aesthetic level.

'Hey! Look at that bollocks, Bill ...'

'What? What?'

'Sitting on top of three fucking kings.'

'I am not.'

'Four, then.'

'Are you calling me a feecker?'

'As well as a fucking alcoholic!'

'No wonder he was winning ...'

'Give me my fucking money back.'

'Oh no you don't ...'

'Jesus fucking wept!'

'He will.'

General dissension descending onto the scalps of these shirt-button speculators. Louis quick to spot the danger of the situation and trying to make a glibby getaway out through the back door. Just as the pot gets knocked off the stove and the jogray begins to fly in all fucking quarters. And even though I'm down a fucking pound or two I don't really want to get in any more trouble with the wobs and only survived The Duck's wedding by the skin of my fucking teeth.

Sleer out into the compound and away across the common with the wild shrieks and howls from the trailer ringing in my ears. Myles' mammy back up out of her bed and laying into them all with a colcannon pounder. And as I turns the twilight corner into Anchorage Quay I sees Ann across the street and she comes. Tears in her eyes and throws her arms around me saying oh Owen! O'Connell is dead!

27

'No!'

'It's true, Owen.'

'It can't be fucking true ...'

'Come with me.'

Drive round to the Hilton where the whole place is sealed off with several wobs standing about outside the door and there's blood on the footpath and bits of O'Connell's fucking brains. Inside the house more uniforms and an inspector called Ireton who sent a runner round to my place when the dead body was discovered. Because he said O'Connell carried my name and address amongst some other things in his inside pocket. Finding Ann at the flat and after some questions letting her stay to wait for me. And sir it looks like suicide. No! Never! You have an opinion of your own then sir? Yes I most certainly fucking have. Homicide of the dirtiest degree! Ann saying oh Owen! What makes you say that sir? Recent circumstances. And sir could you be more specific? No. I'll take my own tut! As you wish and is sir a relative? Closer than that. I see.

Down at the morgue dead-room they asks me to identify this cunt who used to be my best friend and who looks now like some fucking stranger. With only half the head which landed first on the footpath after his fall from a top-floor window. Of course sir it could have been carelessness. A slip perhaps or something. Lots of rubble inside. Very dangerous. And the windows weren't exactly in the safest of condition either. And has he any next of kin who should be notified? I don't know. But I have an Auntie Kathleen in Ireland who knew him once. For those details sir we would be most grateful and of course there will have to be an autopsy. On your fucking arse!

The way home weird with Ann's arm through mine the only reality. We stops for a shock absorber in this little fucking olde worlde pub which I've never seen before in this city and I thought I knew them all. Seeming to be the only building on the street and Ann's voice coming down through a long sound distorter and silence elsewhere around me as these other cunts chats and chinwags with wordless tongues. Is that O'Connell there in the public bar — fist round a full fresh pint? It can't be. He doesn't have a cardigan that colour. But I hears him shouting in my head. Get them in Owen and don't be there 'til you're fucking back. What's that Ann? Aye. And under the plastic sandwich cover is a fucking head. On a bloody platter.

'Did you hear what I said, Owen?'

'What?'

'I have to go back to work.'

'Why, for fuck's sake?'

'There's a new system going live tonight. It's critical, Owen.'

'So am I, Ann. Stay with me.'

'You'll be all right.'

'No, I won't.'

'For Christ's sake, Owen ...'

'They've killed O'Connell.'

'Who have?'

'You know who.'

'You can't say that for sure.'

'I can, Ann. You knows it's true!'

'I'll walk with you to the flat.'

'I'd rather stay here for awhile.'

'You'll only get drunk ...'

'You can't say that for sure.'

'Be better if you don't, dear. Shall I call on my way home?'

'What for?'

'See if you're all right.'

tribe

'You just told me I'll be all right.'

'I don't want to argue now, Owen. I'll see you tomorrow.'

'If I'm still alive.'

'Don't drink too much now. I know it's a shock, but it's not the end of the world.'

It is for fucking O'Connell! And I don't think it will be possible tonight to drink too fucking much. Ann away to her work. Which is most critical and cannot under any circumstances be curtailed. No stopping the fucking systems — even for massacres and murders. And again she says I'm sorry Owen — I really am. But he was warned and brought it on himself and what's done is done and crying now won't change anything. So I sits here alone and unable to fucking move. Although this place is full of freaky horrors.

My glass is empty but I can't get it back up to the bar. Where the titless dibby drotchel smiles and shows her leg to the little cunt who sits opposite with a newspaper over his lap and one hand knuckles white holding onto the fucking table leg while the other wanks madly under the print. Eyes rolling in his fucking head and sinking lower and lower in his seat. Slapping the back of his fucking neck and spitting silver dollars on the vinegar strokes. While all the time outside the window I hears the sound of someone sicking up against the wall. And don't tell me barman that I've had enough to fucking drink or I'll break your face. And this pet mouse in my top pocket says that goes. For your fucking cat as well.

'Drink up now, sir.'

'What?'

'Way after time, sir. Can I have your glass now?'

'Not fucking finished yet.'

'It's a quarter to twelve.'

Not really wanting no trouble I decides I better go. And is it because I've been asleep that I haven't seen the thieving hands of time taking the minutes away? This night warm and a strange scent of lilies rising up from the ship canal and arching across the Broadway. Stop to look at my own image in a shop window. See something strange and unreal — and definitely not natural. Shive on slowly and sense the spectres drifting past me in the dark. And the moon wearing

tribe

earmuffs so as not to hear the fucking screams. Traffic along Trafford Road sending no sound to my deaf brain. Nor the chirpy chatter of these three beors who walks on the footpath in front of me. As I comes closer I somehow remembers the swivel of a derrière and the honeysuckle hair and the peach-smelling perfume drifting back and dragging me delicately again. Into the land of the fucking living.

'Owen!'

'Hello ...'

'What's the matter?'

'Nothing.'

'You look like you've seen a ghost.'

'I've seen several ...'

'You girls go on. I'll catch you later.'

Peggy putting her arm where Ann's was such a short time ago. Her fingers pushing into my pocket and closing on my hand and her light body leaning and her angel face looking innocent and impudent all at the same time. Glad of the unexpected company on this night of black fucking nights. Because Peggy you're my guardian angel and always seems to find me when the need is greatest. Help me concentrate and cast away the fucking monsters from my mind. That threaten to tear the very veins from my body and batter me into fucking oblivion.

'Where are you going, Owen?'

'Home.'

'Wrong way. Follow me.'

'Anywhere, siúcra. Listen, I might look a bit merry, but I'm not.'

'You seem in a sort of dream.'

'And where have you girls been?'

'To the cinema.'

'Good film?'

All about a man who was murdered. By his best friend! And tell me Peggy are we still on speaking terms? Because last Christmas Day you seemed a little cool. At that time Owen I thought there might be some future to our small relationship. Now I see you're back with that Ann again and I know you'll end up with her almost as if it's fate. Still — she says she's glad to see me and she can also see I'm down.

But not yet out. So we'll take the right route to Anchorage Quay and on the way laugh a little with her voice smooth as velvet and the orange lights shining on her highlit hair and passers by peeping at us with a smile. As they slide and says to themselves. The world is not really fucking rectangular after all.

This time we lies on the summer bed with only the street-lights shining on our skins. In the sultry August night we leaves the window open to let in the city smells and the sounds of our little world which I can remember now is still alive. Although O'Connell is dead. No matter what is said or done I'll always have a soft spot for this gracious girl who moves under me and whose hand makes patterns on my psyche and whose bending body knows my own so well after our few short secrets. All thoughts of O'Connell's violent end flowing away on this tide of pleasure which washes over me and makes me cry out little indistinguishable words which floats out through the open window and stays like new stars in the night sky.

Tolui told me that the union of male and female in every human being achieves a new level of consciousness and symbolises the union of opposites in the Universe and unlocks the secret power of nature and the bliss of sexual union becomes the bliss of enlightenment. But I knows when I sleeps I'll dream of familiar fiends and wake all cold and sweating in the morning. To hear someone loudly lashing down the fucking door.

'Owen!'
'Peggy ... oh Christ!'
'I hope it's not her again.'
'What time is it?'
'Four o'clock.'
'In the fucking morning? Hide!'

Peggy pulling herself under the bed. Me falling and farting around the flat. Banging again on the window and I'll brain whoever the bastard is. Fling open the door to find Collins standing on the fucking step. Carpetbag in hand. And brown face bland under his bush-ranger hat.

'Bloody-fucking-hell!'
'It was, Owen. It was.'

In the fucking outback! The cunt pushing past me into the flat and saying is there any fucking tea in the pot? Peggy flying semi-nude from her hiding place and arms all around this thin-framed cunt and lips red all over his horrified face.

'Peggy!'

'Collins, you've come back.'

'Christ, Owen ...'

'Don't fucking blame me.'

'This is a fine fucking thing ...'

'You've been gone two fucking years.'

'I hope you've at least not defiled this flat ...'

'I took the coal out of the bath.'

'You did *what*?'

'Leave Owen alone. He's been good to me.'

'I can fucking-well see that.'

'It's more than you ever were.'

'I was always the perfect gentleman, Peg ...'

'You left, without letting me know.'

'Bought the ticket from a tout. It said sail that day ... or forever stay ...'

'What brings you back, Collins?'

'Bad start, Owen.'

'You don't say?'

'I certainly do. First fucking pub I went into after I landed, they were all drinking out of half-pint glasses. Couldn't settle after that. Took me this long to save up the fucking fare home.'

But now that I'm back I intend to change a few fucking things around here. And at the risk of sounding like a right cunt Owen — I want my flat back. Peggy's grip tightening round the thin fucker's neck and her lips whispering into his ear. Collins' complexion paling a little and saying no you certainly can't move in with me — because young Owen here will have to stay like in the old days. Until some time in the far fucking distant future when he finds a place of his own. But smiling now at this slip of a girl I says of course Peggy you must move in this very minute. Just recently I've become heir to a substantial estate and my executors are sorting out the small print as we speaks. Collins pleading with me as I dresses and I says I'm sure you two would like to be alone so I'll leave immediately — and send a van round for the rest of my stuff at a more convenient time.

The door in Anchorage Quay slamming behind me for the final time as I steps out into the semi-light of this dawning day. With O'Connell's desperate demise again growing large and looming in my head. How can I make amends for the cunt — without getting myself fucking killed as well? Putting all such reckless thoughts to the back of my mind and with my small sack of essentials on my back I turns towards the hatchintan.

And after the hot day which I hopes will sweat all this dangerous fucking anger out I'll take temporary possession of the Hilton until if and when some relatives of the deceased are found. Reigning over it during the interval as pretender in place of its rightful and assassinated sovereign. A phone call to Ann to let her know the news and then clear a little corner in the rubble where I can sit. And sing my songs.

Above me on a branch a small bird whistles. I knows that Peggy's gone for good and on this day it seems to me as if the sun is new-born. As it sticks its head above the high risers and says. Hello you fucking fools. I'm here to fling your little frets away. And lull youse into a false sense. Of credulity.

Black eyes and blue chins for the rest of the working week
and sniggers going around the whole fucking site. Tolui
smiling when he looks at the Duck's lumps and Big Bill
scowling down at everyone with two teeth gone for good and
an enlarged nose. Wifey now with something more to fucking
moan at him about. Myles keeping low and no sign at all of
Louis. Gone off somewhere they said and doesn't want
anyone to see his scars. Both of Black Jake's eyes blinking
now and mad as his fucking Scotch mood. All of them
wanting to know what happened to the sixty-quid stake and
I think definitely a case of insider dealing. And we're sorry
Owen about your friend and we understands why you
doesn't want to talk about that day. But what happened to
that step-lightly Louis? Where was he when the fucking
lights went out? In the dark!

Tom Lee not seeing the humour in the situation and
definitely not laughing at this crew of fucking casualties. Big
problems as well with the racehorses. Gathering from his
scowls that he doesn't see at eye-level with the turf
fraternity who produces all these thoroughbred foals every
year — for the sport of the rich and famous.

'Wild mares' foals every couple of years, Owen. Stud
farms breeds and breeds, them cunts doesn't care what
happens to their horses.'

Telling me it takes many reject foals to produce one
Grand National winner. But the big bookmakers must have

more money and that means more fucking races and the government making millions on the bloody betting tax.

'Some thoroughbreds is starved to death on the lands of the lords and ladies they've made money for. Many is finished before they starts, even at two or three years.'

The Blackberry prepared to trade in these redundant racehorses only in an effort to save as many as he can by preparing them for a less glamorous role in life. But it ain't easy Owen. Because they's mollypeart fuckers and bred to be hot-blooded and some becomes unsound and can't even be ridden. Then they goes to be killed. And ain't it a crying shame?

August moving on after the rest of the year and an autumnal sky overhead as we teach the younger horses to turn before driving by tightening alternatively the side reins. Keeping the long reins over their backs and off the gaskins and hocks of the nervous colts who can panic and kick and some are habitual rearers and won't go forward without a bit and a running martingale. Some will shy away from things and have to be shown that whatever it was won't hurt them. And the thoroughbreds nervous and trembling. Perspiring and tensing their muscles with wide-eyes and in the wild the older mares are the leaders — not the stallions and in the open a wild horse can run for two days and their biological flight distance will be enough to outstrip a wolf or a wildcat and although they're herd animals each one is also an individual.

The coroner having his cut of O'Connell and deciding it was an unascertained cause of death and the police and local press losing interest as there's no mileage now in the fucking matter. Dispatches sent across the sea — but no news yet of any known family. And me sleeping now in the damp dead man's bed. With one eye open and a baseball bat under the pillow in case of unwanted intruders.

'Owen!'

Levesque waving a mobile phone at me from the Land Rover. Unlike Tom Lee the Cajun quite amused at the antics of these silly fucking *enfants anglais*. And all a-giggle inside at the state of the sorry-looking bunch of *bébés bleus*.

'A strange phone call for you ...'

Sending Myles Cashin over to take the bridle of this big black blood from me. And along with it the sweat of the dry day.

'You are in trouble again, *mon ami*?'

'Probably.'

'What for zis time?'

'Setting fire to fucking Saskatchewan.'

'I did not know you were so discerning.'

A strange officious voice on the other end of the mobile. Is that Mr McBride? Maybe — and who the fuck are you? Stanley, Screwback & Squire — Solicitors. Along with my name and address they found a key on O'Connell to a left-luggage locker in Victoria train station. Some correspondence inside and a small amount of cash. And could you come round to our offices at your convenience as we would prefer not to discuss such matters over the telephone? Quite fucking correct too.

Sun smiling for the first time in days as Tom Lee takes me in early to the edge of town. From there a taxi across to the business and professional precincts. Offices of Stanley, Screwback & Squire small but sedate. And a beak-faced cunt in baggy trousers showing me into a small room — where this other ruddy-chopped jovial sort of character wishes me a good handshake day. And please Mr McBride. Would you like to take a chair?

'We have acted previously for the late Mr O'Connell.'

'Oh?'

'In matters pertaining to his property.'

'I see.'

'And it's in the same mood that we now consult with you.'

'Really?'

'Certain documents have come to light indicating that, upon the demise of the late Mr O'Connell, legal ownership of his property in Lord Byron Square transfers to yourself.'

'What about his family?'

'It has now been established that the late Mr O'Connell had no known next of kin. Besides his house, there was a substantial sum in the late Mr O'Connell's bank account. This we have been instructed to pay in total ... to Alcoholics Anonymous. With express instructions that the money be

tribe

used to buy beer, for distribution to the members once a year. This occasion to be known throughout the institution as Skiddledeidlediddledum Day.'

'Are you serious?'

'Quite.'

'What if they won't accept this dubious donation?'

'The money is then to be ceremoniously burned outside the offices of the Inland Revenue.'

'The fucking devil!'

'This we found also, Mr McBride ... addressed to yourself.'

Handing me a small sealed envelope with my name scrawled on the outside. Tearing the fucking thing open I finds inside a fag butt and a few grains of brick dust — and the lines —

> *Owen, I'll be dead when you read this.*
> *Get the bastards to burn me.*
> *I won't be made a meal of by the fucking maggots.*
> *And have a fucking wake for me while you're at it.*
>
> *O'Connell.*

And Jesus Christ you lousy fucking bastard don't worry. I'll give you a good fucking send off.

'The house is no longer within mortgage and our fees have been met. I believe you already have the keys?'

'You believe right.'

'There will be some legal papers to sign and the deeds to be collected. So, if you would be kind enough to call next Monday ...'

'By all means.'

'Good day, Mr McBride.'

O'Connell you dangerous cunt. You've had the last laugh and made a fucking monkey out of me with your fucking house. I'll maybe blow the fucking thing to bits with your own gelignite. Out onto this prosperous pavement with the vultures sitting on top of the office blocks. Wearing words of honour. And the walls built of the best fucking bricks and money for mortar. Down the sidestreets children screaming as their young mother-hoors kick them senseless in fits of frustration.

O'Connell you big fucking bastard. My time is nearly up now thanks to you. I knows Ann is a great girl but even so —

I still don't want to die here in this shitty fucking city. If only she'd come with me to be a bough-house keeper or a beachcomber. Write a computer program that will point us in the right direction. Away from this derelict house and derelict fucking life and promises of creeping fucking disillusionment. Or will we fall into the trap and breed babies to grow up and hate our selfish hearts for being so fucking presumptuous? And who gave you permission to pull me into this pox-ridden world? My son will say as he drives his dagger into my bleeding breast. Who said you had the fucking right to make me? And I'll answer him why a leanbh don't you know? I am the great Yahweh and answerable only — to Judas.

But something inside telling me that I owes it to O'Connell to put his place a little to rights and make it respectable enough for someone to be waked in. So I suppose I ought to take a broom and sweep up the broken glass and tidy this room with the rest of my idle day. Maybe wash the bloodstains off the broken bar and the stale beer from the floor. Tomorrow I might repair that door and clear out some of the rubbish to a skip I seen down the street.

Ann worried all week about the outcome of these legal wranglings and telling me to contest any conditions which might deprive us of our future home and after all Owen — you did have a gentleman's agreement. O'Connell I'll have your bloody bones cremated and place your ashes in an urn on the mantelpiece and at the wake I'll tell the cunts it's the latest thing in ashtrays and then when I'm drunk and under cover of darkness I'll scatter your last fucking shreds over a pile of dog-shite. Because you were a terrible trimmer. And it's what you would have wanted. Who's that knocking on my dream-door?

'Oh Owen, it's terrific.'

'It's a dead man's house, Ann.'

'You're not afraid of ghosts are you?'

'My people don't like that kind of thing. We usually burns the property of the dead.'

'You're not one of them anymore, Owen.'

'No ... I suppose I'm not.'

'And you've already started to clean the place up.'

'Sort of ...'

'You're absolutely sure?'

'That's what they said.'

Then we'll have this place shipshape in no time at all. Did you see that skip down the street? We'll organise some help over the weekend and get rid of this rubbish. That's all very well Ann but before you go any further there's one other fucking thing we must definitely do.

'What's that, Owen?'

'O'Connell wants a wake.'

'Whatever do you mean ... *wants*?'

'A condition of the will.'

Which must at all costs be carried out. If we're to go on passing ourselves off as people of property.

'I think it's bizarre.'

'Like O'Connell himself.'

'I suppose, if we must.'

'We must!'

'Where will it be?'

'Here, of course.'

And never mind millydos — we'll do what we have to do but not right now. Let's go out somewhere because this place is making me claustrophobic. And Oh Owen I'm so happy. And I know you will be too when we're organised and have fixed up this mansion house as our own. Come on now don't be a slowcoach. I promise to pay for the first beer. And as we leaves and locks the door I think I sees a shadow. Across the street.

Sharp increase in serious crime the newspapers say. And all the jails full to absolute overflowing. Can't fit any more in. Have to keep the cunts in the police stations — along with the other criminals. Fatal accidents are also up and O'Connell nothing more now than a statistic. A pile of fucking ash in this little urn on Ann's new wall unit. A few sombre visitors dropping round to pay their respects on this gentle evening. Not knowing what they're letting themselves in for. Because wakes are little known in this atheist country and the English can be pretty fucking peculiar when it comes to celebrating death as if it was dance night in Dukinfield.

Lounge all cleaned up and essential repairs completed. Ann refusing quite categorically to leave the bar where it was. Saying it had an awful effect on the room and what's more it would remind her forever of its mad fucking maker. A discreet cabinet installed instead with a decanter cut by a craftsman and matching glasses — now displaying the Dubonnet and Taylor's port and the Château Tanesse.

All in all a fair few people coming and going. Didn't know the prick was so popular. Milling around and mingling uncomfortably and not knowing whether they're expected to laugh or fucking cry. Some of the neighbours who escaped unscathed from the previous party nervously smiling at Ann. A few other cunts who turn up at all these kind of things to see if there's any free booze and although I've no objection Ann not wanting to risk another row and them maybe break up her new furniture. Mincing from one foot to the other holding teacups and Ann shrugging her shoulders as if to say don't look at me. For I've never before been to a wake and I'm not sure what they do on these occasions.

Gentle glove on the front door. Open it to find the step empty and no sign of life in the lane. Except for a little cunt sitting in his motor car across the street — pretending to read the newspaper. Is the wanker watching us or waiting for some hoor?

'That you, Owen?'

Voice without any form coming from round the corner. Then following it the faltering frame of one of the long lost fucking lodgers.

'Sorry to hear the sad news, Owen.'

'Why are you hiding round there?'

'Tricky times boy. Can't be too fucking careful. We thought the gangsters might be installed already.'

'What the fuck are you talking about?'

'It's all right, lads ... come on.'

Six or seven of the Hilton's previous paying guests streaming from around the corner. All glancing front and back in furtive fright. And Owen we hear you're having a wake for the dear departed O'Connell. And if so it sounds like a dead fucking affair altogether. If you'll pardon the unintended pun. Sorry about that but the only other wake I've ever attended was my father's when I was very fucking young. We should be able to remedy the situation if you'd like us to. Certainly lads. You're very welcome. I was beginning to wonder what I should fucking do next.

'Where's the body?'

'There.'

'Where?'

'On the wall unit.'

'Jesus, Mary and fucking Joseph ...'

'What have you done with him, Owen?'

'It's what the cunt wanted.'

'He'll go to fucking hell for sure now.'

'He'd have gone there anyway.'

Won't be the same without a body. But sure we'll do our best. First thing is to forget the fucking tea and fill up all the glasses with proper drinks and then we'll start off with a few slow songs for the respect — and later liven up this hoolie with a hornpipe or two.

A man called Seamus doing the singing while his brother Billy bangs a stick on the side of an empty beer bottle. Another cunt taking a tin whistle from his pocket and two more of them playing spoons across their knees and up and down their elbows. Drumming to Ann's dismay on the new dining-room table and the laments quickly turning to loud shouts and ho-hoos and the beer tasting better already. Three of the lodgers soon out swinging round the less inhibited ladies and the whole house at last throwing off its morbid fucking mood. One or two of the Travellers turning up — at my express invitation and to Ann's dark and uninviting looks.

Myles and Felix Cashin bringing with them the beautiful Litzy — who they say comes from the Danube Delta down the Black Sea way. Louis also swigging back the large Scotches and The Duck trying to dance with all the women at once. Forgetting for a while about his recent bride. Later on, the lodgers taking a break to lubricate their tonsils and someone putting a compact disc on the portable player. While all the time the little mound of O'Connell's mortal remains looks on in silent sanctioning — as if to say. Amen!

Quarter to twelve and a sudden loud pounding on the front door. Who can that be at this hour? Hope it's not the fucking wobs. Looks of fear spreading on the faces of the lodgers. Felix down with me along the hall to the persistent banging. As the music stops and the floating fear catches hold of the rest of the revellers' hearts. Face at the door familiar. Seen this cunt somewhere before. But no name'll come to me right now. Behind him two gruntys who I definitely knows. One tried to break my fucking fingers at the Star and Garter Steakhouse and the other black cunt grinning and hi there man. You sure fucking fooled us before. Immediately try to slam the door — but Edwin's foot faster and it gets forced back open again.

'Take it easy there, Owen.'

'Who the fuck are you?'

'The name's Patsy ... Patsy Keenan.'

'You killed O'Connell.'

'What a thing to say. Con was me ould mate. Sure, we came from the same parts.'

'Fuck off away from here.'

'Not nice, Owen, me boy. Not nice at all.'

'Get your fucking black boot out of my door.'

'Make me.'

Felix's foot down hard on Edwin's shin. Scream splitting the sinister night air and no sign of life now from the motor car across the street. Myles joining us outside the front door and trying to hold back Bernard the bastard to prevent him from interfering. Felix squaring up to Edwin. Me with this Patsy cunt by the neck and his glibby fist trying to scurf me away as I knees him in the bollocks and says that's for O'Connell you dirty lump of fucking mule shite.

Ann at the top of the hall shouting oh Owen and the lodgers hiding. Don't start all that fighting again and let go of that man this minute. Patsy taking advantage of her outburst and pulling himself away from my grip. Cunt running off down the road to where a black shadow waits with the engine already purring. Revving up and rearing away. Leaving the two tough guys to fend for themselves.

The others help Myles to hold back Bernard as Edwin pulls out his piece of lead pipe and swings it at Felix's skull. Dustbin lid for a shield and the Traveller taking some shelter from the bigger man behind the motor car across the street. Edwin trying to strike across and the lead pipe bouncing off the bonnet and hammering lumps out of the fucking roof. Naked face of the little cunt appearing at the back window. Beside it the screaming mouth of a young hoor. Helpless panic inside the car and a raging fucking battle all around outside. The bodywork being whacked and walloped out of all recognisable shape. Litzy coming lightly to my side.

'I'm sorry about this shite, Litzy ...'

'Felix is your friend, Owen ...'

'Yes.'

'Then, there's nothing to be sorry for.'

Her expressionless face watches as Felix takes a pounding from the lead pipe and I feels the soft pressure of her Romany fingers on my arm for just a second — as Bernard struggles to get away from the other Travellers. Felix staggers against the car and I makes a move to help. But he's back up before I gets halfway across the road and a crashing clout of the dustbin lid to the chest brings the black man to his knees. Another belt across the back of the head and Edwin slips forward onto his face. Felix leaping into the air. Legs bent up under him and the knees pointing down like two fucking pile-drivers as they lands on the small of Edwin's back and the sound of a large bone breaking. Myles letting go of Bernard who rushes across now to drag the semi-conscious coloured man away. Shouting to the Yella Lad that Lionel will hear of this and he can forget about the legitimate fucking fight game.

Litzy goes to help her man as he crosses back bleeding and clothes torn to the crowd. There's a sudden startled squeal of an engine with something gone radically fucking wrong. And the motor car across the road lurches away with the little cunt at the wheel and the girl still screaming through the window. A tooth-grinding of gears and the fucking hub-caps falling off and rattling round in a wide ring. All this unpleasantness having its effect and those of a more nervous nature who haven't already gone now sloping off in ones and twos. Thanks Felix but you really shouldn't have got involved. Ná habair é Owen! As he claps me on the shoulder and then moves off towards his motor with his woman seeing to his wounds. The other Tinkers forming a little circle round him and keeping an eye out in case of ambush.

Lodgers emerging from cupboards and from under the stairs and telling me that this extravagant show of strength could cost me dear. I'm not afraid of them cunts. Then you should be Owen. And don't you know that Patsy Keenan is well known for acts of extortion and armed robbery and even worse — all over the south of England. Especially around London. And a very dangerous fucking man to cross. As O'Connell found out!

And Owen take a tip from us and quit while you're fucking ahead. Because we happen to know that he wants O'Connell's Hilton. He's already after spreading his operations up this way with the Blue Bullet and other establishments and reckons the house would be a good base. And anyway it's owed to him on account of some money that was blown to fucking bits down Wimbledon way — and for which he claims O'Connell was responsible.

'It's my fucking house now.'

'Not according to Patsy.'

'Who the fuck is this bastard anyhow?'

'Comes from somewhere in Galway ...'

'Used to have connections over there ...'

'Always coming and going, up to a few years ago ...'

'Hasn't been back since.'

'What happened?'

'It's said that someone threw him over a clifftop ...'

'And he barely escaped with his fucking brains intact.'

But listen Owen — we may be off now and we hope you'll take our advice and do the same. This cunt has a lot of friends and there's plenty that owes him favours as well. And whatever about yourself — think of the young woman. You wouldn't want to come home some night and find her with her lovely features redistributed to the back of her fucking head. Now would you? But just tell me one thing lads before you leaves. This Patsy Keenan — does he have a wife?

'They say he married a fucking madwoman.'

'And there was a nasty rumour of nymphomania.'

'But he left her ...'

'Long ago.'

'Round about the time ...'

'There was that attempt on his life.'

I thinks Ann we'd better turn out the lights and I'll drive you and your little pink Peugeot home tonight to the safety of your father's world. Because these fuckers are probably right and I doesn't want you here if the cunts come back with reinforcements. Oh Owen — whatever are we going to do? Don't worry theevey-tot. A little light is just beginning to shine for me — and although this Patsy prick might seem to be fucking invincible. I thinks there's a chink in his armour and certainly an Achilles heel which just might prove to be the cunt's downfall.

I'll take O'Connell with me in his little urn. And on the way back climb to the top of the highest building in town and empty him into the wanton wind. Hoping that someday he'll be blown back. To Barna.

30

Sitting now and then over the days with Tolui in the tack-room and he told me I am to be his *nôkor* and gave me *maslo* tea and *byaslag*. He explained that the Mongols have rediscovered themselves and it's time now for him to go home. Said his father was a shaman and could see the soul. He was killed by the Communists when Tolui was a boy so that makes us *aandas* in *tsagaav-sar*. I helped him cut his hair and he hummed a mantra and explained that the cosmic energy of the Universe is brought into play by inhaling and exhaling air. And I felt kind of at peace among the saddleblankets and scawbrigs with this *maitreya* man in front of his horse-dung yog and who can think in Latin and Russian Cyrillic and vertical Mongolian and who knows that every unfulfilled dream is a heartache and the wisdom of the Buddha is a sky without end.

September at an end outside the Hilton and the autumn air bringing with it the brown leaves and a mildness to calm down the madness of the hot summer blood. No sign since of the gangster cunts. Maybe Felix frightened the fucking shite out of them once and for all? But somehow I don't really think so and I've sent a letter just in case across the sea. Better to be on the safe side. Dear Phelim. Please give this sealed note to mad Mary. Which says inside come at once. Now in a position to pay all debts.

'Owen, my *aanda*.'

'Tolui ... I was just thinking about you ...'

Surprised to see this olive-skinned oriental cunt standing on my doorstep. Grinning as he holds out to me a bottle of *baijiu*. Hilton looking at last in a liveable condition. Doesn't know what the fuck's hit it. Fresh smell of paint everywhere and the wallpaper hand picked and paid for with fucking blood. Money being spent left, right and centre on furniture and fancy goods and all sorts of fucking frivolities. Ann in her element. And don't think I'm getting worried lacha but will we have enough cash left for the ceremony?

On top of all that I hears now that the Acquired Immune Deficiency Syndrome was really man-made in some fucking American military laboratory. To be used to rid the world of all fucking reason. Instead it escaped and is running rampant amongst the cunts who thinks they don't deserve it — quite apart from the innocent irons and the junk shooters. Whole world in fucking hysterics.

Felix fully recovered from his confrontation with big Edwin who now apparently occupies a hospital bed and it's widely rumoured that the cunt'll never walk again. The Yella Lad's chances in the legitimate ring however well and truly corbed. Unless he can find another patron. Ann against my better judgement wanting to move in permanently. And if you do mo ghrá dhílis will there be any further reason for the religious rites? I know marriage is seen as superfluous these days Owen but things must be made completely legal. Father of course disapproves but I'm sure he'll mellow when he sees we mean business and come to accept us as a fact of life. But Ann — can we accept him as the same?

Tonight she works late again on some super system which will streamline the future and drag us all screaming into the age of useless information. When will they put micro chips up the mules' arses? And software in the fucking tarmac shovels?

Tolui taking the chair opposite to me. Sipping a small glass of *shimiin arhi*. And I didn't know you *tuins* were allowed to drink. Oh yes Owen. And much more besides. Some mind-numbing celebrity cunt selling soap powder on the television screen. Turn the fucking thing off. Came round he says to see if I'm all right. Because Levesque told him that someone had threatened my life. And his ancestors

were the *Këshig* and as he is my *nôkor* he will defend me
against my enemies. Thanks all the same but it's better if
you don't get mixed up in this. Because your colour and your
current position has enough to contend with in this insecure
fucking country without getting involved in this kind of
white man's shite.

But he says he's afraid of no man and a Mongolian can
kill a sheep just by squeezing its heart. He sprinkles holy
water round the room and chants and smokes a long pipe
with a silver bell hanging from the stem and wears his
father's shaman coat with iron bars sewn into the seams and
spreads his *zad* stones across the floor. He gives me a belt
with three knots tied in it and tells me Owen a person's soul
is kept in his belt and the knots are so no-one can steal it.
And the belt must therefore be buried with me when I die.
He hangs white ribbons from the ceiling and tells me I am
now safe from all misfortune. Then he sits and drinks more
baijiu and smokes his pipe.

'I will soon go back to Mongolia, Owen *aanda*.'

'So you told me, Tolui. You think it's a good idea?'

'Yes. I think maybe when the *ogloonii* of the new year
comes I will go.'

'For a holiday?'

'For ever.'

'You loves Tom Lee's horses too much.'

'You are wrong.'

'What'll you do over there?'

'Buy my own herd.'

'Need a big fucking bonus for that.'

'I have some money. Land and stock are cheap. In
Mongolia the *tugrig* is almost worthless now and it is
possible to live for a long time on a hundred American
dollars.'

'Will the Blackberry let you go this time?'

'He will have to. I want to see my small sons.'

And my warm wife Owen *aanda*. For a man must have
some roots in space and time. Or forever wander the world
as a lost soul. Like you. Why don't you come with me to
Chadān and we'll together herd some good horses. Or down
at Ulaan Baatar or even Ondōr Khan we could laze all day

tribe

in the desert and pay some other poor fools to do the work for us. Lie with the ponies by the shores of Lake Dürge and drink yaks' milk and *ayræg*.

Or in the Mountains of Heaven or on the great Steppe or in the Valley of the Blue Moon or the vast landscape of my land where a man can move freely in time and space. And the dull drone of the insects being all the time eaten by the busy birds and a cool stream at the foot of the hillside and the scent of strange flowers and the colours of this kaleidoscope world all around us. Owen *aanda*. Leave your walls and your cage and come with me. I'd fucking love to!

In his eyes I see the *tuin's* soul which he says will stay for forty-nine days in the *padme* of purgatory when he dies — before he is reincarnated. And also the *taiga* and *hurees* and *hiids* of his high country. And the shining water of the *nuurs* and *harus* and the *maitreya* at the *halga* of heaven. Waiting to step once more into the wickedness of this world to see if we'll this time accept the *unen* of the Universe. And Tolui says he'll show me Owen some day the *Agt* which is the fast track to enlightenment and by learning its principles I will be able to control my breathing and my bloodflow and heartbeat and all the internal forces of my body and will experience the great burst of light which would take several incarnations under other circumstances.

He chants *om maani paadme hum* and some other shaman stuff which he says can make the soul leave the body and experience the lost time before we separated away from the animal world.

'Next year?'

'I only wish it was *margaash*, Owen *aanda*.'

'I hope everything works out well for you, Tolui.'

'And I hope you will also find what you are looking for.'

'Maybe I already has.'

'I will pray for this. But not with these Travelling People.'

'Why not?'

'They are finished. They are just like you now. Only worse off.'

'Things ain't as bad as all that ...'

'Soon there will be no more Tom Lee or Levesque or any of the others. Soon they will all live in houses like you. They

tribe

will forget how to handle horses and how to provide for their families and will live on hand-outs and be like the Aborigines of Australia.'

'No ...'

'Yes. The day is close by.'

'They ain't going to let that fucking happen.'

'They will have no choice. They are simple people, Owen, who do not understand what is against them.'

'It's the fucking politicians ...'

'It is what the world wants.'

'And fucking councillors and fucking officials and all the fucking rest of the cunting cockroaches ...'

'Those people cannot help being what they are. They are ignorant and don't see the consequences of their actions. But everything must conform in the end. Winds of change are blowing even across my own country, which is remote from the rest of the world. So what chance have you got here? Find your place in the Universe, Owen *aanda*. Outsiders will not be tolerated for ever.'

This honey-coloured *chïndamāni* cunt's almond eyes dreaming through the dark window of the flat and his words sounding sinister as he says — I am my children Owen. I am my brother. I am you my *aanda* and also Tom Lee and even Levesque. I am everybody who has ever lived and who will ever live. And so are you. If this world is a terrible place it is our doing and we must endure it. The whole Universe of time and space is one great ox Owen — surviving off itself. I have been and will be everything. There is only me. And you.

'Stop talking through your thóin, Tolui ...'

'You were born, my friend, because of the chance and accidental meeting of your mother and father ... even if the marriage was arranged. You survive purely by the chance of not catching a fatal disease or being accidentally killed or murdered. You will die when some chance circumstance says you must. *Bi oilgoj baina!*'

'Don't let the fucking lamas hear you.'

'Life is not such a sacred thing as you want to think.'

And why you sallow-skinned cunt did you have to come round here to depress me even more than I am already? I don't want to hear your little drops of misguided fucking

tribe

wisdom. Inherited from some fucking confidence *fakïr* or some *aaltän debtër* of fucking doom. I'll die when I decides! But never mind all this nonsense now. What Owen *aanda* about these *kïpchæks* who are trying to break your neck? Think no more of it Tolui. Because if they gets me it'll be because of fucking chance. And then I'll be a victim of circumstance. And if they don't get me it'll be because I myself prevented it and unlike your prophets expect and consider it my right to go on living this little fucking life.

And here. Have another splash of *shimiin aarai* while we talks some more about these things. And Owen *aanda* you must come again to my tack-room for some fermented mare's milk and a chat along these further lines. Because I see that you have wild dreams in your head which are practically unknown in the white man. And maybe I can change your mind. While from across the seas of science comes the sound of strange voices singing. Tomorrow belongs to me.

Felix finding some mop-yawney called Munroe who's an ex-squaddy and bouncer to sponsor him for his first fight in the gloved game. A middleweight bout for a purse of five hundred pounds. But the big money being bet outside the ring and all mine is on the Yella Lad at two to one.

Darkness falling on this converted cinema and Felix's match the third on the programme and his opponent a Moroccan cunt called Menzaleh from the Blue Bullet stable and a protégé of that fucking bastard Lionel's. We all sits here on the ripped-up seats of the old picture-house and waits as the welterweights and featherweights flays the fucking skin off each other. At last Felix enters to an off-key fanfare. He shadow-boxes round the ring with Myles and this Munroe cunt in his corner as seconds. Crowd booing and shouts of piss off you fucking pikey and go home gyppo. Menzaleh approaches the square ring with a swagger and a silver cape with the words Moroccan Murderer on the back. Convulsive cheers as he vaults easily over the ropes and shows off some fancy footwork.

'That lad looks wet behind the ears.'

'Who fucking said ears?'

'Not me, Bill ...'

'It was Louis.'

'I'm warning you, you little fucking louser ...'

The Duck turning up with his hair dyed russet red and for fuck's sake will you look at the state of the cunt. Like a

Gypsy Quentin Crisp. And why Louis is his hair like that? Is it something to do with the equinox? Oh no! It's simply that my sister likes him better that way. The bell rings for seconds out in the first round and immediately the Moroccan running round the ring like a fucking gelding. Felix trying to pin him down but can't as the cunt bobs and weaves like a cat and crouches to avoid the swinging fists.

The Yella Lad taking a few jabs and right hooks in return but none of them seeming to take any effect. Jake saying maybe it's because he's not used to the gloves. Couple of rounds passing without much punching or progress in the ring. Menzaleh doing his ducking and diving and the Yella Lad trying to take the cunt's head off with a frash haymaker. Suddenly in the third the Moroccan gets distracted by his own fucking ego and walks straight into a sideswipe to the jaw. He falls back against the ropes and Felix follows up without mercy. Left and fucking right and blood from the eyes and nose and the ribcage smashed in shite. Menzaleh collapses into the corner and takes a count of ten.

Doctors then seeing to him with the smelling salts and stethoscopes and Felix's arm raised by the referee and the whole room reeling from the boos and jeers of the fucking Gorgios. As we follow the Yella Lad to his dressing room I sees the Bullet maulers furious with rage in a dark corner. Lionel taking tut with the decision and shouting something I can't hear over the noise of the crowd and Bernard looking directly at me with a dangerous grin.

Outside afterwards I walks home alone in the dark night down these streets towards the centre of town. The Travellers gone celebrating but I knows how it feels to have to work in the morning with a huge fucking hangover and anyway — the money I won is for Ann and her ambitions. Footsteps following in the gloom. Catching me closer and I hears the scum-bag voice of that bastard Bernard.

'Hold on there, Henry ...'

'That's not my name.'

'Me and you have something to settle.'

'What would that be?'

'I remember you now ... from the Star and Garter.'

'You've a long fucking memory.'

'Like an elephant. Anyway ... this is for Edwin.'

'Why don't you settle it with Felix Cashin?'

'He's a bit too handy for me. You'll do.'

Wait for no more fucking words but kick him straight and fast between the legs before he can do anything about it. Look of surprise spreading on his face as he sinks to his knees. That's all I needs. Run like a fucking rabbit out into the crowded Oldfield Road and then a quick bus westwards to Lord Byron Square and the dubious safety of the Hilton's bolted door.

Next morning bright and early to the autumn-coloured camp. Me fresh round the fire and the other cunts all sick and sorry and bleary-eyed from the beer. And I told you litchups to go home to your fucking leabas. You're turning into a right fucking ould beor Owen.

At the clover fields we loads some donkeys and horses which have been tamed and trained and now must go to their new homes. A couple of Poitous and an American Mammoth Jack for showing at Stonleigh or Halland and the horses for riding and driving and for the girls and their gymkhanas.

Bloodstock very sparse here these days. Only half a dozen horses and Hercules left now. Mules will be moving out next but first we has to get 'em to work in a team of four for the wagon-pulling. Taking turns to hitch up and drive round the perimeter track of the field. Levesque placing obstacles in the way which the animals and drivers must learn to avoid. And mules as fucking stubborn as ever and some of the cunts even sitting down and refusing to move. Wagons overturning to The Blackberry's delight and hungover cunts with bruises and hurt heads and dehydrated limps to the breakfast pot.

And Levesque with another of his lectures about how mules is man-made animals and don't interbreed in the wild — except for a few feral mustangs in Montana because they says the animals is infertile and only a handful of people in the whole world able to breed 'em. The Blackberry being one and also the Chinese who once bred a horse from a stallion and a mare hinney. And Owen *mon garçon* if you are lucky

tribe

enough to find the hippomane which is sometimes born with a foal it has magic powers and will bring you *bonne chance* for the rest of your life.

Trees beginning to shed their leaves as the sap stops rising and the birds gathering in groups on the bare branches for the launching off down the long airlanes to where the sun has already migrated. Wish I was going with them. Coolness creeping into the air and a small sadness at summer's end. Autumn always makes me restless and uneasy. Like a late Saturday afternoon with everything closing down and shutting up. Leaving at length only a deserted world. All gone somewhere. All with somewhere to go. Except for the poor homeless hicks who wanders about in the snow with footsteps leading nowhere. Until the new spring when they're joined once more by the rest of smug humanity. Sneaking out from their sanctuaries and blending into the background of shifting and shuffling.

Tom Lee asking Levesque to bring out his big pimmock Juno — the puissant percheron. The Blackberry poodling across the paddock all smiles at the sight of this awesome piece of horse-power. Beaming with pride as he goes to meet his great mawkin. Juno suddenly rearing her hair-covered coronets in the air and starting a bucking gallop. Levesque can't hold her and lets go of the reins as the horse heads out of control for Tom Lee. Tolui like a fucking leopard across the paddock fence and round the neck of the giant grai. Turning the mare by her bridle away from the stunned Blackberry and she crashes through the wooden fence into one of the fields. Levesque running with his arms in the air and shouting that the animal was stung in the eye by a half-dead horse-fly.

Tolui clinging on as the percheron bucks and rears but we can see his grip slipping. Shouts of get away from her Tolui! She's safe now in the field and the Mongolian choosing his moment then dropping to the ground. But as he tries to roll away the percheron's iron-clad hoof catches him with a brain-mincing kick to the side of the head. Tolui rolls over several times in the grass and then lies still. All of us through the shattered fence and across to where the twitching body lies broken on the ground. One side of his

tribe

224

face smiling and the other fucking side taken away by the horse's hoof.

'He's unconscious!'

'Jesus Christ!'

'Sure he's not fucking dead?'

'He's still breathing.'

'Call a fucking ambulance ...'

'No time for that. Help me get him into the back of the Land Rover.'

We carries the limp body carefully across to Tom Lee's Land Rover and lays it as gently as possible on the back seat. Cover him with a horse-blanket and another under the back of his head and I climbs in with him as the Blackberry screeches away from the clover fields. The rest of the cunts piling into the pick-up to follow us. Leaving Levesque to catch and tether Juno.

Tolui still and ghost-like in my arms. Crescent growing dim and the old *obo* beginning to fade and leave the field clear for a new cycle of *cakrapuja*. Ninety-nine spirits of the shamans round him now — fifty-five on the right and forty-four on the left as I try to stop the fucking blood that trickles from what's left of his head and ear. Rub the cunt's hands to keep the circulation going. Suddenly a convulsion of cries and kicking. Shout at the bastard to hold on as the desperate last seconds tick out of his footloose life. Dead man's eyes staring up at me and saying. There you dumb white *darüghãchi*. I told you so.

'He's dead, Tom ...'

'No!'

'He's fucking dead!'

And gone. Back to his *yürt* and his yaks and the sun-baked stone of his dream-time land. And the cunt's ghost only will watch his small sons grow in the wind and whisper to his wife. I'm sorry *siafülla*. But I though that in the white man's world things were better than they are here. And although the skins of animals are dear. Life is still cheap. No matter now because I have made some money which will guarantee you a life of little eases and ensure that my sons will not follow in my footsteps to the western world or any other where they say they are more civilised but blow their

tribe

babies brains out every day. And *üljært* I never knew how to tell you in the past. But there is one thing this exiled time has taught me. That is how to say these little words. I love you. Can't stop the fucking salt tears from streaming down my face and so bitter to the taste on my tongue. In this empty little fucking waiting room Tom Lee takes a red handkerchief from his pocket and hands it to me. He says Owen you must not be afraid to cry. Why? Because you'll feel the better for it. Will I? Standing up I leaves the Blackberry sitting there while the fucking doctors tries to establish the cause of death. Which we all know is a circumstantial fucking flying insect. Leave behind the stink of the anaesthetic and walk away. Pass these Gorgio cunts along the footpath who stares out through their idiot mouths in awe and ignorance.

Stride though the streets a mixture of aching and anger towards the trailers of the hatchintan as the drizzling rain turns to downpour. Look up into the steel-grey sky and see a shadow skimming. Is it Tolui on his way to meet the fucking Buddha? Or is it just the darkness in my soul? Don't want to go home and sit in the silent house. Don't even want to drink. Just want to walk forever with the rain lashing down on me to the black heart of darkness of this gudgell-world. And life is not such a sacred fucking thing at all.

Whole camp empty and not a fucking sinner in sight. I staggers about wondering just what the fuck it is I'm looking for. Until I sees the silhouette of Litzy standing alone on her steps. And saying. My sad cold *cudzoziemca*.

32

Wishing now I was away from this shirt-button afternoon of sin. Away in the land of *Chalükyas* or even Cú Chulainn. Anywhere but here on this soft bed with the wild smell of the Danube Delta lingering lightly and laughing at my death-wish. Under other circumstances I wouldn't have given this up for the entire fucking world — with the Romany woman's velvet body vibrating still on the strings of my soul. But I feels now so fucking ashamed.

Clock on the wall of the caravan saying three-thirty and thank you Litzy for your lapse of conscience. Your gentleness and halcyon hands have healed up my little hurt and the perfect shape of your shoulders hovering over me and your sing-song sounds saying things I can't understand and have no need to. Everything so unpremeditated and for a while even seeming somehow right. Until you rise and say softly. Felix. Then I feels the blunt knife of remorse bite a lump out of my brain-dead balls. And I can also see the pain in your fragile face. No more that should or could be said now so without another word I'll sleer away from this haven of hallucination. Like a fucking lizard.

Back at the Hilton Ann in a silent mood. Worrying about the worst coming to the fucking worst. Can't tell her it already has. And how can I work with these cunts ever again? How can I face their simple friendship and Felix's outstretched hand? But I needed something — and can't give back now what was taken in the haste and hurt of the moment.

Ask Ann if she'd like to go out for a little drink. Just to cheer ourselves up. Bits of glass still glinting outside on the street — from the chopped-up motor car. Ann's arm slipping through mine and her head on my shoulder as we drives away into the darkness in search of the nearest friendly light. And in a glum corner with a face like Sydney on a wet fucking Sunday sits Collins. Peggy by his side sipping slowly on a Malibu and pineapple. Haul the cunt headlong up to the fucking bar while Ann sits nodding in a not-too-sure-about way at this person and her impertinent smile.

'You dingo's bollocks, McBride ...'

'Keep your fucking mouth shut, Collins.'

'What about?'

'Finding me with Peggy when you came back.'

'Did I?'

'That's it. Have a pint.'

'Don't know if I fucking ought to ...'

'Suit yourself.'

'On second thoughts ...'

And you remembers Ann don't you? Gidday Sheila. This is Collins Ann. You knows — home from down under. And his one and only passion. Peggy. Hello! Haven't I seen you somewhere before? Don't be so silly dear. Where could it have been Peggy? I get around Ann. And I'm likely to pop up in the most unexpected places. Change of fucking subject quick.

'What was you up to out there, Collins?'

'Out where, Owen?'

'Australia of course.'

'I'm trying to fucking forget.'

Ann looking interested and me growling at the cunt through gritted teeth and tell us what you were working at you fucking wanker. Collins complying with my threatening stare.

'Opal mines in the Great Victoria Desert.'

'Good grief!'

'Lived underground, like a fucking gopher.'

'How gruesome.'

'Had to keep out of the heat and dust. Nearest town was three hundred fucking miles away, called Todmorden.'

'Couldn't be good ...'

'And the beer was like fucking bat's piss.'

And did you Collins know whether it was day or night in your underground hole? I didn't give a fucking toss. And did you have a bidet and a built-in bog? And if so — where did the shite go? And I've heard the crack is good in Kalgoorlie or is it Coolgardie? If you're a fucking Aborigine and likes the raw roo. Keep the conversation on the antipodes to prevent the women talking about dangerous topics and mutual fucking interests.

Miscellaneous lost souls in this long room. Looking for companionship or the chance of a lifetime to cheat. Collins saying at closing time Owen — as no honourable fucking home-coming was arranged what do you say to a bottle of the hard stuff and back to the flat for old time's sake? Ann smiling and that sounds like fun but the flat's not favourite in case it jogs her memory and she has a sudden fucking insight into where she saw Peggy before.

We'll go back to the Hilton if you don't mind because we can't be drinking and driving and we'll get youse a cab in the later on. What say? And Collins have you found any work yet? No Owen — but I wish I fucking could. What's your hurry? I want to start saving for a return ticket to the opal mines.

Immediately realise something is seriously fucking amiss by the splintered wood in the front door. Expensive wallpaper hanging in torn strips from the wall. Ann with hands up to her mouth rushing headlong into the lounge and the rest of the fucking outrage. Sofa slashed and chairs chopped to fucking pieces. Table legs torn off and the cabinet and cut glass of the decanter ground into the spirit-soaked carpet.

'I thought you fucking decorated this place, Owen.'

'The dirty fucking drotchel bastards!'

'Oh Owen ...'

'The scum-sucking pox-ridden shower of cunts!'

'They've been here.'

'Who's been here?'

Attila the fucking Hun. Ann hysterical and hammering the wall with her hands. Hitting out at the table lamps and letting a foot fly at the broken chairs.

'Stay with her, Collins ... until I gets back.'

tribe

'Hang on there, Owen ...'

'Have a fucking drink or something.'

'I have an appointment with my psychiatrist ...'

'Peggy will sort out your problem.'

Blood pounding in my head and driving Ann's car away like a maniac before Collins can protest further. Up to the Blue Bullet as fast as the fucking wheels will turn and come to a screeching halt outside. Down the steps two at a time after pushing past the door cunts without paying. Shouts of hey you fucking bastard come back here.

Big tits smiling at the bottom and can I take your coat sir? Take fucking this. Across the dancefloor to the door marked *PRIVATE* and send this cunt sprawling who stands in my way. Grabbed suddenly by half a dozen hands and about to be poleaxed. Voice from somewhere saying hold on there lads. It's that friend of O'Connell's.

'Owen ... am I right?'

'You fucking dog's vomit ...'

'Nice of you to drop in.'

'Keep away from my fucking house, Keenan.'

'Your house, Owen? Sure what would a Tinker like you want a house for? You'd only shite in the sink and piss all over the walls. You must mean O'Connell's house? Haven't been near it since we were set upon by that bonehead ... what was his name, boys?'

'Felix, boss.'

'Oh aye, Felix. Who does the fighting. Well, Owen, Felix will be hearing from us. And it's lucky for you that Lionel's not here tonight. They say his man Edwin won't walk again.'

'I'll get the fucking wobs onto you ...'

'Hear that? You can take the man out of the Tinker site, but you can't take the shite out of the man. Your little girl ... what's her name boys?'

'Ann, boss.'

'Aye, Ann ...'

'Leave her alone you cunt!'

'Listen, that house of O'Connell's is unlucky. Bit like O'Connell himself. He might even still be haunting the place. I've heard of these ghosts who can throw chairs and things around ... what are they called, boys?'

'Poltergeists, boss.'

'That's them. Jaysus ... if I was you, Owen, I'd clear out of it altogether.'

Shake loose an arm and try to smack this fucking pig across his double-chinned puss. Kicked back to the fucking ground and a knee hard down on the back of my neck.

'I can see you're the type of bugger who won't be told, Owen. Throw him out, boys.'

'I'll get you, you fucking baboon's arse ...'

'Maybe you will, boy, but you'll have to be quick.'

Flung out flailing onto the night-time street. No use in fucking crying to the wobs. Only one last hope left now. And I must also warn Felix before the bastards gets too close to him. O'Connell you curse-of-Jesus cunt. Up there lounging on the Lilo clouds and laughing down at me. Or maybe below in the fucking dungeon bar dibby and dinking. Walk slowly back to the pink Peugeot. Holding a twisted arm and the head ringing from a rain of fists. Sky all a blackness and no stars shining their lights. Except for the silver satellites. Beaming the beautiful pictures across the whole fucking world. And sending message pulses out into the deepest part of the Universe hoping for some acknowledgement from a higher life form. And God fucking forbid that we're the best there is. Went once to see a strongman in a side-show. He lifted me up with one hand and said. Hi boy. What will you do if I don't let you down? Cry!

Ann still hysterical and Collins with one leg out the fucking door for the quick getaway — in case there could be a chance of the cunt getting himself involved in something. Off like a shot as soon as I gets back. Trying to leave Peggy behind. But her faster to the door and arms around his neck away.

'Did you go to the police?'

'Yes.'

'And what did they have to say?'

'They'll take some action at daybreak.'

'What are you talking about, Owen?'

'Need the natural light for fingerprints to be error-free.'

'Owen, this is not a fucking joke ...'

'That I can see.'

And I can also see that things are going to get fucking tougher. Is it all worth it? Maybe we should let them have the fucking house after all. If they wants it that bad. Collins tells me there's a shortage of men in the opal mines. Or we could build a raft out of empty beer cans and float away to the Phoenix Islands. And if you stops crying we'll try to pick up the pieces for now. Put everything possible back in its proper place. If there's no better news forthcoming by the end of the week I'll have to send you permanently home to your horse's fanny of a father. Then board up the windows and break down the fucking walls. Head for the hills with a price hanging on my head and the hounds of fucking hell baying at my heels.

What are you doing now, mother? In your little corner of the golden room. Could be I'll see you sooner than you thinks. Tonight I'm reluctant to go to bed. Maybe in the morning when I wakes. I'll be dead.

Hide here all alone in the high bennet. Hands holding up
the chin and heart cold as the fucking horses' shoes. Light
up another lonely cigarette and then make the feet get
slowly up and stand. Around me the sound of men and
animals and the new October air with silver speckles of
early frost daylight-shining in splendour. The Blackberry
chain-smoking and muttering mouthfuls of abuse against
them Gorgio gobshites who hates their horses. Some of the
thoroughbreds proving unfit to be retrained and now
awaiting the trailer to take them down to the abattoir. The
other pavs putting up windbreaks for the winter shelter
with voices gruff and growling and accusing glances flying in
Tom Lee's direction. Glad in a way that Tolui's not here to
witness this.

The Blackberry shrugging his shoulders and lighting up
another cigarette — having just thrown half the previous
one away. They says a horse knows it's in an abattoir. He
can hear the gunshots — smell the blood. But I suppose it's
kinder to kill an animal than leave it in a field to fucking
starve. And Tom Lee's downcast expression saying I've done
all I can. What else does youse all expect of me?

Had a sudden urge on the way here this morning to head
instead off down to the sea. From there set sail to Santiago
in search of the fifth essence. Otherwise a juggernaut of the
heaviest kind to come flying and kill me outright.
Instantaneously. Without pain or the indignity of lifelong

disability. Deprive that shite Patsy of his small satisfaction. But my feet would only move down the familiar path to the hatchintan. Louis saying sod the cunts Owen and his hand clapping on my back. Growls and grumbles fading away like a spent thunderstorm — replaced by the neighing of horses and the hee-hawing of Hercules.

'Owen!'

'What?'

'Go home. You're no fucking good to me here today.'

The Blackberry telling Levesque to call me a cab on the mobile phone. Asking Myles on my way out how the Yella Lad is and he tells me the whole family left the site the previous night.

'Jesus ... why?'

'How should I know?. He says fuck-all to me these days.'

'Ain't like him, is it?'

'What ain't like him?'

'To leave ... with no fucking reason?'

'He's a Traveller, Owen. And he must have had a reason.'

On the way back to town I sees Felix's trailer across the fields and parked alone in a lay-by. Catch a glimpse of him sitting by the side of the road. Sounds forming on his lips that can't be heard and eyes staring straight ahead. I gets the cab to take a detour and pays the fare and the driver can't wait to be on his way. Half afraid to fucking go near the Yella Lad. But I must.

'Felix ...'

'Owen!'

'What's up?'

'Litzy ...'

'Oh my fucking God!'

'They got to her, Owen.'

'What?'

'The cunts cut her up.'

'Who did?'

'She was lying in the caravan kitchen when I woke ... blood everywhere.'

'Oh fucking God! Oh fucking Jesus!'

'Her face ... her little face, Owen.'

'Is she dead?'

'No.'

'Thank the singing stars.'

'She's down at the hospital ... all bandaged up.'

'What did she say?'

'Nothing.'

'Didn't you hear anything?'

'Not a sound, Owen. I dies when I falls asleep. A fucking bomb wouldn't wake me.'

'All the same, Felix ...'

'They must have come late. She's a light sleeper.'

'I'm so sorry ...'

'Some fucking cunt will die for this, Owen!'

'Let me settle it. It was all my fault.'

'How the fuck will you do that?'

'I've got a way.'

'My way's better.'

'No Felix, you don't know what you're up against. Keep the fuck out of it.'

'I'm already in it, Owen!'

'They won't bother you again.'

'You can stake your fucking life on that.'

'Upon the honour of my father's memory, Felix ...'

'I wants more than that.'

'Like what?'

'A body!'

'I'll give you one.'

'I'll give you until fucking Monday.'

'I'm waiting for reinforcements.'

'Monday!'

Telling me his mammy is looking after the chavvies and offering me a lift the rest of the way to town on this bleak and bloody Friday afternoon. Asking me to come with him to the hospital — and say hello to his little hurt *luciérnaga*. But I couldn't face that right now so I tells him I'm in this terrible hurry and promises to drop by over the weekend. Be impossible to look down into the *anilów* eyes without weeping.

Explosions in my fucking brain and echoes sounding around my ears and my mind trying to work out why the fuck they would slice Litzy up and leave Felix asleep in his bed. Surely he should have heard them. Something not quite fucking right. Should really go and see her but can't make the mind move in that direction. She'll be all right in the hospital I hope.

Nothing I says to myself can change this strange and first-time feeling. Maybe it's a sign that the time has come for me to join a fucking monastery and withdraw forever from the shite-bag world. Sit in my little cell and wank out through an open window. Insist on wearing a blindfold on all excursions outside the safe and sober walls. Tell the post office to re-address my mail to The Model Village where human nature is said to be alive and well and living openly on the streets. Names to call myself coming to mind and the following eyes of the innocent as I sleers away. With his candy. Tolui's words returning now to haunt me and God Owen *aanda* is not responsible for the things men do but we must all account for our own deeds and act according to our karma and people are not born bad — they have to learn it! But everything changes and nothing's certain these days and friends and foes are all mixed up and indistinguishable. Except for some of the fucking bastards. Who'll never be any different.

Have to be careful in Lord Byron Square. Watch out all the time for signs of a fucking ambush. See none of the scum-shites today and safely in the door to the blue envelope on the mat with its Irish stamp and postmarked Galway.

Church Cottage,
Barna.
6th Oct.

Dear Owen,
Received with interest your urgent
message. Regretfully, however, it is impossible
for me to travel at this time. The banns have
already been posted and I intend, in six weeks,
to marry your cousin, Phelim.
Yours platonically,

Mary

PS You are, of course, cordially invited to
attend the celebrations.

tribe

Feel my face turning pale and an extra beat to the fucking heart. Hand shaking as I searches for a notepad and a desperate urgency driving this pen across the paper.

Use no ink now. But fucking blood.

> *The Hilton,*
> *Lord Byron Square,*
> *Manchester.*
> *8th Oct.*

> *Dear Mary,*
> *Appreciated your heart-warming epistle and*
> *delighted to welcome you into the family, albeit at a*
> *distance. Don't mean to be a fly in the ointment,*
> *but I think it might be prudent to finalise matters*
> *with your first husband before taking on another.*
> *Expect you Sunday night, if not sooner.*
> *Yours in discretion,*

> *Owen*

> *PS Must decline your cordial invitation, due*
> *to circumstantial pressure.*

Bullrushing down like a deranged dimmock to the post office and your fittest and fastest strato-cruiser fucking courier service please. An urgent invitation which must at all costs arrive no later than first light tomorrow morning. Leave it to us sir. Provided you don't mind paying for the privilege. Expense is of no fucking consequence.

Mary late on Sunday night drumming lumps off the fucking door with flailing fists. Phelim panting up the hall at her heels — carrying a couple of hurriedly packed bags. So what in the name of the suffering Christ is this all about Owen? I've brought with me in one of the bags a machete. Just in case it's a fucking joke.

'Put the kettle on, Phelim, like a good lad.'
'Where might it be, Owen?'
'In the kitchen.'
'Of course.'

The blond-haired yawney stoaching round the Hilton in search of the kitchen. Mary still standing and staring hard at me. Eyes on fucking fire.

'What did you bring that dummel for?'

'He happens to be my betrothed.'

'How come?'

'It was in the stars.'

'Anyway ... I needs your help.'

'Again?'

'Aye.'

'And what's this about repaying all debts?'

'A barefaced lie.'

'You bastard ...'

'Patsy Keenan is alive and well.'

'I know.'

'You can't marry Phelim.'

'Patsy won't make trouble.'

'I will.'

The mad eyes flaring and the fists clenched in an eruption of rage. A small movement under her blue raincoat making me step back in hair-standing horror. But instead of an instrument of murder she drags out a litre bottle of duty free. Sitting heavily on the shattered sofa and the voice soft now and saying.

'What do you want from me, Owen?'

'Your secret.'

'What secret?'

'Why does he leave you alone?'

'He's afraid of me.'

'Make him afraid of me.'

'Why should I?'

'Because I owes you.'

And I might not live fucking long enough for you to collect. Phelim back in with a tray and teapot and tripping over a broken chair leg. Mary's finger moving to her lips and her left eye winking. Say no more for now and we'll leave discussion of the details until a little later on. I knows time ain't on my side but it'll be good to relax for an hour or so and sip a drop of this dark Irish malt. And tell me cousin how is my little mother making out? And her bird boy.

'On the pig's back, Owen.'

'What is?'

'The best bacon.'

'I see.'

'Sure, they've already built half the bungalow and Tim's a dab farmhand altogether.

'Only one little cloud, Owen ...'

'What's that, Phelim?'

'They wouldn't let her put your father's ashes in the consecrated ground.'

'He'd probably be happy about that.'

'Something about the circumstances of his death.'

And nobody was sure at all whether or not he'd received extreme unction. Or for that matter had ever been baptised. For although he was an Irish-born man no records could be found to categorically prove he was ever in his life a Christian. And what Phelim about this thing called benefit of the doubt? Oh aye — the priests had it.

'This wedding is very sudden.'

'We've known each other well for a long time, Owen.'

'How well?'

'Well enough.'

'And is Auntie Kathleen in full favour?'

'She has to be ... there's a baby on the way.'

'Good God ... how many months?'

'Three or four, we think. Conceived in July or August.'

Sacred heart of the divine fucking Jesus! What was that the ould duckerer said?

'Mary has money.'

'How much?'

'Enough to make things tolerable.'

'Mary tells me, Owen, there's some trouble.'

'Does she?'

'I think it's terrible altogether ...'

'It is?'

'All this aggravation over a few turkeys.'

'Phelim ... only I was with Owen on the day he got lost, and that's the time in question. Isn't it, Owen?'

'Oh aye ... of course!'

'But Mary, he was in Ireland ...'

'It makes no matter, Phelim. The law is a quare thing, especially English law.'

tribe

'What I'd like to know, Owen, is why they accused you of turkey rustling in the first place.'

'Picked me out of a line-up.'

'And they come down hard over here on crimes of that nature.'

'Oh aye, I've heard the British public is easily outraged.'

Over the rights of dumb fucking animals. So it's just as well I've got Mary as my witness and alibi. Save me from a long fucking stretch in a top-security wing. Pour some more of that whiskey into my tea and we'll talk of old times. Build a little fire of hope in my heart to warm your weary selves by its fickle flame. Plots already pouring through my mind for mad Mary to murder Patsy Keenan. Hasn't said she'll help me yet but I thinks she will. Root the cunt out and put a final end to all his extortions. Hoping that Felix will wait before unleashing all fucking hell and even more that Litzy will say nothing under the influence of anaesthetic to incriminate me and draw tight again this noose round my neck which I've only just now managed to loosen.

'What are these English girls like, Owen?'

'That's lovely! And you nearly married!'

'I was only asking, dear.'

'Well don't!'

'Mary and I may go to court tomorrow, Phelim. Will you stay here and mind the house?'

'Can't I come too?'

'I needs someone here in case of callers.'

'What kind of callers?'

'Karen's kind.'

'You can count on me, Owen.'

'Who's Karen?'

'Nobody, dear.'

Just for Christ's sake keep your yud down and don't open the fucking door to anyone. Because it might be the bogey man looking for blood. Or bollocks!

Make a mental note to send a secret and anonymous donation to the Society for Retired and Starving Rent Collectors. Provided of course the eventual outcome of all this is satisfactory and secure. Phelim lashing the bottle round and into the teas and onto the table and some splashing down on the floor. Don't want to be too blurred tomorrow so I'll be off to my bed soon. You two can take that room over there. Certainly not. Separates please until after the ceremony.

And I don't believe in anything I fucking hears anymore. And what I sees sometimes make me wonder if the world is not after all. Completely fucking witless.

34

Side door of the Blue Bullet drab and clat-coloured in the trespassing daylight. Opening a little crack now and a hesitant hair-pinned ould hoor peering out. Unlit cigarette butt and a yellow duster dangling.

'We're not open, ducks.'

'We know.'

'Don't open 'til tonight.'

'We wants to see the manager.'

'What for?'

'We're the new dancers.'

'Don't think he's here yet.'

'We'll wait in his office.'

'What sort of dancing?'

'*Double entendre.*'

'That's nice.'

Follow this ould drotchel down the stairs. I hope he won't mind my dears. And we hopes so too. Lionel arriving a little later and surprise on his face when he sees us sitting there drinking his Scotch. I immediately recognises the cunt's crombie coat from the Star and Garter. Mary pulling a number five iron from the bag of golf clubs in the corner. Reaches for the telephone but stopped with a scream and several broken fingers from a belt of Mary's báiní. Then she pulls the flex from the wall like it's done in the films and wraps it round the cunt's neck. Face turning blue and tongue out learing for the life-saving air.

No sign yet of the heavies. Worlys all still in bed wanking themselves more stupid. Some fucker up there is on my side at last. I hits the higgler hard in the stomach and he doubles over in two. Mary relaxes her stranglehold and throws him into his chair.

'We want to talk to Patsy Keenan.'

'Well he's not fucking here, is he?'

'We can see that. Where is he?'

'Down fucking London, I suppose.'

'When will he be back?'

'You're that fucking joker, aren't you ...?'

'What's his address?'

'... O'Connell's friend ...'

'I think I know where to look, Owen.'

'Do you Mary?'

Lionel laughing at us as if to say you poor stupid sods. Mary scurfs him straight in the face with the golf club and he falls backwards onto the floor. Blood flowing from his broken nose. Lionel blates and holds his face with the claret coming through his fingers. Reaches inside his pocket for a mobile phone. But Mary snatches it from his hand and smashes it to bits against the corner of the desk. We can see we won't get any more information from this cunt so the madwoman ties him up with the telephone cord and gags him with a scarf from around his neck. Then we finds a cupboard and locks the litchup into it.

'What if he gets out?'

'There's no one here but that ould cleaning woman, Owen ...'

'She might hear him ... he might manage to warn Patsy ...'

'Then we could walk into an ambush!'

'Holy Christ!'

'What else do you want me to do?'

'I don't know ...'

'I could kill him?'

Oh my good God! Manage to persuade her to leave Lionel alive. At least for now. Have to hope that no one finds him until we've finalised our business. Otherwise I may say a final few prayers for my simple soul. Mary shouting back to the manager and tell the bastard Patsy if you do manage to get hold of him before us that mad Mary's on her way. To finish the job she started many years ago.

Mary with a memory of her husband's old haunts and a quick taxi at the nearest rank and negotiations to drive us with all haste down to London. Sitting on the back seat I watches this woman who I hardly knows and wonders what in the whole fucking world is happening. Where is this vehicle taking me and what in the name of Jesus will be waiting at the other end? Never a cunt for the complicated issue and always only after the simplest of lives. Caught up somehow and blown like fucking smoke — as we hurtle along the motorway. Knowing that this thing has to be seen through to the bitter end no matter what. Gone too far to turn back now.

Bald taxi cunt looking in his rear-view mirror and speaking with a stammer. Staring down Mary's cleavage as she adjusts the buttons of her blouse. Keep your eyes on the road you cunt! Her teeth flashing favours as she smiles back at the garm's glibby face. Nice out now. It certainly is.

Conversation after the briefest of formalities turning to sexual perversion and the taxi cunt asking Mary all sorts of questions about phobias and fetishes and fixations. And one in particular which belongs to a friend of his who likes to strip naked at the supermarket and sit in the freezer with the birdseyes and fucking beefburgers. What could the cure be? Her being as she told him a world renowned neuro-surgeon and expert on extreme cases. Just been summoned specially to save the life of a Saudi in the city of London. Who suffers severely from delusions of deity and the dreaded be-all and fucking end-all disease.

'The terrible embarrassment of it ...'

'Not to mention the court fines.'

'And the fucking frostbite.'

'So sad.'

'And curable?'

'Only by constant curry poultices.'

Dropped off at an address in Eversholt Street. Nerves on a knife-edge as Mary forces the door and we enters the building illegally. At least they say you don't hear the sound of the bullet that bags you. Be some small consolation to Ann when they invite her down to identify my cold corpse.

But after a cautious search of the apartment no Patsy to be found. And what now? Maybe that cunt Lionel's managed to raise the alarm and there's a gang of them waiting with guns around the corner. Be beaten to death and thrown into the Thames with concrete shoes on our crippled feet. How the fuck did I get myself into this?

Follow quickly the madwoman down an escalator to the underground at Euston which Mary navigates with a fresh and easy familiarity. Tube train on this Victoria Line platform pushing the asthmatic air before it and sending dust swirling all around as we jumps on before the doors can trap an arm or a leg — to be later mutilated along the flying tunnel walls. Can imagine all sorts of molestations down here after dark. Hoors and homos and pimps and procurers and perverts of all kinds.

Speed through the three short stops to Green Park. Change there for the Piccadilly Line — pausing only to stare in amazement at the rest of these peculiar passengers. Can see this city is certainly cosmopolitan. With its begging babies and multicultural misfits. Could all be due to the political volatility flowing from the collapse of the Eastern Bloc and the re-drawing of national boundaries in the emerging Central European democracies. People on the move everywhere. Looking for love. And London and Dublin and Paris and Düsseldorf full of cliques and clans and spicks and spans and all sorts of others. Leading to further racial strife on top of the established turmoil. Send all the buggers back to where they belong!

Head on at full throttle a further seven stops westward to Hammersmith. Back up the escalator and almost having my arse severed by the automatic fucking ticket gates. Glad to get back into the daylight. Know now what it must have been like for Collins.

Mary silent across the Broadway and stepping with confidence through the blaring traffic and cursing cab drivers. With me following nervously and darting glances all around in case of collision with some homicidal maniac. Maybe a distant cousin of the fucking Krays. Or a soldier of Diamond Jack Sloan. Crowds pushing and crushing in the King Street. To make things worse an unseasonably strong sun shining down on this excitable city. Smells of the side-street fruit stalls and the café savouries all a-mingle with the dug-up sewers and the seeping scum. Take a right turn into Leamore Street and then left along Glenthorne Road.

Side door by a shoe shop. Number two hundred and twenty-fucking-two. Always been an unlucky number for me. Sinister. Suspicious. Surprised by the look of the place that it's not been raided by the fucking flying squad. Or even the Sweeney Todd. Maybe it has. Mary producing a key from her pocket and with a finger up to her shushing lips we lets ourselves in. Steep stairs ascending in the high picture-walled hallway. Hear some cunt moving about overhead. Heart pounding like fucking mad. Head light. Mary's hand moving to her bag and a faint feeling sticking the tonsils to the back of my throat as she takes carefully out. A heavy-looking hand gun.

'Jesus fucking Christ!'

'Shhhhh ...'

Move up slowly. Me hiding low down behind her in case of a sudden fucking crossfire. Footsteps fast across the ceiling and then stopping dead at the top of the stairs.

Patsy's face frantic with fear. Staring into the barrel of Mary's loaded automatic with the spreading look of a mortally wounded man. Two suitcases dropping from the cunt's strengthless arms which the milky lich intended to carry outside. To his waiting car. Suddenly he kicks the luggage down the stairs scattering shirts and socks and sending me sprawling. Mary managing to side-step the suitcases and she moves forward with her face set. Regaining my feet and up quickly after her to the top of the stairs with the fucking heart left down at the bottom.

The madwoman with her gun held at arm's length. Searching from room to room. What if he's got a weapon as well? This whole fucking thing is well outside of my thread of life and I'm too young to die this way. Noise from behind a big wooden bureau and the pounding inside my chest speeding to a pace no man could stand. Mary screaming and a shot from the gun as I lie on the floor trying to protect my delicate brain from flying shrapnel. She drags Patsy out by the hair and flings him to the floor. Knee down on his neck and the gun pressed against his forehead.

'Don't shoot! Don't shoot me ...'

'Why shouldn't I, you shite-bag?'

After he's finished pissing on himself she gets me to pull him to his feet and pushes him ahead of her into a large room with roof beams and fashionably bricked walls and off-white carpets and sterile chromed steel furniture. Glass-topped tables scattered at random and pictures by Picasso and Paul Gauguin and a few Pellegrini caricatures. The dealer in me mentally estimating a fair few fucking pounds' worth in this one room alone. Never think it from the outside of the kip. Camouflage!

'Thought I'd forgotten about this place, Mister P?'

'Leave me alone, Missus M ...'

'All done up like a ponce's palace, eh?'

'What do you want from me?'

'It'll make a nice shrine for you!'

'Now listen here, Missus M ...'

'No use trying to plámás.'

'I've not bothered you, have I?'

'No.'

'I've kept my side of the bargain.'

'To an extent.'

'What in God's name does that mean?'

'You've been bothering Owen here.'

'I never knew he was a friend of yours ...'

'Not just a friend — family!'

'Bejaysus ... you're joking!'

'So you see now what you've started.'

'I'll leave him alone in future.'

'Oh, you'll do that all right.'

'Holy mother of God ... don't shoot me, Mary ...'

'I have to now.'

'Why? Why?'

'I want to get married again.'

'Do! Do! To who ... him?'

'What difference does it make?'

'None whatsoever. I'll come and give you away myself.'

'That wouldn't look too nice, now would it?'

'What's the problem, Missus M?'

'You are.'

'Sure now, how am I a problem? Aren't we divorced?'

'The priests don't believe in divorce.'

'Then, don't tell them.'

'I couldn't be party to such deception.'

'Course you could ...'

'And what about Owen?'

Ah sure this fella here is an Englishman and wouldn't be worried about such things. You're not a nark now are you Owen? Might be. Patsy with a may I picking up a cordless phone and push-buttoning a number and smiling at us through the beads of fucking sweat. Hello there Lionel. Didn't expect to be speaking to me again so soon. Is that right? No — your message conveniently came too fucking late and maybe you didn't expect to speak to me at all? What? Is that right? Took you two hours to get out of the cupboard — OK OK! Now listen here. Lay off the Hilton lot. What? Because I fucking said so. If you don't there'll be some serious trouble. No no — not them. Worse than that! Oh there is — take my fucking word for it. I'll explain to you some other time. Good-bye now Lionel and I'll see you get sorted out. Phone down gently and all smiles over to the liquor cabinet.

'Would youse like a drink?'

'You're sure now this mistake is all over with?'

'Of course, Missus M. You know I'm a man of my word.'

'What about my smashed up furniture?'

'Owen boy ... I'll have it all replaced. Only the best quality.'

Mary with a small smile and Patsy sighing with relief and a big blue and white hankie out to mop his brow. Gun going back into the bag and listen here you bastard we don't want your drink but we are tired and hungry. But sure say no more. There's a little place up West called the Cannibal. Just off Lower John Street. And scribbling something on a card and saying take this and order anything you like. Stay for the show and if you want a room that can be arranged also. I'd love to come up with you but there's this important business pending with my physician. See if he can give me something to stop me shaking. As well as that there's a coffin to cancel. And don't forget you lump of dogshite. If we don't see you —you won't see us!

Outside in the taxi which Patsy politely ordered she takes my arm and says there. I've done it for you. And I asks — why Mary is the cunt so afraid of little you? As we travel up West she tells me of her family who has a long history of being hard men and the blood-line goes right back to Brian Boru who drove the fucking Vikings home to Valhalla from the shores of holy Ireland. In recent times Owen my money and my loyalty have lain with a noble cause which wouldn't normally piss up against the likes of Patsy. If you take my meaning? Oh I believes I do. And I'm beginning to see the light. And sure even though there's peace now and the politicians have taken over — the fundamental basics are still in place and that man knows it would only take one word from me and a long arm would reach out and when the smoke cleared he'd be confined to a wheelchair for life. On account of having no kneecaps. That's if he was very fucking lucky. He knows as well that all his men and maulers couldn't protect him from my people.

'But, Mary ...'

But fucking nothing! We'll talk no more about implications or instigations or unpleasantness of any kind. Cruising after a while into the neon centre of this swinging city. With its waxworks and big shop windows and winos and beautiful-looking women.

Taxi dropping us right outside the Cannibal where this big brute on the door welcomes us with open arms. And yes sir no need for notes. We've had a phone call. Actually — we've had several. All anxious as to your safe and sound arrival. With strict instructions to call back expressly as soon as you've been installed. A secluded table for a shameless meal that would feed half the leary fuckers out on the street. And sir it's a little early for the show but there's a room upstairs at your disposal. And of course sir and certainly madam you may have enough champagne to sicken a horse.

After a little picking of the teeth and chasing down the wine with big brandies we takes our leave followed by impressed looks of polite regard. Up in the room a red bed with carpet of the same colour and a little window with red curtains looking out over Golden Square. And we pops a cork

tribe

and laughs with hands excitedly pulling at clothes. Her blouse in bits and my shirt ripped to shreds. Lips crushing over my ear and her tongue trying to lick out the blind and punch-drunk fucking brain. Fingers feeling the weight of my balls as she lies now legs astride my chest and my nose stuck halfway up her arse. And Mary in a low voice saying Owen. It's time now for the calling in of all my notes.

35

Catching later the last train home and darkly down to Lord Byron Square.

Suspect silence from the Hilton. Wonder if Phelim's already in bed? See suddenly the black Mercedes under the street light and Lionel with his hand and nose bandaged stepping out and saying I'm sorry Owen. Despite Patsy's instructions one of the lads was a little over zealous. The cunt's sacked now of course and severely fucking reprimanded as well and anyhow — it's not entirely my fault.

'Where's my cousin?'

'Down at the hospital.'

'How is he?'

'Battered.'

'Badly?'

'Well ... a bit.'

Mary's hand reaching for the gun. Have to restrain her from blowing half the fucking street to bits. Lionel trying to hide behind the wing-mirror of his Mercedes.

'Who did it?'

'This bollocks called Bernard.'

He was one of my fucking best Owen. Qualifications of the highest standard for this kind of work. Good grudge-carrier. And a back-stabber of the most dangerous fucking kind. Be difficult to replace him. But how was I to know the cunt had a personal spite to settle with yourself that would interfere with the phlegmatic fucking nature of the job. I certainly hope Patsy won't find out about this Owen and I've already arranged for a man to see you about some new furniture of the very finest sort. And will pay for professional decorators to do out the whole place. Feeling brave now with Mary by my side and I catches Lionel by the lapels of his crombie.

'Tell me the fucking truth now ... was it Bernard who cut up the Yella Lad's wife?'

Lionel shaking me off and a surly look spreading on his face. I have the cunt where I wants him and he hates me for it.

'The what lad?'

'Litzy.'

'Litzy who? What sort of a name is that?'

And I haven't a fucking clue what you're talking about but I'll give you a grudging lift over to the hospital in case you grass me to that fucking pleb Patsy. Mary dragging me into the back of Lionel's car before I can say any more and the cunt telling me as his driver races us across town that he doesn't know any lady named Litzy nor anything about an ambush and the earlier threats against Felix Cashin were just a bit of bravado and not to be taken seriously. And anyway none of his men would go near the Gypsy camp for fear of their fucking lives. But now that you mention it Owen — Bernard told me before I sacked him that a young woman ran from your premises in a state of near fucking hysteria just as he pulled up outside.

'What young woman?'

'Didn't recognise her, I'm afraid. Said she was driving a pink Peugeot ...'

'Did the bastard touch her?'

'Definitely not! She drove off down the street screaming something like rape.'

Phelim propped up in a pillowed bed. Head bandaged and arm slung in a white round-the-neck sling. Smiling through some loose teeth as we walks up the ward. Begod it's about time. And did it all go well in the dock Owen? What? Oh aye. An unconditional acquittal and Mary with arms all around her bruised buachaill.

'How are you feeling, cousin?'

'Nearly fucked. But I've told them I'm not staying here.'

'Doctor says there's nothing too serious ...'

'Doesn't say much for the English hospitality.'

'Why did you let him in?'

'I didn't!'

'How did this happen then?'

'The woman left the door open.'

'Tell me about the woman.'

'Mind you, I put up a fair fight. But sure, I was already in a sorry state ...'

'Tell me about the fucking woman, Phelim!'

'I thought it was you-know-who, Owen.'

'Did you not ask her who she was or what she wanted?'

'Said she was the mistress of the house and I know what mistress means, Owen ...'

Phelim lowering his voice and whispering she just screamed her head off — when I leapt on her. And sure bejaysus it was half her fault because she kicked me in the balls before she bolted and wasn't I nearly crippled when the boyo came through the door to finish the job? Must have been her accomplice.

Mary trying to overhear the whispers and inside her handbag a finger tightening on the trigger. Holding me personally responsible and promising a terrible fucking vengeance on the perpetrator of this assault on her espoused and me trying to convince her it was all a horrible mistake and I'd sort it out myself. Finally an underpaid and badly harassed nurse coming to end the argument. Mary being allowed to spend the night at her future husband's side because he suffers from these terrible nightmares and if I'm not here he'll keep the whole ward awake with his roaring and screaming. Little nurse ordering me out and walking down the sterilised stairs I falls across Felix. Hands deep in pockets and all the lights out in the cunt's eyes.

'Owen!'

'Felix ... you're here late.'

'So are you.'

'Been to visit a sick relative.'

'Did you sort our fucking problem out?'

'Aye, it's all done. We'll get no more trouble.'
'I still wants a fucking lich, Owen!'
'Tomorrow. How's Litzy?'
'Why don't you come and see for yourself?'
'I don't think so ...'
'She won't talk, Owen.'
'Visiting time must be over ...'
'Hasn't said a fucking word since it happened.'
'Shock, I suppose.'
'Fuck visiting time.'

Felix's grip like a pit-bull terrier on my arm. Can't shake the fucker loose as he drags me down this corridor to the private and lonely little room where Litzy lies. Surrounded by flowers and sleeping. Face and neck all bandages and her slight brown arm outside the covers shuddering as Felix takes it and says. Banríon mo chroí. Look who's here. Dark dream-time eyes opening and in them pure fear and turning her head away as she sees me. To stare at the bare wall.

'It's all right ... It's Owen.'

Strange and shocking sensation freezing over my body like fucking ice as I stands here. Room growing cold and converging on all sides as gradually it dawns on my dim fucking brain that she did it to herself. It wasn't the cunts from the Bullet.

I sees now the full scenario and her sobs saying that for some strange reason she did it herself! I can't fucking speak but wants to turn her round and tell her that these things sometimes happens to people. And it's just like shaking hands if looked at in its proper perspective. A little love on a lonely day. Who could begrudge it? I can only hope in my heart and soul that whatever little fucking demons was lurking in her head has now gone for good. Seen off by the smell of anaesthetic and the sight of Felix's baleful frown. Maybe it's a custom with these Carpathians to mutilate themselves after adultery. Us English is much more civilised and takes it all in our stride. Except for the occasional fucking axe-murder. And the odd beating to death with iron bars. Felix trying to turn her over.

'Leave her, Felix.'
'Talk to her, Owen.'

'Litzy ...'

Very slowly she turns her head and looking up at me her mouth opens in an attempt to talk. I puts a finger to my lips and says shhh. Don't speak. It's all right. I smiles and Felix sits beside her on the bed. Arms around the thin shoulders. Bruised hands gentle on the small bones. Kisses her forehead.

'Owen's sorted everything out, ain't you, Owen?'

'That's right.'

'There won't be any more trouble.'

'Litzy ... I'm sorry. Sometimes strange things happens to people when they're off guard. And all the words we says afterwards means nothing. But it's not the end of the world. We has to keep living to put things right again. Do you understand? There's not a thing we can do about it if we're dead. We makes amends in other ways — to the people we loves.'

After looking at me for a long time she finally nods and turns to the Yella Lad. Small frightened soul looking out through the dark circles and without a sound her eyes say. Felix. Tiny spark of hope but at least there's something there now and I can hope that maybe a little sanity has been salvaged from the confusion of the past few fucking days.

My hand on Felix's shoulder and a last look back at this *gospodyn* girl. Off then quick out the door before I pushes my fucking luck too far. Stretched as it is like thin ice over a thawing pond. Ready to crack at any fucking moment and plunge me balls deep into the freezing water. Every cunt in fucking hospital these days. Either injured or visiting the injured. And all on my account. I really ought to ring Ann now to explain. But it's too late to run the risk of her natchy father answering the phone. Give her a call tomorrow at the office. Say how do you do? Get an answer from the computer. Who? Her lover and guardian angel on the line. Have to leave a message as she can't under any circumstances be disturbed. Well just tell her time. Is now on her side.

Wake in the morning covered in sweat and shouting. Climb out of the dark bed and after three cups of black coffee trudge across town to the hatchintan. The Blackberry saying I hope Owen we're going to get some decent work out of you today. Had a few personal problems Tom. We Gypsies can't afford those Owen. But I knows you'll be glad to hear they've all been sorted. Felix back on the site and his mood a little lighter. Still insisting on revenge and wanting satisfaction for the small scars that will be left on his Litzy's face. But at least Owen she's talking. Said last night after you left. My lovely *lubíc*.

Think now of nice things to make the mind wander as we drives out of the campsite towards the grais. Juno gone from the clover field as it would be unlucky to keep her after killing Tolui. Tom Lee bringing on a couple of white Andalusians to take her place in his broken heart. But things is not the same without the Mongolian pav and though nobody speaks of it I knows they all feels the same as me. This day dragging a little as I'm all the time anxious to get my last fucking problem out of the way. Must first say goodbye to the relatives.

Five-thirty in the afternoon and Phelim self-discharged from the city hospital. Cunt tied up with sticky tape and told to take things easy. Mary saying don't you worry a leanbh. Because I used to be a trained nurse in my younger days. Before becoming a gangster's moll and later on an attempted murderess. Shaking hands and Owen are you sure you can't come to our wedding? It'll be a great affair altogether. With at least a twelve-gun salute from the quare fellas and all sorts of things could happen. That's what I'm fucking afraid of! And anyway it seems I'll soon be in the same situation myself. Isn't that just amazing? And shall we come to yours? It'll just be a small ceremony and I'll be in touch. Take my best wishes with you and Phelim my sincere apologies for that bit of a hiding you took on my account. Say no more cousin because it's given me a greater insight into the English psyche.

Taxi calling to take the cunts away. Shout the waving goodbyes down the street after the speeding car. And when it turns the corner a strange and unexpected loneliness touching my lukewarm heart with its cold fingers. Somehow I can't help feeling that Phelim will need more than all the luck in the world that I wished on him. Be a much wiser man the next time we meet. Mary saying she knows time is

tribe

not on her side but with the help of God the baby will be born healthy. And the first of many others. Be some fucking chavvy! Come out wearing a shoulder-holster and carrying the genetic traditions that made her family infamous. Have three strange numbers etched into the back of his skull and be the terror of the entire Connemara countryside. Perhaps be the beginning of a new and dangerous tribe of outlaws. To terrorise the west coast of Ireland and strike fear into the hearts and souls of all who cross their path. Have the American fucking tourists coming over specially to pose beside the cunts and say they knew their old daddies.

Onto the telephone again and Lionel I knows you shite that everything's been settled but I needs a last piece of information. And what the fuck do you want now? This cunt Bernard you sacked for insubordination. Where does he live? Somewhere called Stanhope Street.

36

Maybe I will go to Mongolia some day. Start in the south at the Great Wall and tramp north across the Gobi Desert and the sea of grass they call the Steppe. Stop beside the turquoise waters of Lake Telmen and chant a mantra and sing a sutra for the soul of the long-lost Tolui. Then meditate on the duality of all things before taking off again to spend the rest of my short life in the great Daa Kure. But first things first.

Sky dull overhead and a dead sort of light fading away in front of the descending night. Quiet in this section of the city as we turns the Land Rover into Stanhope Street. Twenty-two — and I can't get away from that fucking number. Where Bernard the bastard lives with his ageing ould mother who thinks the sun shines out of his evil arse. And his fucking father who was once in the armed forces though now retired and living on the memories of a less tolerant time. When a man could be as prejudiced as he liked without the worry of being called to book by some group of bleeding-heart liberal fucking losers.

Big dog barking in the hall. A shuffling of slippered feet and down boy down. Kindly sort of face and a curlered head peeping out from behind the security-chained door. But I knows it's just a disguise and that this ould hoor would gladly bring back the fucking death penalty for shoplifting. What d'you want him for? I owes him money. In that case you'll find him at the end of the avenue in the local friendly snooker hall. This could be more dangerous than I fucking thought. Hope I'm up to it. Dad shouting from inside who is it? A friend of our Bernard's. Didn't know the young cur had any. Do call again son and we'll have some tea and talk about my little baby boy. Ta-ta now. And thanks again. Back into the Land Rover beside Levesque.

'Well?'

'End of the street ... where that light is.'

'Shall I come in with you?'

'No! Just keep the engine running.'

'Be careful *mon ami!*'

Outside the pool hall. Head fucking pounding. Slip off a shoe and sock and then the brogue back on over the bare foot. Darkly up to a vacant table just inside the door. Shove a couple of colours and the white for weight deep down into the sock and stand still until these cunts moving in the semi-shadow above the table lights become familiar. Spot the bastard at the other end of the hall.

Don't like this situation. Too fucking dangerous. Under normal circumstances I wouldn't set foot inside this fucking place. Nor come near these savages. But the Yella Lad wants his pound of flesh and if I doesn't give him someone he might start making enquiries. Bernard or me! And as nervous as I am now I'd rather be here than facing Felix. This cunt deserves it anyway for kicking the shite out of poor Phelim. Only problem is how to get the grunty back to the site. Without getting myself masafangled. Maybe I should have let Levesque come in with me. Too late now and anyway it's not the Cajun's problem.

Silently slip closer. Moving stealthily from one table to the next. Until I'm right up close to the cunts. Hasn't spotted me because of the gloom and the concentration on the game. What now? Ain't really thought this out. Serious chance here of getting fucking crippled and left in a wheelchair for the rest of my misguided life. Three other tough-guys with Bernard. Don't like the look of the litchups one little bit. Might be maniacs or psychopaths or serious crime squad for all I fucking know. Wish O'Connell was here. He'd know what to do. Or maybe the cunt wouldn't. Look at the fucking mess he got himself into. Game coming to a close. Now or never. Tap the cunt on the shoulder and he turns round. Just in time to see my face before the sock swings hard into his fucking snout. Hear the sound of teeth smashing and Bernard spitting blood onto the floor. Then he looks back at me and grins like the bear that found Goldilocks in his bed. Holy fucking Christ! I'm dead and buried. Ugly faces all round in this gloom full of growling ganja-heads.

Swing the sock around my head a few times and they fall back a bit. Won't be able to keep the cunts at bay forever. Wish I was an innocent child again. Away from all this hatred and haranguing of each other. When all things was bright and beautiful and lived forever. Bernard lunges and I just manages to keep out of range of the butt-end of his pool cue. Cunt circling the table after me. Followed by his friends.

'You got a bit of a nerve, eh, Henry?'

'You beat up my cousin.'

'Who?'

'At the Hilton ...'

'That silly cunt?'

Bernard laughs and spits more blood and bits of teeth. Swing the sock again and this time catch the big bollocks on the side of his head. Staggered him that time but he keeps his balance and coming after me. Sending his shifty shite-heads back round the other way to cut off my retreat. Rest my hand on the edge of this table and he brings the cue butt down hard — breaking several of my fingers. Hurts like hell but I won't please the shite to scream.

'Just like old times, eh, Henry?'

'What fucking old times?'

'At the Star and Garter.'

That's another one I owes the bastard. Backed into a corner now and what fucking possessed me to come in here in the first fucking place? Be the next one down at the hospital. In intensive care. If I'm fucking lucky.

'*Mon ami!*'

Heads turning to look at Levesque and this will be my last fucking chance. Hit Bernard on the head again while he's not looking and this time the eyes glaze over and he slips down onto his knees. Blood from the nose and mouth dripping onto the fag-end floor. Thought the cunt would never keel over. There you puss-sucking sack of shite — now you know what fucking hit you. Rest of the gudgells in two minds whether to kick the living shite out of me or make a move on Levesque. Cajun approaching slowly with a rigger chain in his hand. Two against three now.

Odds a bit more even. Fingers on my left hand already beginning to swell and the pain shooting up my arm to the pounding heart. Bernard trying to get back to his feet and calling me a cunt through the bubbles of blood. Dope-heads hesitating. Too blown away on skunkweed and sulphate to give too much of a fuck about Bernard now. Certainly not wanting a wallop of the sock or Levesque's chain. The Cajun at my side and saying *vite! Il faut ficher le camp*! We drags Bernard in the direction of the door — swinging his fists at us so I swipes him again. Semi-conscious now and much more co-operative. Other fuckers following at a safe distance. Still undecided about whether to charge us at the expense of a severe hammering from the sock and the rigger chain. Or suffer the wrath of Bernard whenever he gets back from wherever we're taking him. If he gets back. Second option finding more favour with the slags who growl and bark like the dirty dogs they are. Out onto the dark street and bundle the barely conscious Bernard into the boot of the Land Rover. Levesque letting out a low sigh.

'*Mon Dieu*! We did it.'

'I'm still not fucking sure how. Just get the fuck out of here quick!'

Levesque speeding across town and not slowing down for traffic lights nor roundabouts nor any other such obstacles. Eventually stopping the Land Rover outside the site gate and helping me to drag the howling Bernard up the compound. Then he disappears into the black night before Felix comes in bare feet to his trailer door. Lights going on all around and a circle gathering. I hears in the distance Levesque accelerating away.

'What's this?'

'Your body.'

'It's that Bernard cunt ...'

'Aye.'

'Was it him?'

'I has it on good authority.'

'Are you fucking sure, Owen?'

'Check with the Blue Bullet if you wants.'

'I'll take your word for it.'

Turn away and walk back out through the site gate to the sound of bones breaking and Bernard's pleading screams. And somewhere in a New Orleans suburb an alligator has eaten a pet poodle. Apart from that the news is of genetic cloning for the superhuman race and super currencies to keep up with it all. Be able to shite gold fucking bars. As well as already cautious plans for the coming Christmas. And cowardice!

'Where in God's name have you been?'

'Doing his job for him.'

'Don't get smart, Owen. That cousin of yours nearly raped me.'

'How do you know he's my cousin?'

'That's what he told the police.'

'You didn't involve the wobs ...?'

'I came back with the police and found him in a pool of blood. How d'you think he got to the hospital? They tried to blame me for his injuries. Father really had to pull some strings to sort it all out ... and what's happened to your hand?'

'The gangsters done it but don't worry — they came off the worst.'

'Have you been to the hospital?'

'Aye, seen to by a sister.'

'My poor Owen, does it hurt?'

'Let's get married, Ann.'

'We *are* getting married.'

'I mean right fucking now ... tonight.'

'Be serious, Owen.'

'Never been more so, Ann!'

'We can't get married right now.'

'Why the fuck not?'

'You know why not.'

'No I don't.'

'What was your cousin doing here, Owen?'

'Came to invite us to a wedding.'

If we can't elope then at least let's eat. All of a sudden I've got an appetite like a leary rooker. And if you likes Ann I'll tell you the whole seedy shiteing story. Leave out of course the incriminating bits and all irrelevant details and keep things simple and to the point. But first ring out for a couple of pizzas with everything on top and several shivers of garlic bread thrown in. For good measure. And I means what I says about marriage. Oh Owen! Don't be so silly. There's a time and place for everything. And besides there are arrangements to be made and cakes to be baked and dresses to be altered and function rooms to be booked and all sorts of other things as well.

But Ann — I've had enough fucking hardship and have decided to concede defeat. Want only now to lie in a soft bed and never again have to get out of it to face all the fartology of this lousy fucking life. Cover my head with the continental quilt and curl up like a foetus in the feathery womb-warmth. Waiting my time to fall head first back into this howling world.

'Are you sure it's all over, Owen?'

'On my father's bones.'

'Oh ... isn't it wonderful!'

And I knew all along Owen that despite everything we'd win through in the end. All set up now to stare hard at this fucking wankerworld and say. You big blating bollocks! We've taken all you can throw at us and we're still fucking standing. Oh Owen! Isn't it great to be alive at last?

And after skoffing the chuck we don't stand on ceremony to slip out of these inconvenient clothes and tiptoe to the bedroom — because there's no fireplace in the Hilton only the central heating-radiators. Which haven't the same narcotic effect when lying there making love. Will it ever be the same again? Or will we become civilised and slope off to this special room which is smiled on by polite society for the flinging over of the leg and the doing of all these little intimate things. Never again to fall down animal-like on the very spot where the mood manifests itself. Ann's arms opening and also this door. Which leads to a brave new world. Of sobriety.

tribe

37

Sky overhead scowling down on this black morning. Soft November rain falling to wash away the blood and bitterness. Ann loaning me the car today and I hopes the cunts don't laugh at the colour. Park up on the road outside the hatchintan and notice a curious lack of smoke on the skyline and no sounds at all of moulders revving up nor pavs growling at this beginning of another little life-precious day.

Reports in the papers of economic upturns and downturns and swings and roundabouts and political fucking trapezing. Tolui now only a little red moment in the back of my mind. See him sometimes as a tiny speck high up on the *taiga* with his stallion and his snow-leopard. But stay away from me you low-lying spirits and let me at least be happy now as I takes the final few short steps to inevitable insanity. Big sign outside the camp saying —

THIS SITE HAS BEEN ACQUIRED BY GREATER MANCHESTER COUNCIL AND DESIGNATED FOR CAR-PARKING FACILITIES AS PART OF AN OVERALL DEVELOPMENT OF THE AREA FOR THE INFORMATION TECHNOLOGY INDUSTRY.

All empty inside. Completely deserted. Trailers and lorries and men and women and chavvies all gone. Not one single sinner left. Louis! The Duck and Myles — all gone. Where? I can't be fucking left here all alone. They wouldn't leave me here on my own. Don't leave me! There must be a message. Some fucking sign? Shiving round the empty site I can find nothing. No indication or trace of the people who lived here such a short time ago. Maybe the cunts is out at the clover fields.

Rain caressing my face like gentle tears as I heads back to the car and drives away down the M62. Hoping as I push the accelerator pedal through the floor that I'm not too late. Overwhelming sense of anxiety driving me forward and for no reason I sees Ann's face before me — half sympathetic half relieved. Down along this dejected road. No birds singing and a soft moan to the wind. Smoke spiralling as I approaches the clover fields. There is some higgler still here. Park the Peugeot and vault over the gate to see Levesque standing in front of the burning tack-shed. Flames licking at the sky and sparks ascending into the atmosphere. No animals to be seen and the fields forlorn and friendless.

'Where the fuck's everybody, Levesque?'

'All gone, *mon ami.*'

'Where to?'

'I don't know. Some other camp, I suppose.'

'What about you?'

'My plane waits to take me back to Calcasieu Lake. I leave in a couple of hours.'

I looks up at the black smoke spiralling and knows it's a fucking funeral pyre. Tolui's body has been flown back to Mongolia and it's our custom to burn all belongings. Cunt'll be laid to rest somewhere in his Altayn hills. With all the family filing by and throwing orchids and incense after him. Tears dropping down which soaks like blood into the dusty soil to wait for that future time when the terrible wound will heal. And leave behind only a scar.

'Why did they go?'

'They had to ... no choice. Council closed the site down.'

'Isn't there such a fucking thing as notice?'

'Only need to give twenty-four hours by law.'

And what matter anyway *ma monnaie*? Here today gone tomorrow. The present is a fleeting thing — if it exists at all. A day or an hour or a second — there really is no present. Only past and future. Once the future appears — it straightaway becomes the past. There is nothing in between

tribe

and life therefore is a complete illusion. Jesus Christ — another fucking philosopher!

'Are they all gone?'

'Except for Felix. He's moved into a bungalow outside town for his *famille*. They, at least, are finished with the road. I'm sure you'll see him sometime.'

Levesque says I should go now because there's nothing left for me here. Places of death should be avoided as they are unlucky and I turns to stare into the leaping flames for a long moment. Offering the Cajun my hand he claps me on the shoulder and says Owen. No goodbyes. We never say goodbye because goodbye is forever. *Au revoir* then as I looks once more into the fire before leaving him standing there — a macabre figure. Not turning at all as I walks away up the road. In case I might like Lot's wife be turned into a pillar of fucking self-pity.

Somewhere I knows the sky is blue and the world is wide open. Won't be long until I can sit on a park bench and stare up at its mystery and think of all the things there must be out there in the Universe. Besides this dirty little planet full of wankers and wishful-thinkers and even fucking worse. Set sail some day on a first-class star to the heavens. Stop off at exotic places like Proxima Centauri and Saturn and the planet Strom. Never again come back down to swim against the stream of shite in this fucking sewer world.

Voice of all recent acquaintance echoing in my head on the drive back to town. Light from the sky grey and iron-like. New winter closing in. Birds all gone south and the cold air forecasting frost. Greasy heat hitting my face from the doorway of this city chippy. And there standing in the counter queue is pretty Peggy.

'Hi Owen!'

'Peg ...'

'Ann not cooking for you these days?'

'Not today.'

'I would.'

'I know. Collins working yet?'

'In a shite factory I hope. Not seen him for some time.'

'Maybe he's had an accident?'

'I don't care anymore, Owen.'

'Could be lying crippled in some hospital.'

'He's gone again. I know it.'

'What are you going to do?'

'Nothing.'

'He might come back again in another two years.'

'He needn't bother.'

'It's still his flat ...'

'Not any more.'

Catastrophe for Collins. Peggy's been to see the Council. Told the cunts she's Collins' common-law wife and has lived in Anchorage Quay for many years. Said they could check with the opal mines in Australia if they didn't believe her. Now deserted by the bastard and as she's paying the rent and council tax she should by right be the lawful sitting tenant. Council clerk intoxicated by her pink perfume and making the necessary arrangements and putting all the paperwork in her name. He was very nice about it all Owen. It's her fucking flat now!

'Wonder where the cunt's gone to this time ...'

'Hell, I hope.'

Or back to the underside of the fucking world. Told me about some glibby cunt he heard of who makes his own money and prints his own postage stamps and pays no taxes and is absolute ruler over a little acre of land. Could be that Collins has ambitions in that area and means to stake a claim over some isolated corner of the Great Sandy Desert. Maybe put up a barbed-wire fence and become self-sufficient in the reptile rearing or maybe the manufacture of kangaroo-skin coats. And yes madam. It's the latest thing from the house of Collino on the outskirts of Sturt Creek.

Have a string of models marketing his products all over the world and his fucking fizzog on the cover of all the fashion magazines. Once as boys we broke into an off-licence together. Crowbarred the door and in the dark grabbing the first crates we came to then several miles down the road at full pelt with our arms full and lungs bursting. Under a street light we sits down and drinks until we're dibby and then sicks up on our shoes. Drinking more and repeating the puking process. I passed out but Collins stuck with it until all the cans were empty and a river of reasy choking up the channel. And if ever in his little corner of the world he does make the big time it'll be because of such dogged fucking determination.

Kiss Peggy goodbye and her smile saying pay me a visit sometime. When there's a lull in the storm. Or when they're all about you again with the big sticks to break your bloody neck. Come then and lie between my legs and never mind the niceties of this bear-baiting bastard of a world. I appreciates her unspoken offer and can see it's all in honest level-headed lust. But I'm booked on a trip to obscurity and it'll be a hot day in heaven when the boat again berths and I can run without any shoes down the gangway and shout. Syzygy!

Blue envelope on the mat inside the front door. Another Irish stamp but this time my mother's small handwriting.

> Barna,
> Galway.
> November

Dear son,

Just a little line, hoping you are well. As
we are all fine here T.G. Heard only this morning,
after the event, that you had a visit from your cousin
and his surprise of the year bride. It all happened
shortly after that party when you were over here.
I don't suppose they told you, but she's up the pole.
Your Auntie Kathleen nearly had a coronary. Swore
it wasn't Phelim's. But she's a headstrong bitch ...
Mary, I mean. Said youse can take a blood sample
if necessary and swore blue murder it was definitely
the fault of this family. And, sure, Phelim's a bit of a
sap on the side and said it was probably his all right.
And when a Bank of Ireland deposit account was
mentioned with in it over two hundred thousand
pounds, sure your Auntie Kathleen had second
thoughts. Nobody knows where she got the money
from. Some say it belonged to her crook of a husband
before his disappearance and he never came back
to claim it. The priests were a bit worried on that
score until she produced a death certificate dated

some time since and signed by an English doctor.
Anyway, they're married now and living in her house
up by the old church. Phelim seems happy enough.
But then, he's easily pleased. I'm not so sure about her.
But the baby is due in a few months and the doctors
says it's a son and I suppose she's hardy and can't pick
and choose anymore.

Timmy is as happy as Larry over here. He works the
land with his uncles and sure isn't he the white-
haired boy round here now that Phelim's moved out?
He's built himself a hut out by the bay and sometimes
he stays out there for days on end. Says the birds
come to visit him and they talk to each other all night
long. He says they've taught him how to fly and
he's busy building himself a set of wooden wings
so's he can jump off the clifftop and soar with them
over the waves. I don't say anything. Sure, I suppose
he's not doing any harm and it's keeping him happy.
Not to mention the birds.

I'm grand meself and I've settled back down
nicely here. My little bungalow is coming along a treat
and they says I can move in sometime in the spring.
Only one fly in the ointment and that was with them
ould pharisees of priests who wouldn't let me put your
father's ashes in the consecrated ground. So I told
them all to feck off. That he was a better man and had
more balls than the whole lot of them and their Pope
and cardinals and bishops all put together. Needless
to say that got on their nerves and there was talk of
excommunication. But I didn't care. Your Auntie
Kathleen had a word with them unbeknownst to me
and I'm sure that money changed hands. So they
said no more. I have the ashes here and I'll keep them
safe until it's time for me to go meself. Then I'll swallow
them stirred in a glass of stout and outsmart the hypocrites
after all.

Must close now because there's a commotion outside
the house and someone's shouting that Tim's up a tree.
Dropping something on people's heads? I can't hear. I
know you're not one for the letter writing Owen, so I've
told Desmond's Willow to keep an eye on you and let me

*know all when she writes. I may go because there's murder
going on outside.*
Bye for now,
Love,

Mammy.

PS Sad about that chap O'Connell. You must miss him.

Fold back the paper along its crease and replace it in the
envelope. Stopping the Celtic calls and the sound of the
waves washing in my ears. And the wild cries of the curlews.
Smell of salt air and seaweed subsiding and the heart now
all a-pounding and a-pumping blood faster than the brain
can bear. And the face of the ould duckerer haunting the
room. Telling me I must didge along and dingle as I can from
now on but always keep a twipper of docity in me no matter
how unkind life comes.

Sit in the studio as Ann now calls it and shake this tiny
sorrow from my half-entranced soul. Thoughts flying wild all
over the known world and even in places not so popular until
all track of time is lost and landfall lies far far away.

Sudden slamming of the front door sending the sense
stoaching back into my yawney brain. Ann's slow-motion
voice from somewhere dull and distant. Footsteps falling
into the room and a blinding flash of electric light-bulb.

'Owen! Jesus ... you startled me.'

'You're a bundle of nerves.'

'Can you blame me? Why are you sitting in the dark?'

'Must have dozed off.'

'Who's the letter from?'

'Mother.'

'That's nice. What does she say?'

That she read a report in the *Connaught Herald* which
said that the fucking yanks are going to make it compulsory
for the biblical account of creation to be taught in all
southern schools. They reckon Darwin was a homosexual
Iranian Ayatollah. Ann doubting if my mother was ever
interested in evolution. On the contrary. She's constantly
scanning the horizon for a sign of my father. And how would
she know him? By his big toe. Stand up and have a stretch.
Kiss Ann on the faint perfume forehead and rub the sleep

tribe

out of my eyes. Trip over yawning the cold chips on the floor. Ann picking them up with a frown and carrying them to the kitchen.

'Must be the day for parental communication.'

'Oh aye?'

'Daddy rang me today at work.'

'Had he a question which only the computer could answer?'

'Owen ...'

'Am I animal, vegetable or mineral?'

'Listen to me ...'

Machine tested to the full capacity of its fucking chips and finally prints out — pass! But apparently the cunt wants us to come round on Sunday for dinner. And maybe it's time now to compromise. Need another fucking job and if his offer is still open. You'd never know.

'Both of us?'

'Of course.'

'I hope somebody felt his forehead.'

'Don't be unkind, Owen. I think he's finally ready to accept the inevitable.'

'He's always accepted you, Ann. It's me the lich has trouble with.'

'You will be nice, won't you?'

And could you qualify that characteristic? Polite and patient. You forgot pimmocky. But I'll do my very best and try to be what he wants me to be. A man for all reasons! And although I doubts it perhaps the ould prick has some good points. If so I'll show him a few of mine and there might be just a slim chance that we'll communicate. Breaking to Ann the news of the Travellers' unceremonious eviction and she sympathises and says at the same time she's glad. You were becoming too much influenced by them Owen. And what about when we're married and people ask me at a dinner party or other social engagement what you do? How could I say — why my husband's a Gypsy! And apparently her computer company is one of the ones relocating to the site. Be more room for the fucking machines. And now's the time to talk seriously to father about that job with the paper. Oh Owen!

tribe

Won't be long now 'til Christmas comes again. In the aftermath of this long and dangerous year. Will the next be even longer — and even more detrimental to the delicate life-thread? And the year after that? Where will we all be in ten years' time? Or ten thousand? In the post-natal pains of a new yuga-kalpa? And what about black and white and all the colours in between? Especially in summer with the fucking suntans. Will good triumph over evil or evil over good? And who knows these days which is fucking which?

Cunts all soon be driving around in diamond Daimlers and the nano-technology and molecular self-assembly and bio-chips churning out zillions of tiny little tractors for the dawning of a bland-new day. Must be a way I'm sure to go through this light-weight life in a more dignified fucking manner. But how? Be very surprised to hear that no cunt's yet found the secret. Sometimes I thinks I have the answer. Sometimes it's almost there — so close I can smell it. Then the terrible awesomeness of it all crashes over my mind like a tidal mirage and it's gone. Back to its star-bright stratosphere. And dark reality returns. Tell me please! Send me an anonymous note. Or give me a sign like a shining star up there in the sky. Or a pointing finger of fire. Boss a lightning bolt down the chimney of the Rose and Crown. Illuminating all along the bar and sending a pool cue singing through the window. Follow it out and where it lands half sunk in the soil we'll gather round hands joined and eyes cast upwards to see the smoke-trail letters in the sky saying. SHITE. You crowd of cribbled cunts will never amount to nothing. And we'll sing and thank our lucky fucking stars.

Coffee pot percolating in the kitchen and the television screen flickering its subliminal message at me. Clock ticking ten-past-eight and my hazy head clearing to let in the light of this real *real* night. See Ann smiling and the other images fading away like ghosts in the gloom. Until only all that's left are her eyes. In them I sees my own face looking back like a lost dilling waiting to be found. The recent names I can't remember now. Except for Ann. Ann! Calling with a faint voice from somewhere on a sea-lashed shore. Rain outside the window playing with the night. And if it ain't wrong. It must be right!

tribe